"WHAT HAVE WE GOT?" KIRA ASKED.

"Ensign ch'Thane found him at Quark's," Ro said. "He's making his statement now."

As she spoke, they started through the door that led to the holding cells, Ro leading the way. "The soldier was unarmed and offered no resistance; he was carrying a pack of ketracel-white cartridges, but nothing else. He asked to speak to you, claiming that he's here on a peace mission—"

Kira couldn't help a sneer as they turned into the holding-cell area. *A peaceful Jem'Hadar. Right.* At least she knew now why she'd felt watched, but that small relief was heavily overshadowed by thoughts of what he could have been doing all this time; he had to have been hiding on the station since the attack.

"—and that Odo sent him."

They stopped in front of the only occupied cell, Ro nodding at the guard, excusing her with a few words of direction—but Kira barely heard them. She could only stare dumbly at the soldier, overwhelmed with feelings of loss, of anger and disbelief—and a tiny seed of hope.

Odo . . .

(handwritten notes)

(a little Aussie 3½ yrs
KRYSIA)
WOODS
Female
instructor 973
w/ Lotus 417
Beverly 97 09
PMU
LESSONS

STAR TREK: DEEP SPACE NINE®

A V A T A R
BOOK ONE OF TWO

S.D. Perry

Based upon STAR TREK®
created by Gene Roddenberry,
and STAR TREK: DEEP SPACE NINE
created by Rick Berman & Michael Piller

POCKET BOOKS
New York   London   Toronto   Sydney   Singapore   B'hala

An *Original* Publication of POCKET BOOKS

POCKET BOOKS, a division of Simon & Schuster, Inc.
1230 Avenue of the Americas, New York, NY 10020

A VIACOM COMPANY

STAR TREK is a Registered Trademark of Paramount Pictures.

This book is published by Pocket Books, a division of Simon & Schuster, Inc., under exclusive license from Paramount Pictures.

ISBN:0-7434-0050-X

First Pocket Books printing May 2001

10 9 8 7 6 5 4 3 2 1

POCKET and colophon are registered trademarks of Simon & Schuster, Inc.

Cover art by Cliff Nielsen
New logo design by Michael Okuda

Printed in the U.S.A.

CLOSE TO HOME

McPHERSON   closetohome@ucomics.com   8-4-01

With prescription drug prices rising exponentially, many drugstores now provide armed escorts to assure that customers reach their cars safely.

For Myk, who puts up with me on deadline.

ACKNOWLEDGMENTS

Star Trek is a great big place, and a lot of people contribute, so:

This book wouldn't have been possible without the kindness, creative improvements, and/or information provided to me by . . .

Paula Block, at Paramount, for her tremendous support. Keith R. A. DeCandido and David Henderson, who helped compile the time line. Doctor Joelle Murray, for a few physics definitions that I *think* I understand (Joelle: you rock). Cliff Nielsen for his brilliant cover art, and Mike Okuda, for the new logo design (sharp, eh?). Jessica McGivney, for always believing. Also, Rob Simpson, who was there at the story's conception . . . and of course, my editor, Marco Palmieri, who is a creative force behind these books but tries to avoid taking credit.

On a more personal note, I need to thank Steve and Dianne Perry, Doctor Les Goldmann, and Myk Olsen, for their moral support . . . and to every brave writer of *Star Trek* technical journals, encyclopedias, chronologies, and companions—without you, I'd still be writing the outline.

One meets destiny often on the road taken to avoid it.

—FRENCH PROVERB

LINEAR TIME

THE DISTANT PAST

• Over the course of ten thousand years, the people of Bajor discover nine mysterious artifacts that sometimes convey prophetic visions. Called "Tears of the Prophets" or "Orbs," they are believed to have originated in the Celestial Temple, the legendary home of Bajor's gods, the Prophets.

2328

• The Cardassian Union conquers Bajor. Eight of the nine Orbs are confiscated for study. The ninth, the Orb of Prophecy and Change, is successfully hidden by Bajor's spiritual leaders.

2332

• On Earth, Benjamin Sisko is born, the child of Sarah and Joseph Sisko. Unknown to anyone at this time, Sarah is actually the host for a noncorporeal entity from the as-yet-undiscovered Bajoran wormhole, who has brought about the exact circumstances necessary for Benjamin Sisko to exist.

2345

• A liquid lifeform of unknown origin is discovered adrift in the Bajoran system's Denorios Belt. It is later found to be a shape-shifting sentient being, and accepts the name Odo.

2346

• The Cardassians construct space station Terok Nor in orbit of Bajor. It becomes the seat of the Occupation under Gul S.G. Dukat.

• To ensure the survival of her husband and children, Kira Meru becomes the comfort woman of Dukat. She is never reunited with her family.

2347

• On Bajor, seven-year-old Ro Laren witnesses the torture and murder of her father by the Cardassians.

• Richard and Amsha Bashir subject their six-year-old son Jules to illegal genetic enhancement. The boy later changes his name to Julian and keeps his enhancement secret for many years.

2354

• Ensign Benjamin Sisko meets joined Trill Curzon Dax at Pelios Station. Their friendship continues through Dax's next two hosts.

2355

• On Bajor, twelve-year-old Kira Nerys, daughter of Meru, joins the Shakaar resistance cell to fight the Cardassian Occupation.

• Jake Sisko is born to Benjamin and Jennifer Sisko.

2358

• Ro, after living all her life in Bajoran resettlement camps, attends Starfleet Academy.

2360

• Quark opens a bar on Terok Nor after spending eight years as a cook on a Ferengi freighter. Among his staff are his brother Rom, and Rom's young son, Nog.

2364

• While serving aboard the *U.S.S. Wellington*, Ensign Ro disobeys orders during a mission on Garon II, resulting in the deaths of eight members of her away team. She is court-martialed and sentenced to the Starfleet stockade on Jaros II.

2365

• Odo comes to Terok Nor and begins arbitrating disputes among Bajorans, leading to Dukat recruiting him for a murder investigation. In the process, Odo meets Kira, with whom he will eventually fall in love, though he keeps that secret from her for many years.

• Dukat makes Odo the station's chief of security, replacing a Cardassian named Thrax.

2367

• The Battle of Wolf 359 between a Borg cube and forty Federation starships claims 11,000 lives—including Jennifer Sisko. *U.S.S. Saratoga* first officer Lieutenant Commander Benjamin Sisko and his son Jake both survive. Sisko is subsequently assigned to the Utopia Planitia Shipyards on Mars, where he becomes part of the *Defiant*-Class Development Project, a starship designed specifically to fight and defeat the Borg.

• Curzon, seventh host of the Dax symbiont, dies. The symbiont is transferred to Jadzia.

2368

• Ro is freed from prison in order to carry out an illegal covert mission for Starfleet Admiral Kennelly aboard the *U.S.S. Enterprise*. Instead, she exposes Kennelly's duplicity. At the request of Captain Jean-Luc Picard, her rank is restored and she is assigned to the *Enterprise*.

2369

• The Cardassian Union withdraws from Bajor and abandons Terok Nor. As Bajor regains its independence, a provisional government and an armed militia are formed. Bajor applies for Federation membership, and invites Starfleet to administrate the station as a Federation starbase with an integrated Starfleet and Bajoran crew. Terok Nor is renamed Deep Space 9.

• Cardassian exile Elim Garak, former intelligence agent of the Obsidian Order, is left behind on the station during the withdrawal. He remains an enigmatic station resident, living as a tailor.

• Commander Sisko is made commanding officer of DS9, with Major Kira reluctantly serving as his first officer and liaison with Bajor. Lieutenant Jadzia Dax is assigned as science officer. Lieutenant (j.g.) Dr. Julian Bashir becomes chief medical officer. Former *Enterprise* transporter chief Miles O'Brien is made chief of operations. Odo stays on as chief of station security.

• Sisko meets Bajor's spiritual leader, Kai Opaka, who tells him he is the Emissary long foretold in Bajoran prophecy, the one who will open the gates to the Celestial Temple.

- After experiencing the Orb of Prophecy and Change, Sisko and Dax discover a stable wormhole in the Denorios Belt, linking the Alpha Quadrant to the Gamma Quadrant. The wormhole is also found to be the home of noncorporeal entities who exist outside of linear time. DS9 is moved to a position proximate to the wormhole, and becomes a major center of commerce and the exploration of the Gamma Quadrant.

- The Bajoran faithful believe the wormhole is the Celestial Temple, and that its inhabitants are the Prophets. Sisko is hailed as the Emissary, a role with which he is never completely comfortable.

- Opaka is killed on a planet in the Gamma Quadrant. Nanomachines previously introduced into the planet's biosphere revive her, but also make it impossible for her to leave.

- Ro leaves the *Enterprise* to receive Starfleet advanced tactical training.

2370

- Minister Jaro Essa and Vedek Winn Adami conspire to seize power on Bajor and oust the Federation. The coup fails, and Jaro is disgraced, but Winn emerges unscathed.

- Kira and Vedek Bareil Antos become romantically involved.

- Ferengi trade expeditions to the Gamma Quadrant first encounter rumors of a powerful civilization known as the Dominion.

- The Federation and the Cardassian Union sign an historic peace treaty, leading to the creation of a "Demilitarized

Zone" between the two powers. As a result, several Federation colony worlds are ceded to the Cardassians, but many of the colonists refuse to be evacuated.

• In response to Cardassian hostilities against Federation colonists still living in the DMZ, and believing they have been abandoned by the Federation, some of the colonists organize an armed resistance and become known as the Maquis. They consider themselves freedom fighters, but are generally regarded as terrorists.

• Winn is elected kai of the Bajoran faith.

• Lieutenant Ro returns to the *Enterprise* and is assigned to infiltrate the Maquis. Finding herself sympathizing with their cause, she turns against Starfleet and joins them. Over time, many other Starfleet officers do the same.

• The Dominion makes first contact with the Federation when Sisko is detained by Jem'Hadar soldiers in the Gamma Quadrant. At the same time, a Jem'Hadar strikeforce destroys the Gamma Quadrant colony of New Bajor and the *U.S.S. Odyssey.*

2371

• To meet the Dominion threat, Starfleet assigns the prototype *U.S.S. Defiant* to DS9. To assist in the defense of the Alpha Quadrant, the Romulan Star Empire equips the *Defiant* with a cloaking device.

• The Federation attempts unsuccessfully to open relations with the Dominion. The Founders' homeworld is discovered, and Odo learns that the Founders are his own kind, a species of changelings.

• Bashir learns that the Jem'Hadar are a genetically engineered species dependent for their survival upon a crucial isogenic enzyme that their physiology cannot produce naturally. The enzyme can only be obtained through the intravenous delivery of the chemical compound ketracel-white, which is created and rationed by the Dominion to maintain its control over the Jem'Hadar.

• The Cardassian Union and Bajor sign an historic peace treaty, negotiated by Bareil, who dies during the final stages of the negotiations.

• With Sisko's sponsorship, Nog becomes the first Ferengi to apply to Starfleet Academy.

• Grand Nagus Zek of the Ferengi Alliance obtains the Orb of Wisdom from the Cardassians and returns it to Bajor.

• The Cardassian Obsidian Order and the Romulan Tal'Shiar intelligence agencies hatch a covert plan to destroy the Founders' homeworld. The Founders learn of it and annihilate the combined fleet.

• While hunting sabre bear on Kang's Summit, Klingon General Martok is abducted and replaced by a Founder.

• Jake Sisko introduces his father to Kasidy Yates, a civilian freighter captain. Sisko and Yates later become romantically involved.

- Former resistance fighter Shakaar Edon is elected First Minister of Bajor.

- Sisko is promoted to captain.

- To save the *Defiant* and prevent the outbreak of a new war with Tzenkethi, Odo kills a Founder impersonating a Federation ambassador. It is the first time that one changeling has killed another.

- Dax and Bashir are promoted to lieutenant commander and full lieutenant, respectively.

- On Cardassia, the civilian Detapa Council overthrows the Cardassian Central Command and what's left of the Obsidian Order.

2372

- At the instigation of the Founder impersonating Martok, the Klingon Empire invades Cardassia. The Federation objects, and in response the Klingons withdraw from the Khitomer Accords, ending their alliance with the Federation. Hostilities between the Klingons and the Cardassians, and between the Klingons and the Federation, continue for over a year.

- Lieutenant Commander Worf, former security chief of the *Enterprise,* is assigned to DS9 as strategic operations officer and commander of the *Defiant.*

- Bashir discovers that it is possible (though exceedingly rare) for a Jem'Hadar to be born without a dependency upon ketracel-white.

- Nog leaves DS9 to attend Starfleet Academy.

- Fear of changeling infiltration leads Admiral Leyton to attempt a Starfleet *coup d'etat*. It is thwarted by Sisko.

- While on Earth, Odo is surreptitiously infected by the autonomous covert organization Section 31 with a virus intended to wipe out the Founders.

- Kira and Shakaar become romantically involved.

- Yates is arrested for smuggling supplies to the Maquis. She is convicted and sentenced to six months in a Federation prison.

- A pregnant Keiko O'Brien is seriously injured. Bashir is able save the unborn child, but only by implanting it in the body of Kira, who volunteers to carry the child to term.

- Odo is found guilty of murder by the Founders and, as punishment, is made a "solid." In the process, he unknowingly infects the Founders' Great Link with the genocidal virus created by Section 31.

2373
- The Founder impersonating Martok is exposed and killed on Ty'Gokor.

- Worf and Dax become romantically involved.

- The Cardassians return the Orb of Time to the Bajorans.

• Bashir is abducted by the Dominion and replaced by a Founder.

• Cadet Nog returns to DS9 as part of his Academy training.

• Yates completes her prison sentence and returns to DS9.

• After suffering a neural shock, Sisko experiences visions that lead him to unearth the Bajoran city of B'hala, lost for millennia. At the same time, premonitions of disaster compel him to persuade Bajor to delay its imminent entry into the Federation.

• Kira gives birth to the son of Miles and Keiko O'Brien, who name the child Kirayoshi.

• Odo finds an infant changeling, but it dies of radiation poisoning. Upon its death, its remains are absorbed into Odo's body, turning him back into a changeling.

• The Cardassian Union joins the Dominion after months of secret negotiation between the Dominion and Dukat. A massive Dominion fleet enters the Alpha Quadrant to assume direct control of Cardassia. The Klingon Empire and the Federation renew their alliance. An attempt to destroy Bajor's sun by the Founder impersonating Bashir is thwarted.

• Worf and Garak rescue the real Martok and Bashir from a Dominion prison in the Gamma Quadrant. Martok becomes the Klingon Empire's official representative on DS9.

• Bashir's genetic enhancement is exposed, but he is allowed to retain his status in exchange for his father's voluntary imprisonment.

• Kira and Shakaar end their romance.

• Working together, the Cardassians and the Jem'Hadar exterminate the Maquis, leaving few survivors.

• Open war with the Dominion breaks out. At Sisko's urging, Bajor signs a non-aggression pact with the Dominion. As Dominion forces take DS9, all Starfleet personnel withdraw from the region. The station is renamed Terok Nor and put under the joint command of the Vorta Weyoun and Dukat, with Kira, Odo, and the rest of the Bajoran staff still intact.

2374
• With the aid of a resistance group on the station led by Kira, Starfleet forces retake DS9. Dukat is captured. At Sisko's insistence, the Prophets prevent Dominion reinforcements from coming through the wormhole, but the entities warn Sisko that their intervention carries a price.

• Dukat's former aide-de-camp Damar is promoted to legate and made the new leader of Cardassia under the Dominion.

• Nog earns a battlefield commission of ensign.

• Martok is made Supreme Commander of the Ninth Fleet.

• Worf and Dax marry.

• Dukat escapes Starfleet custody.

- Section 31 attempts to recruit Bashir. Although he refuses to join, the organization will continue to consider him an operative.

- Betazed falls to the Dominion.

- With the aid of Garak, Sisko manipulates the Romulans into allying with the Federation and the Klingons against the Dominion.

- Kira and Odo become romantically involved.

- Dukat makes a pact with the Pah-wraiths, the enemies of the wormhole entities. Using Dukat as their vessel, they seal the wormhole, killing Jadzia in the process. The Dax symbiont survives.

- En route to Trill aboard the *U.S.S. Destiny,* the Dax symbiont takes a turn for the worse, necessitating an emergency implantation into Ensign Ezri Tigan, a Trill who never intended to be joined, but reluctantly becomes Dax's ninth host.

- Kira is promoted to colonel.

2375

- On the planet Tyree, Sisko discovers the Orb of the Emissary and learns that the wormhole entities were responsible for his very existence. This previously unknown tenth orb also reopens the wormhole.

- Ezri Dax is promoted to lieutenant (j.g.) and is assigned to DS9 as a counselor.

- The disease created by Section 31 starts to manifest among the Founders.

- Ensign Nog loses a leg in battle on AR-558. The limb is subsequently replaced by a biosynthetic leg.

- Dukat has himself surgically altered to pass as a Bajoran in order to turn Winn against the Prophets, and to use her to unleash the Pah-wraiths.

- Sisko and Yates marry. Shortly thereafter, they conceive a child.

- The Breen ally with the Dominion. Fearing for Cardassia, Legate Damar rebels against the Dominion and forms a Cardassian resistance.

- Sisko sends Kira, Odo, and Garak to the aid of Damar's resistance. To help Kira gain the Cardassians' acceptance, Sisko grants her a Starfleet commission with the rank of commander.

- The *Defiant* is destroyed in battle against the Dominion and the Breen at the Chin'toka system.

- Odo begins to manifest symptoms of the disease ravaging the Founders.

- Worf kills Klingon leader Gowron in honorable combat and names Martok the new chancellor of the empire.

- Bashir extracts the cure to the Founder disease from the mind of Section 31 operative Luther Sloan. Sloan commits suicide, but Bashir succeeds in curing Odo.

• The *Defiant*-class *U.S.S. Sao Paolo* is assigned to DS9 under Sisko's command. Special dispensation is granted to rechristen the ship the *U.S.S. Defiant*.

• Bashir and Dax become romantically involved.

• Zek retires and appoints Rom his successor as Grand Nagus of the Ferengi Alliance.

• Federation, Klingon, Romulan, and rebellious Cardassian forces fight to retake Cardassia from the Dominion and the Breen. In retaliation for the Cardassians' betrayal, the Female Changeling orders the entire planetary population put to death. Odo provides the cure for the disease and his return to the Great Link in exchange for the Dominion's surrender, but at least 800 million Cardassians have already been executed.

• Dukat and Winn go to the fire caves of Bajor to unleash the Pah-wraiths. Sisko stops them, but at a cost. Winn is killed, and Dukat becomes trapped with the Pah-wraiths. Sisko joins the entities in the wormhole, but promises to return.

• O'Brien transfers to the faculty staff of Starfleet Academy on Earth. Worf is made Federation Ambassador to the Klingon Empire. Garak returns home to aid in the rebuilding of Cardassia. Nog is promoted to lieutenant (j.g.). Kira returns to her Bajoran rank of colonel and becomes commanding officer of Deep Space 9.

2376

THREE MONTHS LATER

PROLOGUE

At night, when the tunnels of B'hala were empty, dust swept through on tireless winds. The night breezes were relentless in their irregular keening, the soft, lonely sounds trailing over heaps of dry and crumbling soil, lingering in the corners and dark spaces of the long lost city. Like the gentle cries of shades and spirits lamenting the daily disturbances of their tomb.

Sometimes, particularly at night when he couldn't sleep, Jacob Isaac Sisko thought he might like to write about those ancient spirits—a short piece of fiction, or even a poem—but those instances were few and far between. For the first time in years he had put aside his writing padd, and for the time being, at least, he didn't miss it much. Besides, by the end of each day, he was usually too exhausted to do more than eat, pull off his boots, and crawl into his cot, the sheets heavy with dust in spite of the air recycler. His sleep was deep and peaceful, and if he dreamed, he didn't remember upon waking.

Last night, though . . .

He wasn't quite ready to think about that; he concentrated instead on the small patch of dry and faded earth beneath his fingers, on the feel of the brush in his hand as he carefully dusted. Behind him, Prylar Eivos droned on about some of the recent discoveries in the southernmost section of the dig, his ponderous voice seeming to draw the very life out of the tunnel's cool, recycled air. Eivos was a nice enough man, but probably the most dreadfully dry of all the student overseers; the aging monk seemed to be perfectly happy with the sound of his own voice, regardless of whether or not the content was relevant to anything. Jake tuned in for a moment, still brushing at what would almost certainly turn out to be yet another pottery shard.

". . . but there was one figurine among the rest that was carved out of jevonite, which is nothing short of extraordinary," the prylar said, his tone suggesting that he'd devoted great thought to the matter. "As you know, it has always been believed that jevonite could be found only on Cardassia . . ."

Jake tuned out again, paying just enough attention to know when to nod respectfully. From farther down the tunnel he could hear the soft hum of the solids detectors and the repetitive *chunk* of manually worked picks and shovels. They were pleasant sounds, a bright counterpart to the nights of ghostly crying from ancestors not his own. . . .

He *was* feeling a bit on the poetic side lately, wasn't he? It was strange, unearthing fragments from an ancient culture, and stranger still that the culture wasn't even his—

—Dad's, though, in a way, and in the dream—

He shut that thought down before it could get any further, afraid of the concomitant feelings, afraid of what he might uncover. And he realized that, beneath the soft bristles of his brush, a sliver of color had appeared, a dull red against the lighter soil.

Jake waited for a break in Prylar Eivos's oratory.

". . . but then, quantum-dating of the jevonite artifacts unearthed at the site proves indisputably that they actually predate the First Hibetian civilization," the monk stated firmly, and took a deep breath.

"I think I've found it," Jake said quickly.

The prylar smiled, stepping forward and crouching, using the tunnel wall as a support. He pulled his own brush from a fold in his robes and whisked the remaining soil from around the piece with practiced ease. As Jake suspected, it was another broken clay shard. For every intact relic that was uncovered at B'hala, there seemed to be about a billion broken ones.

And they all have to be catalogued.

"Let's see what we have here . . . ah, very good, Jake!" The prylar stepped back, reaching for one of the innumerable trays on the nearby cart. "And how gratifying—it's kejelious, one of the most important materials used during the Sh'dama Age. Have I ever told you about kejelious? I don't know if anyone truly appreciates how versatile it can be, when the liquid ratios are altered . . ."

Jake nodded, smiling, seeing no point in reminding the monk that he'd already heard all about the virtues of the stuff, twice. Eivos really was a nice old guy, and seemed to be genuinely excited about the work—though for the first time in all his weeks at B'hala Jake found himself feeling disappointed, gazing at the slender fragment as the monk eased it from the ground.

Maybe because it's not what you came here to find, his mind whispered, and it was another thought that he pushed away—but not so quickly as he might have only a few days before. Things were changing whether he liked it or not, and though he knew it was inevitable, had known for some weeks, a part of him was still fighting to avoid the next step.

Acceptance.

When the prylar suggested that they break for a meal, Jake was relieved. He hurried away, suddenly eager to be out of the tunnels where the dead were dust and wind, where his father was a ghost that could only be longed for.

It was late in the afternoon before he thought of it again.

The dream, Jake. Last night.

He felt a tingle at the back of his neck, a subtle shiver of remembered dream-reality—something about the wormhole . . .?

Jake sighed, still not sure he wanted to remember. Not sure he was ready, in spite of the fact that he'd been having trouble concentrating for the last several days, really. He was alone in one of the smaller catalog rooms, a constant, soft drone of activity filtering in through several openings that had once been windows; he leaned back in his chair and closed his eyes, breathing deeply.

As far down as they were, second level up from the

tunnels, it was always pleasantly cool, and although a lot of the volunteers preferred to work in the larger, climate-controlled areas, he liked the fresh air. Usually it kept him alert, but he'd been daydreaming since lunch. Well, since breakfast, technically, although working with Prylar Eivos would make an android's mind wander. . . .

Jake opened his eyes and returned his attention to the shard he'd been handling, one of several from the area he thought of as the Kitchens, over at the northeast end of the partially unearthed city. Number, 1601; Designation, C/Utensil. The familiar numbers and keys of the database portable flew; he hardly had to look at the container tag, knowing from the curve and distinctive blue color that it was another one of the goblet sets. He'd catalogued at least thirty of them in the last few days, all from the same coordinates. Standard estimation comments from Prylar Krish, noted date of extraction . . .

. . . and had he been in the wormhole with his father? It seemed so distant, but he thought that the dream had been about him and Dad, together, flying . . .

Jake set the piece of clay aside, knowing that he had to stop dancing away from the truth of things. Away from the gentle physical and mental repetition that his time at B'hala had been about, and towards why he had come.

To accept the fact that I have to go on without him.

The hesitant thought, so simply worded on the page in his mind's eye, struck him as a little trite—but no less true or powerful for that. When no paralyzing sorrow came, he allowed the thought again, accepting the heaviness in his throat and chest. For now, at least, he had to make a life for himself.

It hurt, but there was also a forced quality to it. Or, not forced, but . . . deliberate. He knew what had to happen, what he was supposed to do, but he didn't *feel* it yet.

But Dax said that's normal, didn't she? That it could be a gradual thing, or all at once. Ezri had been very straightforward about what he might experience, telling him not to underestimate or belittle his loss, and to keep his expectations to a minimum. He'd talked to her a few times, before and after leaving the station, carefully skirting any real conversation about his father. When he'd told her about his intention to join the B'hala excavation, she'd suggested that not thinking for a while might be exactly what he needed; in the almost nine weeks since he'd started, Jake had come to agree wholeheartedly.

He'd been invited just about everywhere on Bajor after his father's disappearance. Like Kas, Jake had politely turned down each hopeful request—to speak at schools, to lead prayer groups, to extend blessings over everything from local harvest festivals to the openings of new business ventures. Kasidy had received twice as many offers; he was the Emissary's son, but Kasidy was carrying the Emissary's unborn child, a somehow more miraculous connection. They'd shared a quiet laugh about it the last time they'd talked, some small joke that was more affectionate than funny. Jake loved her for that, and had been glad to see how well she looked. Kasidy had the celebrated pregnancy glow about her, even if her eyes were a little sad.

You're still dancing, Jake, avoiding the inevitable—

Jake scowled at his inner voice. If it was inevitable, why rush? It wasn't like he was on a schedule.

Although he hadn't realized it at the time, getting away from the station had been the best thing he could've done. The initial invitation to visit B'hala had been extended by a branch of the Order of the Temple, the prylars who primarily worked the dig, and had been offered as a chance to experience Bajoran history first-hand. Being the Emissary's son surely had plenty to do with it, but Jake appreciated the less-obvious wording. He knew that B'hala had been a special place for his father. And the fact of it was, the station had been too empty without Dad, and the looks of sympathy—or worse, the well-meant platitudes from the Bajoran segment, about the Emissary's great calling—had only served to remind Jake of just how much he missed his father. Kas had been great, and his friends, especially Ezri and Nog, but B'hala had been what he needed. He'd heard about the volunteer program—usually open only to religious initiates—on the second night of what had started as a four-day visit, and had only been back to the station once, to pick up a few personal items.

He'd had time here. Time to not think, to categorize shards and books, to run artifacts between scholars and techs and prylars and vedeks. In the mornings, there were the digs, while afternoons were usually for cataloging. Occasionally he helped out the students who hand-cleaned and preserved the crumbling stones from the many small temples that dotted the city, each etched with secrets from thousands of years past.

For all the sense of community, there were enough people milling around for Jake to feel anonymous—well, more so than on the station, anyway. Besides the initiate program, there was also a large, semi-organized group of research scientists on site. Mostly they were Bajoran archeologists, although there was a handful of recently arrived Vulcan chronologists and a few assorted off-world theology groups—not to mention a constant trickle of the faithful, devout sightseers who came to pray and meditate in the long shadow of B'hala's central *bantaca*. Jake generally avoided the spire during the daylight hours, as uncomfortable as ever with being recognized—

"Jake Sisko?"

Jake blinked, then smiled amiably at the small Bajoran woman in the doorway. *Speak of the devil,* as his grandfather liked to say. He still felt uneasy with the semi-reverent attitude that so often accompanied his name—when spoken by a Bajoran—but it was actually a relief to have his meandering self-analysis interrupted.

The stranger wore a prylar's robes, and was very obviously a member of the dig; short, silver hair contrasted sharply with her deeply tanned skin, and she had the look of leathery strength that he'd come to associate with the lifelong archeologists who had come to work at B'hala. She didn't look familiar, but there were always new people coming to the city.

"Yes?"

The monk stepped inside, and in the few seconds it took her to cross the room, Jake decided that she was nervous about something. She walked stiffly, her expression polite but blank, her hands clutching at the shoulder strap of a well-worn satchel.

She stopped in front of him and seemed to study his features, her pale eyes intent with some emotion he couldn't place. Jake waited for her to speak, interested; a break in routine, with a vague air of mystery. . . .

Give it up. She probably wants directions, or an entry reading.

The prylar smiled, revealing small white teeth and deeply etched laugh lines. "My name is Istani Reyla. I'm—I was one of the main overseers with Site Extension."

Jake nodded. Beneath the seemingly casual working atmosphere at B'hala was a well-organized system of committees and unions; Site Extension made the decisions about where to dig next and sent in the first documentation people, mostly scientists or vedeks with years of archeological experience. Interesting job; Jake had heard they'd recently excavated the oldest shrine yet discovered, in the ruins beneath B'hala.

"Nice to meet you. What can I help you with?"

The prylar reached into her bag and pulled out a narrow, loosely wrapped bundle, vaguely tube-shaped. The careful way she handed it to him suggested that it was exceptionally valuable or fragile. The package was very light, the cloth it was wrapped in organic and extremely soft.

"It's a . . . document of sorts. Very old. If—it may be—I believe it's important that you—" She grinned suddenly, and shook her head. "I'm sorry, it's been a long week." Her voice was low and musical, and Jake noticed how tired she seemed. There were dark circles under her eyes.

So much for intrigue. He smiled, setting the bundle on the counter in front of him. She seemed nice, if a little odd; *scientists.* "I understand. I have these dishes to go through, and there's a tray of jewelry ahead of you,

11

but I can run it through the translator after that. There's kind of a backlog for the main computer, but if you don't mind a simple text, I should have it done by—"

Prylar Istani shook her head, her grin fading. "No, it's for you. It was written for you, for the son of the Emissary. I believe that unequivocally. Please, don't share it with anyone until you've read it. Whatever you decide to do after that . . ."

She took a deep breath, meeting his gaze squarely. Her own was bright and sincere. "Read it, and think about it. Trust your heart. You'll know what to do."

Without another word, she turned and walked out.

Jake started to stand, then sat down again. *That* was interesting. After nine weeks of quiet and routine, he wasn't sure what to do . . . besides the obvious.

He peeled back the soft, fibrous covering, conscious of his heart beating faster at the sight of the tattered parchment inside. "Very old" was an understatement, though Istani surely knew that. Jake hadn't become an expert by any means, but from his weeks of cataloging, he'd seen enough to make a layman's evaluation. By the uneven texture of the single page and the light shade of ink, it was the oldest document he'd yet handled. And he'd dated writings 23 millennia old.

He looked back at the suddenly boring sprawl of pottery bits he was supposed to finish and decided he couldn't wait. There was a text translation program back at his field shelter, the very one that Jadzia had augmented during that crazy "Reckoning" business over a year ago; new symbols were being added all of the time. He was ahead of schedule, anyway, and it wasn't as though anyone was waiting urgently for his next filing.

He marked where he'd left off with a tag and quickly straightened the work counter, excited about the mini-adventure—until he realized that he was looking forward to telling Dad about it. To seeing his eyes light up with interest, and the slight smile he'd wear as he listened to Jake recount the facts.

Jake took a deep breath, releasing the sorrow and anger as best he could, deciding that he'd worked on his acceptance of truth enough for one day. He had a mystery to unravel—and though he would not have admitted it out loud, he could not help the small but desperate hope that somehow, in some way, whatever he uncovered might tell his heart something about why his father had had to go.

. . . battles fall and fail, and there is a time of waiting, the space between breaths as the land heals and its children retire from war. The Temple welcomes many home, the faithful and the Chosen.

A Herald, unforgotten but lost to time, a Seer of Visions to whom the Teacher Prophets sing, will return from the Temple at the end of this time to attend the birth of Hope, the Infant Avatar. The welcomed Herald shares a new understanding of the Temple with all the land's children. Conceived by lights of war, the alien Avatar opens its eyes upon a waxing tide of Awareness.

The journey to the land hides, but is difficult; prophecies are revealed and hidden. The first child, a son, enters the Temple alone. With the Herald, he returns, and soon after, the Avatar is born. A new breath is drawn and the land rejoices in change and clarity.

Jake rubbed his eyes, wincing at the hot and grainy feel of them, too excited to care much. It was late, hours after he normally went to bed, but he couldn't sleep. He sat at the ancient chipped desk in his small field shelter, the translation and the original in front of him, writing and rewriting the text's story in his mind. He'd lost count of how many times he'd read it, but if it was true . . . if he decided to believe it . . .

. . . everything changes, and how can I not believe it? How can I deny what's in front of me?

He'd already verified an approximate age, making it a credible artifact. To get an exact date, he'd need access to equipment in B'hala's lab complex; they had a sensor there for detecting the degradation of cytoplasmic proteins in plant cells, used specifically for pounded root parchment. It was amazing, how well-preserved most of the ancient Bajoran writings were, the materials treated by some method long lost to Bajor of the present; even the oldest books seemed to have held up better than many stone carvings from only a few centuries ago.

The remnant in front of him was way beyond "old." His tricorder had only been able to run a basic biospectral analysis, but that still put it as written between 30 and 32 millennia ago—putting it in the era of the tablet that had correctly foretold the Reckoning.

And what it says . . . the son goes into the Temple and comes back with the Herald, the lost messenger who communed with the Prophets—and in time to witness the spiritually significant birth of an alien child.

The translator's dictionary said that avatar meant "embodiment of revelation" in the document's context. The word for herald, *"elipagh,"* could also be translated as messenger or proxy, as carrier or bearer of news—and as *emissary.*

The son, him. The *elipagh,* Benjamin Sisko. The

Avatar—Kas and Dad's baby, conceived in wartime, due in . . . five months, give or take. He'd have to get a ship, go into the wormhole by himself . . .

" 'Prophecies are revealed and hidden,' " he said softly, and rubbed his eyes again. Was that meant for him? Did it mean that a revealed prophecy would be hidden, or that there were things that wouldn't be revealed? Maybe it wasn't a prophecy at all; a lot of the ancient writings contradicted one another, or foretold things that had never happened.

But . . . it feels right. True. He wasn't Bajoran, and didn't share the Bajoran faith—but he'd seen and experienced enough not to doubt that the Prophets, whatever they really were, had an interest in the destiny of Bajor, and he knew from his father's encounters with the wormhole beings that feelings counted for a lot. It *felt* true, and he couldn't shake the distinct feeling that he was meant to see it.

Jake shook his head, not sure where to put such an overwhelming thought—that millennia ago, someone had foreseen *him*. And written about it.

He'd already tried to track down the prylar, but she was gone, or hiding. He wanted to know more, to ask her so many things. According to Site Extension, Prylar Istani Reyla had signed herself out for an indefinite leave of absence the day before. She'd been working alone in a newly excavated section of the tunnels, beneath B'hala's foundation. The ranjen Jake had talked to obviously thought highly of her, commenting several times on both her dedication to the Order and her reputation as a scientist. Jake had been careful not to ask too many questions; until he decided what to do, he planned to take Istani's advice.

Think about it, and trust my heart. Easier said than done, when all he could think about was that his father might be waiting, expecting Jake to come and bring him home.

He was too tired to think about much of anything anymore. Jake carefully wrapped the ragged parchment up and slid it into the top drawer of the desk, then stood and stretched. He had to try to get some sleep.

He crawled into bed, tapping the manual light panel at the head of the cot and pulling the dusty coverlet to his chest in the sudden dark. He doubted he'd be able to fall asleep right away, but it was his last coherent thought before he drifted off into an uneasy slumber— and he dreamed again of Dad, dreamed that the two of them were flying through space without a ship, his father laughing and holding his small child's hand as they swam through the infinite black.

The freighter was Cardassian, of an older class, and everyone on board was about to die.

I'm dreaming, Kira thought. She had to be, but the awareness brought no relief. The details were too real, the sensations too vivid. She stood at the entrance of a large cargo bay, the curved and heavy lines of the ship obviously Cardassian, the kind once used to transport laborers and plunder during the Occupation. And in front of her, sprawled amidst the broken crates and overturned bins, were a few dozen raggedly dressed Bajorans and a handful of Cardassian soldiers, gasping for air, many of them already unconscious, bathed in the dull glow of the ship's emergency lights. Life-support failure.

She clamped down on a flutter of panic, inhaling deeply—and though she could breathe easily, she had to clamp down even harder, her senses telling her that she couldn't possibly be asleep. The air was cold and sharp, and she could smell the fading scents of sweat and fear and watery katterpod bean gruel, the smell of the Bajoran camps where she'd spent her short childhood. It was dark, the only light coming from emergency backup, casting everything in deep red shadow, and the only sound—besides the pounding of her heart—was the hopeless, laboring beat of slow asphyxiation, a chorus of strained and pitiful hisses.

She stepped into the storage bay, afraid, struggling to stay calm, to try to make sense of what was happening.

The clothes, the Cardassian's weapons, the very status of the Bajorans—Occupation. And from the bulkiness of the guard's uniforms, probably from before she was born.

Kira stepped further inside, feeling old defenses rise to the surface, grateful for them. Though bloodless, it was as terrible a death scene as any she'd witnessed. Except for the struggle to breathe, nobody moved. Most of the Bajorans had huddled into couples and small groups to die, clinging to one another for whatever pitiful comfort they could find. There were several children, their small, unmoving bodies cradled in the thin arms of their elders. Kira saw a dead woman clutching a pale infant to her breast and looked away, fighting to maintain control. The Cardassian soldiers were in no better shape; they still gripped their weapons but were obviously helpless to use them, their gray, reptilian faces more ashen than they should have been, their mouths opening and closing uselessly. The image of fish out of water came to her, and wouldn't go away.

Kira turned in a circle, dizzy from the helpless terror she saw reflected in so many eyes, so many more glazing as they greeted death—and saw something so unlikely that the disaster's full impact finally gripped her, sank its dark teeth into her and held on tightly.

Two young men, slumped together against the wall to her right, their stiffening arms around each other in a last desperate need for solace, for the consolation of another soul with whom to meet the lonely shadows of death. One was Bajoran. The other, a Cardassian.

What's happening, why is this happening? Her composure was slipping, the things she saw all wrong—foreign to her mind and spirit, a nightmare from without her consciousness. She was lost in some place she had never known, witnessing the final, wrenching moments of people she'd never met. *Stop, this has to stop, wake up, Nerys, wake* up.

A new light filtered through her haze of near-panic. It filled the room, coming from somewhere above and toward the back of the cavernous space. It was the pale blue light she'd always thought of as miraculous and beautiful, the light of the Prophets. Now it threw strange shadows over the dying faces of the doomed men, women, and children, combining with the emergency lights to paint everything a harsh purple.

She felt herself drawn toward the source of the light, breathing the air of her youth. For some reason, she couldn't pinpoint the light's origin. It was bright enough, and well defined—but there was a sort of haze at the back of the bay, obscuring the exact location. It was like looking at a sun from under deep water, the light source shifting and unsteady, far away. Kira walked on—and then she was in the haze, like a mist of darkness, and the light was as bright as a star's, only a few meters in front of her.

Nerys.

A voice, spoken or thought, she wasn't sure, but there was no doubting its owner—and there he was, emerging from the dark like a spirit, like a *borhya*. He stepped in front of the light and was enveloped by it, his face serene and aware, his deep gaze searching for hers. The Emissary, Captain Sisko. Benjamin.

He's been waiting for me. . . .

Colonel Kira . . .

Kira, this is

". . . is Security. Colonel?"

"Go ahead," Kira croaked, and opened her eyes as she bolted up, instantly awake. Her room. Her bed. A man's voice on the com . . . Devro?

Dream, just a dream but it was so—

"I'm sorry to wake you, Colonel, but there's been an attack on board the station." It was definitely Devro, newly assigned to security, and he sounded excited.

Kira sat up, blinking, forcing herself to leave the dream behind. "What happened?"

"Ah, I don't have the details, Colonel, but it appears that at least one person was killed, possibly two. The lieutenant said that she'd meet you at Medical D."

Autopsy facilities. Kira felt a rush of anger. Quark's, it had to be, and he was going to be sorry this time. There had been several drunken riots in his place in the past few months; no fatalities, but it had only been a matter of time. Just two weeks before, a female Argosian had stabbed one of Quark's servers for mixing up a drink order. He'd been lucky to survive.

I told him to start cutting them off earlier . . . and where the hell was security? After I specifically ordered higher visibility on the Promenade?

"On my way," she said, and Devro signed off. The computer informed her that it was 0530, only a half hour before she had to get up, anyway. She swung her feet to the floor but sat for a moment, eyes closed. Bad news after a bad dream, after a whole series of bad days. Frustrating ones, anyway, with the station's overhaul running past schedule; she had enough to do without having to worry about the continuing stream of die-hard revelers on the station, still looking for a party to celebrate the end of the war. Or having to babysit her new security chief, a woman to whom inconstancy was no stranger.

She dressed quickly, her anxiety growing as her mind began to work, as she woke up and considered the possibility that Quark's had nothing to do with the incident. Maybe she should talk to Jast about trying again to request a few additional security details from Starfleet, just until things settled a little. . . .

. . . *wishful thinking. Might as well have her ask for a few dozen Starfleet engineers while she's at it, and the backup tactical and science cadets to fill out the duty rosters, not to mention medical.* They'd have as much luck requesting a new station made out of gold-pressed latinum. The Federation's postwar reconstruction efforts meant that Starfleet's resources were spread thin, almost to the point of being ineffectual in some places. Not to mention their humanitarian work, the aid being extended to independent worlds and cultures that had been damaged by the war. Politically, it made sense— the new allies and friends they were making meant potential new Federation members, and if that meant that facilities like DS9 had to run overextended and under-staffed for a while longer—well, those facilities would just have to make do with what they had.

Some of us more than others. As if they didn't have enough to do, DS9 had also been designated the official coordinator for the multi-societal relief efforts to Cardassia, which meant extra work for everyone on staff. With supply and aid ships from over a dozen worlds arriving and departing daily—supplemented by an ever-changing number of freelance "ships for hire"—there seemed to be a near-constant stream of problems great and small. Add to that a strange new emotional climate on the station, like nothing the colonel had ever experienced. Although Kira had faith in the good intentions of her people, with the overwhelming majority of the station's nearly 7500 inhabitants being Bajoran, she wasn't so certain that DS9 was the best choice for the restoration effort, regardless of their position and capacity.

First Minister Shakaar had disagreed, arguing that Bajor's willingness to take point in the relief efforts would be an important step toward rapprochement with the Cardassians . . . as well as in Bajor's renewed petition to join the Federation. "Besides, Nerys," Shakaar had said, "you were there. You saw what it was like. How can we *not* help them?"

The question, so gently asked, had left Kira unable to argue as she recalled the carnage and destruction the Dominion had wrought. There was a time, she knew, when she might have looked on Cardassia's fate as a kind of poetic justice. But thinking back on the blackened, smoking ruins, the corpses that lay everywhere, the shocked and vacant faces of the survivors . . . It was no longer possible to view them as the enemy that had raped Bajor for half a century.

But while convincing Kira of the role that Bajor, and

DS9 especially, was to play in the healing of Cardassia had been relatively easy . . . the Bajoran populace was another matter. A Bajoran installation providing aid to the Cardassian homeworld? Irony was seldom so obvious, and the atmosphere of reluctant, often grudging charity from some of the Bajorans aboard the station was less than ideal.

At least Starfleet had given her Tiris Jast. The commander had already proven herself able to work miracles when it came to administrative matters, among other things; after a somewhat rocky start, Kira's new first officer had turned out to be a definite asset.

It wasn't until Kira checked herself in the mirror on the way out the door that she thought about the dream again, and was surprised by the sudden loneliness she felt, the loneliness she saw in her tired reflection. *Was it just a dream? And if it wasn't, what meaning was she supposed to take from it?*

It would have been nice to talk to Benjamin again, under any circumstances. . . .

"Get moving, Colonel," she said softly, straightening her shoulders, her gaze hardening. She was the commanding officer of Starbase Deep Space 9, arguably the single most important outpost in the Alpha Quadrant, and there was a matter on board requiring her immediate attention. How she felt about it—or anything, lately—was of secondary consideration.

Will of the Prophets, she told herself, and taking a deep breath, she stepped out of her quarters and started for Mid-Core.

The colonel marched in looking alert and fully rested, like always, making Ro Laren wonder—and not for the first time—if the woman ever slept. Ro herself had been dragged out of bed on four hours of sleep, and was feeling it; her days of catching a few moments here and there and calling it even were long gone.

"Report, Lieutenant."

Brisk and efficient, undoubtedly Kira's finest qualities; Ro could respect her, at least. Too bad it didn't seem to be mutual.

"At this point, it appears to be a botched robbery attempt," Ro said. "Two dead, the victim and the perpetrator, both Bajoran civilians. Dr. Bashir is conducting the autopsies—"

"Where did it happen?" Kira interrupted. "The attack?"

"Promenade, in front of Quark's. I've got people talking to the witnesses now . . ."

The colonel's eyes had narrowed slightly, and Ro hurried on, remembering their last terse encounter. "There was a strong security presence in and around Quark's, as you, ah, *suggested,* but it didn't seem to matter. He stabbed the woman in front of a crowd, took her bag, and ran. Two of my deputies chased him to the second level, where he attempted to jump one of the railings. He fell badly, he died."

Kira nodded. "Who was he?"

"We don't have an ID yet. He came to the station yesterday, but apparently he was using a false name. He wasn't much of a thief, whoever he was; there was nothing in her bag but a few personal items. The woman was a monk, a Prylar Istani Reyla; she'd only been here two days, which makes me wonder if he somehow came after her specifically—"

Ro broke off, surprised at the change in Kira's demeanor. The color had drained from her face, and her eyes were wide and shocked.

"Reyla? Istani Reyla?" Kira whispered.

Ro nodded, uncomfortably aware that Kira knew the victim. "Yes. Colonel . . . are you all right?"

Kira didn't answer. She turned and walked away, headed for the door that led into the autopsy room. Ro hesitated, then followed her, wondering if she should say something else. Something comforting. She and Kira didn't get along, but they weren't exactly enemies, either. Shar had been pushing the idea that they were too much alike—both strong, stubborn Bajoran women with histories of following their own rules. . . .

. . . and if I was also judgmental and blindly pious, we'd definitely have something in common.

Ro sighed inwardly as she stepped into the autopsy room, reminding herself that she'd rarely been accused of open-mindedness. Besides, she'd only been on the station for six weeks, and although she didn't feel the need to prove herself to the many doubters on board— and doubted herself that it was possible—she was aware that even a grudging acceptance would take time.

Dr. Bashir was speaking softly, standing over Istani's body as Kira stared down numbly at the woman's still face. Ragged circles of blood radiated from several wounds in the old woman's chest, staining her monk's robes a dark, shining crimson.

". . . several times, and with an erose blade. The atrioventricular node was destroyed, effectively severing neuromuscular communication between the chambers of the heart. Even if I'd been standing by with a surgical team, it's unlikely that she could have been saved."

Ro saw the pain in Kira's wet gaze and immediately

regretted her unkind thoughts. It was the first time she'd seen the colonel display any emotion beyond impatient irritation, at least in front of her, and it had the instant effect of making her want to leave, to allow Kira some privacy with her pain. If Ro had just lost a friend, she'd hope for the same consideration.

Kira reached out and gently touched Istani's face with the back of her hand. Bashir's demeanor changed abruptly, from subdued respect to open concern.

"Nerys, did you know her?"

Kira's hand trembled against Istani's slack cheek. "At the camps, when I was a child. At Singha. She was a good friend to my parents, and after my mother left . . . she was a good friend. She watched out for us."

The doctor's voice became even softer. "I'm so sorry. If it's any help to you, I don't believe she suffered."

The three of them stood for a moment, Bashir's words lingering in the cool, sterile air, Ro feeling out of place as a witness to Kira's grief. She was about to excuse herself when the colonel began to speak again, almost to herself.

"I've been meaning to contact her, it's been . . . five years? The last time we spoke, she was on her way to Beta Kupsic, for an archeological dig."

Ro couldn't stop herself. "Do you know when she got back?"

Kira looked up and seemed to collect herself, straightening away from the body. "Just before the Peldor Festival, I think, for the Meditation for Peace; the Vedek Assembly called everyone home. That was five months ago."

Ro nodded, biting her tongue. She knew when the Peldor Festival was. "Did you know she was coming here? To the station?"

Kira shook her head. There was another awkward silence, for Ro, at least, and then the colonel turned to her, seeming entirely in control once more. "I expect a full investigation, Lieutenant, and I want to know what you find as soon as you find it. I'll expect your initial report before the end of the day."

"Yes, sir," Ro said. Her first real case; a flutter of anxiety touched her and was gone. She was ready.

"If there's anything I can do . . ." Bashir started.

The colonel managed a faint smile. "Thank you, Julian. I'll be fine."

She nodded briskly at Ro and walked out of the room without a backward glance, as composed as when she'd entered.

She had to admire the woman's self-control. Ro had lived through resettlement camps, and knew something about the kinds of bonds that could be forged under dire conditions. When she was with the Maquis, too . . . the friends she had made and lost . . .

"Was there something else you needed, Lieutenant?"

Not impolite by any means, but the doctor's voice had lost its former warmth. She supposed she should be grateful it wasn't open hostility; her history with Starfleet wasn't going to win her any friends among its personnel.

"No, thank you, Doctor. I'm sure your report will answer any questions I might have."

Bashir smiled civilly and picked up a padd, turning away. Her cue. Ro started to leave, but couldn't help a final look at Istani Reyla. Such gentle character in the lines around her eyes and mouth; to have survived the camps and the war, to have lived a life devoted to humble faith, only to die in a robbery . . .

What would a prylar have worth stealing? Worth being murdered for?

That was the question, wasn't it? Istani's bag was locked up in the security office, and Ro decided that she needed to take a closer look at its contents. She wasn't going to give anyone a reason to doubt her appointment to DS9; they didn't have to like her, any of them, but she *would* do her job, and do it well.

"Doctor," she said, as way of good-bye, and left him to his work.

Kira was on the lift to ops when it hit her. She acted without thinking, slamming her fist into the wall once, twice, the skin breaking across two of her knuckles. No pain, or at least nothing close to the boiling darkness inside of her, the acid of sorrow and loneliness grasping at her heart. She was sick with it. Reyla, dead. Murdered.

She let out a low moan and sagged against the wall, cradling her wounded hand. For a second, it threatened to overwhelm her, all of it—Reyla; the dream, like some dark omen; the fading memory of Odo's arms around her when she felt alone, so alone . . .

. . . deal with it. You don't have time for this, and you will deal with it, and everything will be as it should be, have faith, have faith . . .

Kira took a few deep breaths, talking herself through it, letting go . . . and by the time she reached ops she was through the very worst of it, and prepared to bear the weight of another day.

2

Although he was only three minutes late, Kasidy was already waiting when Bashir got to the infirmary, sitting on the edge of one of the diagnostic tables and chatting with Dr. Tarses.

". . . and I'll want to do some planting in the spring," Kasidy was saying, her back to Bashir as he approached. "Kava, I think. If I'm not too fat to bend over by then."

Bashir noted the readout over the bed with a practiced eye as he joined them, pleased with the slight weight gain since her last checkup. Perfectly within normal human parameters. "In five months you'll be big as a runabout, I imagine," he said. "Bending over shouldn't be a problem, though standing back up might take work."

His listeners laughed, and Julian felt his spirits lift. Getting up early to conduct autopsies was not his idea of a pleasant morning, and for Kira's friend to have been murdered . . .

Poor Nerys. Bad enough to lose someone important, but practically, the timing couldn't be worse. Kira wasn't always good at delegating responsibility, too often overburdening herself, and the current upgrades to the station were no exception. With the Federation and Bajor both re-organizing their resources and personnel—along with practically everyone else in the Alpha Quadrant—DS9 had been operating understaffed anyway; technical support personnel were in short supply, and even with Jast to take over arrangements with Starfleet, Kira wasn't smiling as much as she used to. The look on her face when she'd touched her friend . . .

. . . *Ezri should speak to her, professionally. Assuming she can find the time in the next year or two.*

The slightly sour thought surprised him, although only until he remembered the reason. Ezri had already been gone when he'd gotten the call that woke him, off to help Nog with some engineering conundrum. Again. Funny, how quickly he'd gotten used to having her beside him when he woke. And how much he missed her when she wasn't there.

Tarses handed over the shift report and said his good-byes, leaving them in relative privacy. Both nurses on duty, Bajorans, stayed a respectful distance away—although he would have to speak to them about the beaming glances they couldn't seem to help shooting in Kasidy's direction. He knew that the Emissary's wife didn't care much for the attention, resigned to it or no.

Julian pulled up a chair and sat, calling up Kasidy's charts on a widescreen padd. It had been two weeks since he'd seen her last, for a topical rash she'd picked up on her last run to the Orias system. It had turned out to be an extremely mild allergic reaction to a shipment of Rakalian *p'losie* that had gone bad, thanks to a malfunctioning refrigeration unit.

"So. Tell me how you're feeling these days." He glanced at her hands. "No more bumps, I see. I assume you're staying away from Rakalian fruit?"

Kasidy nodded, smiling. "Absolutely. In fact, I'm staying away from the cargo holds altogether. Other than that, let's see . . . I feel pretty good, I guess. Still no more morning sickness. I'm a little tired, even though it seems like I'm sleeping at least ten hours a night. Oh, and I've recently developed a craving for anything made with ginger root, of all things."

Julian ran the bed's diagnostic against a hand-held tricorder's as she spoke, careful to keep the screen away from her line of sight; Kasidy insisted on keeping to a family tradition regarding ignorance of gender prior to birth. The child's sex was listed in the upper left corner, along with the series of numbers that suggested textbook normal development for the fourth month. Both she and the child were doing remarkably well.

"I guess I shouldn't be surprised," Kasidy continued. "Ben loved ginger. He said . . ." Her smile faded slightly, her hands moving to her belly. "He said there was no such thing as a good stir-fry without ginger."

Julian nodded, setting aside his tricorder and focusing his full attention on Kasidy. "I remember. He made it for me once, with Bajoran shrimp. It was wonderful."

Kasidy smiled crookedly, still holding her lower belly. "I've been thinking I should take up cooking. I never wanted to, before, but I set up the kitchen just like he wanted. It seems a shame to let it go to waste."

Sisko's dream house, in the Kendra province on

Bajor. He'd bought the land just before the end of the war, and Kasidy had decided to build the home he'd designed and live there until his return. Through Kira, Julian knew that she'd agonized over the kitchen, about everything from whether or not to put in a dividing wall to what kind of appliances Sisko would want.

"It's finished already?" Julian asked. "Last I heard, there was some problem finding the right kind of, ah, cooking device."

"Quark came through," Kasidy said. "Don't ask me where he found it, either. Original wood stoves are hard to come by these days. As for the rest of the house, you'd be surprised how quickly things go when everyone on the planet wants you to get settled in."

"That's all right with you, isn't it?" Julian asked gently.

"Most of the time. They care about him, too, in their own way."

She seemed a bit melancholy, but not actually depressed. Under the circumstances, it was the best he could hope for. Having one's love whisked away to fulfill his own spiritual destiny couldn't be easy, particularly with a baby on the way. Love could be such a tenuous thing, running from emotional ecstasy to fear of loss and back again in a matter of days, hours, really. There were times he felt so connected to Ezri, so elated with what they had, that it was hard to accept the distance that could grow up between them sometimes, as sudden and strange as . . .

". . . a robbery on board. Julian?"

He started. "I'm sorry, I'm a bit distracted this morning. You were saying?"

"I said that the station seems different now. Even

dangerous sometimes. Did you hear about the robbery?"

"Yes. Two people were killed, I'm sorry to say."

Kasidy shook her head. "There are just so many strangers here, lately. I really think this move will be good for me. For us."

Julian smiled. "I think that anything that makes you happy will be good for you, and the baby."

She patted the swell beneath her fingers. "Me, too. Another two weeks and we'll be setting up house. We'll be visiting a lot—I'm still part-time with the Commerce Ministry, at least until the big day—but Bajor will be home."

A positive note to end on. He stood up, and was about to tell her to check in before she left, when she asked him a question he wasn't sure how to answer.

"So, distracted, huh? How *are* things going with Ezri?"

"I'm—fine. Well, I think." He felt suddenly flustered, and sat down again. Kasidy's kind expression was inviting, and he hadn't really had a chance to talk about his relationship since—since Miles had left.

Has it really been that long? He shared so much with Ezri, it hadn't occurred to him to talk *about* her with anyone. And things were going well, weren't they?

Julian took a deep breath, and started talking. And quickly discovered that he had more to say than he thought.

As usual, there was a lull in business as the last of the late-night drinkers straggled out and the early breakfast crowd chirped in, but there was a fifteen per-

cent drop from the day before, which meant Quark
wasn't happy. It was those damned security guards,
hassling his clientele and the staff for details about the
murder. Not only had he lost half of his breakfasters to
T'Pril's—although why someone would dare Vulcan
cuisine first thing in the morning was anyone's guess—
he'd had to offer several of his less reputable customers
free drinks just to keep them from fleeing. So when he
saw Ro Laren walk into the bar, he wasn't nearly as
charming as usual; as entirely awe-inspiring as she
was, fifteen percent was enough to shrivel his lobes.

"How about you tell your people to leave my customers alone?" he snapped, in lieu of a greeting. "If I
remember correctly—and I do—the incident occurred
outside, on the Promenade. Not in here."

Ro sat at the bar, her lean body bent toward him, a
slight, curling smile playing across her lips. "And a
good morning to you, Quark. Would you do me a favor
and take a look at this?"

Still smiling, she dropped a slip of paper on the bar
and leaned back, crossing her arms. Quark ignored the
slip and studied her for a moment, not sure what she
was up to. He'd heard a lot of interesting things about
Ro, of course, practically everyone on the station had,
but he hadn't had much of a chance to interact with her
on a professional level. From the stories that had preceded her arrival, he'd expected DS9's new head of security to run around throwing tantrums, stealing
Federation supplies, and shooting people—but so far
she'd been a disappointment, employing almost Odo-
like tactics to interfere with his less than legal enter-
prises. She'd already managed to re-route several
contraband shipments, and with Rom gone and Nog too

busy to help his own uncle, Quark had been forced to actually buy a program to further randomize his security code generator.

At least Ro doesn't gloat about it. And unlike her predecessor, she's not in love with Kira. Nowhere close. The friction between the two women was already well-established, a definite point in her favor; between that and her looks, Quark wasn't quite prepared to write her off as a liability.

"Of course," he said, picking up the slip of paper and mustering his most seductive smile. "Anything for you, Lieutenant—"

He saw what was on the slip and his smile froze; his name and a series of numbers, written by that Bajoran monk. She'd promised that she would commit her storage code to memory and destroy the hard-copy scrap, but it seemed she'd gone and died before getting around to it. Aware of Ro's close scrutiny, he casually dropped it on the bar and shrugged, silently cursing. The woman was dead, but there was his reputation to consider.

"Doesn't mean a thing to me. Where did you say you found it?"

"I didn't."

He waited, but she didn't elaborate any further, only gazed at him serenely, ever smiling. Quark shrugged again, wondering how much she actually knew.

And to think, my nephew could have been security chief . . .

"I really have no idea," Quark said finally. "Maybe she was going to meet someone here, that's why it says my name, and those numbers—could mean a time . . ."

He realized his mistake before Ro could point it out, and did his best to cover. He had to start getting to bed earlier; these late nights were killing him. "I mean, I assume this is something about that murdered woman. Isn't it?"

"Give it up, Quark. I found it in her bag and you know it, and you also know what it means." Her dark eyes sparkled. "You already owe me for not telling Kira about that shipment of phaser scopes."

Quark feigned innocence. "What phaser scopes? Really, Lieutenant, I don't know—"

Ro moved so fast he didn't have time to react, reaching across the bar and taking a firm hold of both his ears—not hard enough to hurt, but pain was imminent. Quark froze, shocked, afraid to breathe. She leaned over, so close that her soft voice tickled his left tympanic membrane, arousing in him a strange combination of excitement and terror. Her tone was as firm and unyielding as her grasp.

"Listen carefully, Quark," she half-whispered, sweet and deadly at once. "I don't have a problem with your petty schemes to make money, and unless you're dealing in something dangerous or unethical, I'm often as not willing to look the other way. I'm not Kira and I'm not Starfleet and a victimless crime is just that, right? But if you don't tell me what I want to know when I ask for it, I'll teach you new meanings of the word 'sorry.' And what I want to know right now is what *you* know about Istani Reyla. Make no mistake, this is not open to negotiation."

She abruptly let go, leaving him stunned but unhurt, and in the time it took him to catch his breath, Quark decided two things: one, that it was in his best interests to tell her about the monk—she'd really only paid him a pittance, anyway—and two, he was halfway in love.

Kasidy walked back to her quarters slowly, thinking about Dax and the doctor. She didn't know either of them as well as Ben had, especially Dax. . . .

. . . *but some things never change, and probably never will. Ah, love!*

Kasidy grinned. The look on Julian's face had been so sincere, so entirely heartfelt as he talked about Ezri, and the "problems" so normal. He worried that they thought differently about some things, and said she sometimes seemed bored by his work. He felt lonely sometimes, and didn't know what she was thinking. He said she wanted to be alone occasionally, and that he did, too, but was afraid for them to spend too much time apart. Every now and then, he felt overwhelmed by emotion for her—and every now and then, she got on his nerves, and what did *that* mean?

The brilliant doctor was certainly clueless in some ways, and Kasidy suspected that Ezri, for all her lifetimes, was probably on the same ship. They were in love, that was all. In love and finding out what that meant, once the initial shine wore off. Falling in love was easy; maintaining a relationship was work, no matter how emotionally or intellectually developed the participants were, and it wasn't always fun.

"I just want us to be happy. I don't want things to become dull for her. Or me," Bashir had stated, so honestly that Kasidy had been hard-pressed to keep a straight face. And he'd been visibly distressed by her advice, that there was no way to set everything up in advance, to avoid mistakes before they happened—that it would take time to learn about each other, to let things unfold.

In a way, being smart probably made it harder; Kasidy imagined that they were both trying to reason out their differences, to logically define their roles in each other's lives. To decide how to feel.

And nothing's more frustrating than having feelings you didn't decide to have.

Kasidy stopped walking, struck by the intensity of the memory. Ben had said that, not long after they'd become a regular thing. He'd been teasing her about something, she couldn't remember what, exactly, although she recalled that they'd been in bed together, talking. He had a way of doing that, of gently pointing out to her the most basic truths in life—things that she'd learned, that they'd both learned but sometimes misplaced. It was the miracle of their time together, that capacity for understanding the truth that they'd been able to share. . . .

The sense of loss flooded through her, so like a physical pain that she had to close her eyes. *Oh, baby, I know you had to go, but I miss you so much, I want you here, with me—*

Kasidy felt tears threatening, and hurriedly walked on, firmly telling herself that she would not cry, would *not,* not in public. She even managed a smile and a nod for a Bajoran couple passing by. She'd had no real choice in the matter about giving Ben up to the Prophets, but her feelings about it, at least, she could keep as her own.

My feelings. As if anyone else would want them.

It had become a full-time job for her just to keep track, so many things were changing. The connection she already felt with the baby wouldn't allow her to be truly unhappy; she was already in love with the small life, and that love kept her from descending into real sorrow—but in all, it was a very strange time for her. Most days she felt strong, positive about a future that would allow for her and Ben to be with each other, with Jake and with their child. But there were also moments that she felt a kind of emptiness inside, a fear for what could be—that too much time would pass and he would return a stranger to her, their paths so far apart that they wouldn't even be able to see each other. He was with the Prophets, after all, experiencing things she couldn't begin to imagine. And as the Emissary, what if he came back and then was called away again? What further sacrifices might they have to make? When those thoughts welled up, she felt like everything she was doing was madness—leaving her job, moving away from everything she'd known to wait for a man who might not return for months, even years. . . .

. . . *and that's okay. That's okay because my life will be as full as I want it to be, because I had a life before I met Benjamin Sisko and I have a life now.* Two lives, she amended happily, and felt the slow, heavy warmth in her lower belly, where their child slept and grew. . . .

Her hormones were certainly in an uproar. She felt vulnerable to herself, to the wanderings of her own mind in a way she never had been before. It was almost funny; from amusement to tears and back again, in the time it took her to walk from the turbolift to her quarters. She thought she might be able to relax once she actually moved off the station and got settled on Bajor. She could hope, anyway.

As she walked into her quarters, she realized suddenly that she was tired. Tired and in a state of mild chaos. She was a strong, independent woman, on the verge of beginning a new life for herself—but at the moment, she thought she might like to go back to bed.

Maybe with a cup of tea, and some of those ginger cookies . . .

That sounded good. Kasidy yawned, and decided that there wasn't anything on her slate that couldn't be put off for another couple of hours. If she could nap, get away from her own turbulent moods for a little while, so much the better.

"Oh, kid," she said, smiling, patting her lower belly as she headed for the replicator. "You're really something else."

3

The colonel had not been happy with the status reports, although Shar had the impression she just wasn't happy, not this morning. He'd hardly finished listing the various systems and subsystems that were still off-line before she'd disappeared into her office, and she hadn't come out again. Not that he could blame her, given how things were progressing.

Short-range shield emitters, down. Tractor beam emitters, down. Six of the RCS thruster modules were being re-paneled, almost half of the ODN system still needed re-wiring, and the entire computer network was running on one processing core without backup. In short, the station was barely functional.

Shar sat cross-legged on the floor of the engineering station next to a partially disassembled console checking plasma power levels and half-wishing he hadn't offered to work a double shift. He didn't need as much sleep as most—about half as much as a human or Bajoran—but it had been a long week and he was tired. The constant low-level drone of conversation, of tools clattering and the occasional soft curse, was making him sleepy, and he could honestly say he'd run enough system diagnostics to last him a lifetime. Everything had to be checked and triple-checked.

This climate isn't helping much, either. The station's common areas were set to 22 degrees Celsius, 18 percent humidity; cold and dry by Andorian standards, making him long for the comfort of his quarters. Even after Starfleet Academy and a year on the *U.S.S. Tamberlaine*—with a primarily human crew—he still couldn't get used to the environmental conditions.

Shar tapped a key on the padd next to him and saw that he still had two hours to go. He briefly considered finishing with the console and leaving early—Kira and Jast had both urged him to take on half-shifts, if he insisted on working extra hours—but a look around made him decide against it. Everywhere, stacks of partially wired sensor panels leaked from gaping console chasms, the men and women in front of them certainly as tired as he. They were already three days past the original deadline for finishing, and he estimated it would be another four before everything was back up and running. And that wasn't including the *Defiant;* Lieutenant Nog's last report had suggested at least another week.

If the SCE would just send a few more people . . . Typically, DS9 boasted thirty-five resident engineers from the corps, plus an affiliate group of almost as many techs from the Bajoran Militia. But in spite of Starfleet's assurances about more help coming soon, the station had been running with less than half that number since the war's end. Anyone with any engineering experience was being put to work.

Including Ensign Thirishar ch'Thane, science officer; if that isn't desperate, nothing is. He wasn't an egotistical person, or at least he hoped not, though he was aware of his worth in his field—top of his class, already published several times over, and assigned to DS9 just four weeks earlier; only his second assignment, too. When he'd first graduated from the Academy, he'd been fought over by some of the best Starfleet scientists working. But he wouldn't pretend to be any mechanical genius; when it came to the physical application of his abilities, he thought "clumsy" was probably most apt.

"Taking a break from your troubles, Ensign?"

Shar started, realizing he'd been staring blankly. He looked up into the teasing gaze of Commander Jast and smiled, pleased to see her, to hear her distinctively accented voice. Although she was considered cold by some, he liked Tiris Jast; there was something about her, something inspiring. She projected strength and confidence, as would any good commander, but there was also an unapologetic frankness in her manner that was rare in higher-ranking Starfleet officers. She openly discussed her feelings as well as her ideas, and not for any effect; she appeared to simply believe in expressing herself, whether or not it was diplomatic to do so. An interesting person and a superb officer, Shar considered himself fortunate to be working with her.

Besides which, she knows what it's like to suffer these conditions. Jast was Bolian, but came from a similar environment. In the short time that he'd been aboard, they'd commiserated more than once over the chill aridity of the station.

"Commander. No, sir. I'm just a little tired, nearing the end of my shift."

Jast shook her head. "Your second, I imagine. What have I said to you about working doubles?"

Shar nodded, trying to recall the exact phrasing. "That I'll end up freeze-dried if I don't get back to my quarters occasionally. Sir."

"That's correct." Jast glanced around, then leaned closer to Shar, speaking low. "I know things are in disarray . . . but I think you could probably slip away, if you hurry. No one is looking."

Shar grinned, fully aware that she was granting him permission to end his shift early, and relieved that he was starting to recognize it when she was being humorous. Jast was like that; she could be as officially Starfleet as they came when necessary, but didn't flaunt her rank once she became acquainted with those under her command. Or at least in his observation.

"If it's all right, sir, I think I'll stay. The colonel wanted to get as much of ops finished today as possible."

Jast nodded toward the science station, where several people were working. "Remind me why you're not handling the sensor arrays, Shar."

Shar held up his hands, flexing his long—but somehow incapable—fingers. "The work is a bit too delicate for me. I'm sort of acting as a . . . technical consultant."

"Sir," Jast added, her eyes twinkling. "You'll get better with practice, Ensign. Perhaps you should take up a musical instrument, or some sort of cloth-weaving. Work on improving your dexterity."

"Yes, sir." Now he wasn't sure if she was being serious or not. Humor was still difficult for him. Andorians smiled often, but primarily looked upon it as a diplomatic tool; they were a serious-minded people, and he was no exception. From his time in Starfleet, however, he'd come to appreciate humor in other species, whereas most Andorians viewed too much laughter as frivolity. Or witlessness.

The commander certainly *seemed* amused. "Carry on, Ensign. And no more extra shifts for a few days, all right?"

"Yes, Commander. Thank you, sir."

Jast headed for Kira's office and Shar picked up the diagnostic padd again, glad that she'd taken the time to speak with him. Although still quite new to the station, he already liked everyone he'd met—Jast, Colonel Kira, Ro Laren, Ezri and Prynn and Turo Ane . . . Even Quark, whose hard-hearted reputation preceded him, had been very friendly, going out of his way to offer discounts on Andorian delicacies in his bar. Shar was pleased with his assignment to DS9, and hoped very much that he wouldn't be forced to leave.

The thought was a shadow, a darkness. He pushed it away and went back to work, losing himself in the simplicity of the display screen's tolinite matrix, tired but happy to be where he was.

Kira was on an audio channel with the *Aldebaran*'s first officer, a pleasantly efficient woman named Tisseverlin Janna. After giving the lieutenant commander an update on station repairs and a rundown on expected arrivals and departures, Kira dutifully listened as Janna briefly went over the day's scheduled off-duty boarding parties. She also had several questions about the station's environmental control capabilities, particularly in the holosuites. The *Aldebaran*'s two Denebian crewmembers were up for leave, and were hoping to be able to get out of their suits for a while; it seemed the *Aldebaran*'s holo facilities couldn't manage the intense conditions they required for more than an hour at a time.

"I'm sure Quark has a program," Kira offered, her voice sounding far away, as if someone else was speaking. "We had a freighter crew come through just a couple of months ago, and they had a Denebian on board. He spent a lot of time at Quark's."

Janna said something about how grateful the two ensigns would be, and started telling an anecdote about one of their suits leaking heated slime in the captain's ready room, but with their business concluded, Kira's thoughts were already elsewhere. She liked Janna, but she wasn't in the mood to talk. She needed to work, to move, to not dwell on Reyla. A friendly chat would bring her too close to letting her guard down, and having to force polite laughter was probably beyond her current capabilities. Although she'd gotten a lot better at it since taking command, diplomacy had never been her strong suite.

When Jast showed up for their daily progress meeting, Kira, relieved, apologized for having to cut Janna's story short and quickly signed off. Jast waited patiently, padd in hand, looking as composed and calm as always.

"Good morning, Colonel," Jast said. "I'm sorry I didn't get here sooner, I spent the last few hours dealing with the *Defiant*'s computer refit. Have you had a chance to look over Nog's proposal for expanding the tactical capacity? You know, I was concerned when I first met him, he's so young, but his ideas are quite innovative."

Kira nodded. "He inherited something of his father's technological genius."

"Ah, the Grand Nagus. Rom, isn't it?"

Kira nodded again. *What do I say about the murder? How do I start?*

Jast accidentally saved her, her bright countenance fading to solemn. "I haven't had a chance to read any reports on what happened this morning, but Ezri mentioned it. Terrible. Anything Starfleet should know, or was it a civilian matter?"

Kira cleared her throat. "Ro is looking into it. At this point, there doesn't seem to be any motive beyond robbery."

"Good. It's a sorrowful affair, but with the state of things, we don't need another Federation complication. I've already worn out my welcome with Starfleet on our behalf; they keep telling me that we'll just have to wait for more techs, that with the *Aldebaran* keeping watch we don't need to hurry with the weapons arrays . . ."

Kira felt she was putting up a good front, but Jast must have seen something. She frowned, the raised ridge that ran down the center of her face wrinkling. "Colonel . . . what is it? What's wrong?"

With the huge responsibilities that they shared, the commander had become a friend in a relatively short period. Jast had been hard to get used to at the beginning, their relationship initially somewhat adversarial, but Tiris had finally relaxed. She'd made an effort to see how things worked at a deep space station, and started accommodating. Kira had come to respect the woman's honesty and sincerity, and thought Jast was coming to feel the same.

On the other hand, she and Jast were still at the foundation level of a friendship, and . . . it just didn't feel right, not yet. Besides, Kira had come to pride herself on the high degree of professionalism she had reached with all of her new officers; it made things easier, having a clean separation between the private and professional areas of her life. Bad enough that she'd already slipped in front of Ro Laren, of all people, who had been obstinately unfriendly since the day she'd arrived. . . .

"I don't know if Ro can handle the investigation," Kira said abruptly, answering Jast's question with a partial truth. "She's never done anything like this before, and what if it wasn't a robbery? I thought security would work out for her, but I may have been wrong. She hasn't even been able to identify the killer yet."

Expressionless, Jast watched her for a moment—and then spoke slowly, as if choosing her words carefully. "She is new . . . but maybe you should see how things progress before you consider replacing her."

Kira was surprised. "You're in Starfleet."

"Yes, and I know her history," Jast conceded. "Her Starfleet file actually makes rather interesting reading, especially once you realize what's missing from it. But there are multiple truths to a story, and for all of Ro's . . . missteps, she's also not afraid to cause a disturbance in order to reach her objective. That's why she was sent here, wasn't it? It would seem to me that you'd want someone in security to be headstrong, even aggressive sometimes. And she does have the tactical background."

She had a point, though Kira found herself reluctant to recognize it. It wasn't just Ro's past, although Kira was anything but reassured by her record—her Starfleet career had been a disaster, marked by bad calls and questionable choices. Many of the Starfleet people in the crew considered her a traitor and a criminal twice over, and being forced to work alongside her because the Bajoran government had insisted on her assignment to DS9 was doing nothing good for the tension level on the station. There was also her abrasive manner, and her obvious disinterest, even scorn, for her own heritage, her own cultural beliefs.

Our cultural beliefs. Ro didn't hide her rejection of the Prophets, in everything from conversation all the way down to deliberately wearing her earring on the wrong side, as if she was daring anyone to object . . . maybe Kira *was* letting her personal feelings about Ro influence her ability to evaluate her performance.

Kira sighed, deciding that it could wait for further analysis. Picking herself apart after the morning she'd had was more than she could stand.

"I want to be fair," Kira said. "And it's not as if we have anyone to replace her with." They didn't, either. Nog had acted as head of security for a couple weeks after Odo's departure, but it had been a temporary measure . . . much to Quark's eternal disappointment. Nog was much better suited to engineering, anyway.

"It's your territory, of course," Jast said. "As for our ongoing upgrade frustrations, why don't we go to an early lunch and work through a new schedule? Nog insists that things will progress faster if we regulate the EPS conduit outflow for the next few days."

Jast smiled suddenly. "Maybe we can have Quark make us up a couple of Black Holes. Just to enhance our creativity, of course."

In spite of how very wrung-out she felt, Kira found herself smiling back—and thinking that perhaps it wasn't too soon, after all, to think of Jast as a good friend. The Prophets knew she needed as many as she could get.

With the *U.S.S. Aldebaran* working its sixth day of sentinel detail for the space station, the bridge wasn't overly crowded or overly busy. The helm and science officers weren't present, and communications was represented by a second-year cadet, one of several trainees currently earning hours on the *Aldebaran.* Captain Robison was in his ready room, probably catching up on paperwork, and although Tiss Janna occupied the captain's chair, she looked as distant-eyed as everyone else on duty—excepting the cadet, of course, who stared intently at his console panel, watching for any incoming calls. Trainees; it was sometimes hard not to pat their heads, they were so adorably vigilant.

Thomas Chang, the *Aldebaran*'s counselor for just over seven years, wasn't officially on duty, but he spent a lot of his off hours on the bridge. He enjoyed the atmosphere of efficiency, liked watching the people he'd come to know so well as they applied their talents. Of course, watching them during downtime could often be just as interesting . . . but then, finding people interesting was how he'd come to be a ship's counselor.

Pretending to be absorbed in the contents of a science

digest, Chang surreptitiously watched the men and women around him, occasionally tapping at the padd in order to deflect suspicion. He didn't want to make anyone uncomfortable . . . and besides, it was part of the game, trying to figure out what someone might be thinking about just by watching them, their gestures and body language. Shannon liked to joke that it was the Romulan in him, driving him to spy on the unwary. Because he was falling in love with her, Chang always laughed—but he couldn't help feeling a vague sadness when the topic came up, recalling the story of his great-grandmother's capture, and how that story had haunted him as a child. That the Romulans eventually released her, and that her life had been happy and full ever after . . . it couldn't take away the memory of hearing the awful truth for the first time, that a brutal man had once hurt her—and that that man's blood ran in his own veins. . . .

It seemed that he wasn't above a little daydreaming himself; Chang let the unhappy feelings go, letting his attention wander back to the pleasantly directionless analysis of his friends and co-workers. Tiss Janna, for example; from the softly calculating gleam in her eyes, the way she kept pulling on a lock of her curly dark hair, Chang imagined that she was thinking about those green opal-and-quillion earrings that the Ferengi bartender had shown her the first night they'd arrived at DS9. She wanted them, but wasn't willing to pay the obnoxiously high price that the bartender had quoted. Even now, she was thinking of a counteroffer . . . and perhaps imagining what Lieutenant Commander Hopping Bird would say about them on their next date.

Chang shifted in his chair, casting a sidelong glance at the officer in question. Mike Hopping Bird, chief tactical officer and Tiss's recent love interest. Only a few people knew, of course; Chang had heard it from Mike himself, and had been pleased. Mike and Tiss were a good match, and although they probably wouldn't let their romance be widely known, Mike was going to give it away if he didn't stop gazing at her with such obvious and ardent affection. It wasn't much of a jump for Chang to guess what Mike was thinking about, particularly considering his own developing relationship with Shannon.

There was a definite rise in the number of romantic relationships on board . . . and, Chang imagined, all across the Alpha Quadrant. There were innumerable statistics and psychological studies he could cite to prove his point, but put simply, as Captain Robison himself had said, "It's an end-of-the-war thing."

Not that everyone was after romance. Kelly Eideman, the dynamic young woman currently slouched comfortably at the engineering station, had already been to DS9 three times to play dabo, and had done fairly well . . . although Chang couldn't rule out a romance there, either. Some of the dabo girls at Quark's were extremely attractive. As practical as the junior grade lieutenant was, however, he imagined that the slight smile she wore was for the clacking spin of the wheel, and the delighted cries of the watching crowd over each dabo win.

He didn't care much for dabo himself, but Shannon had been pushing for them to try out one of DS9's holo-suite programs, one recommended to her by Dr. Bashir. It was for some sort of combined gambling-restaurant-entertainment center, set on Earth in the mid-20th century, and there was a game called baccarat that Shannon very much wanted to try. Shannon, a researcher on the *Aldebaran*'s medical staff, had been corresponding with Bashir off and on for several years, debating something or other about chromatin formation, and had been excited to meet him. The doctor had turned out to be a very personable young man, and was apparently involved with the station's counselor, one Ezri Dax. Dax was Trill, a species that Chang found to be highly perceptive as a general rule, and although he hadn't met her yet, he was interested in hearing her take on Vanleden's newest theories about focus charting—

"You're just pretending to read, aren't you?"

At the sound of Tiss's voice, Chang looked up guiltily. Tiss was smiling playfully.

"What an odd question," he said. "What else could I possibly be doing?"

He tried, but couldn't keep a smile from creeping up as he spoke. As well as he'd come to know so many of the crew, they had come to know him. The thought was warm, inspiring a sense of belonging, and although he'd been caught out at his guessing game, he didn't mind a bit.

Tiss started to answer—and then Lieutenant Eideman was standing and turning, running to the helm even as Mike Hopping Bird's usually calm voice was rising to a near shout.

"Commander, the wormhole—it's opening!"

Then Tiss was moving, calling for on-screen, calling for bridge personnel as Captain Robison strode from his ready room, head up and eyes bright as he moved to his chair.

Chang felt an instant of cold shock, watching numbly as the brilliant colors spread out in front of them. The wormhole hadn't opened since the last of the Dominion forces had returned to the Gamma Quadrant three months ago, and although the *Aldebaran* had been assigned to guard DS9 against any possibility of attack during their repairs, no one on the ship had really expected anything to happen.

Thomas Chang swallowed his disbelief, hoping desperately that nothing *would* happen, refusing the idea that they might be in trouble. And even as he accepted that he was in denial, the first of the ships came through.

They were just finishing up their informal meeting when both of their combadges trilled at once. Outside Kira's office window, men and woman were jumping to their feet, dropping tools and running to their half-assembled stations. On Kira's desk, an incoming call blinked urgently; the *Aldebaran* was hailing.

Kira and Jast both stood, turning to look out at ops. Shar's voice spilled into the room, the young officer speaking quickly as he looked in at them from his position on the main floor.

"Colonel, Commander—three Jem'Hadar strike ships have just come through the wormhole in attack formation, weapons and shields up, and they—they're heading for the *Aldebaran*."

No.

It was the unthinkable, the reason she'd put off upgrades for so long. Now, after three months of dead silence from the Dominion, it seemed that someone had decided to make contact, just when the station's defenses were at a minimum.

"Red alert. Battle stations," she ordered. "Shar, send

out a distress call, lock off nonessential systems and get me everything on our weapons. I need to know where we are *exactly*. Implement emergency shelter protocols, try to get us visuals on the main screen, and tell Nog to get the *Defiant* ready, *now*."

She nodded at Jast, who took her cue and hurried out of the office and across ops, toward its transporter stage. Kira reached for the blinking light of the *Aldebaran*'s call, already calculating the kind of damage they could expect if the ship couldn't stop the fighters, her mind flooded with too-recent images of burning starships and a growing dread. *No tractor beams, limited shields, all of the new tactical systems that aren't even assembled yet—*

Kira felt sick and put it aside, praying that things weren't as bad as she feared, suspecting that they were worse.

4

"... and, considering all of *that,* do you think it could increase the energy dissipation effectiveness of the hull plating, in the event of shield envelope disruption?"

Ezri sighed, wondering if she could just pretend to be asleep. Probably not; she was on her back beneath the flight control console, but Nog could see her face if he turned around . . . and she *had* encouraged him into a conversation.

Next time, I'll be sure to suggest a topic. Nothing so vague as, "What's on your mind, Nog?"

"Honestly, I'm not sure," she said, reaching up into the ODN bundle that swayed above her face and twisting two of the wire patches together. Ensign Tenmei would have to integrate them, she had the fiber torch, but she was below, working on the pulse phaser assemblies. It would have to wait. "It sounds good to me, Nog, but that's really not saying much."

The problem was that Tobin Dax, her second host,

had been a theoretical engineer two centuries ago; not only were the memories hazy, technology had progressed more than a few running steps past Tobin's experience. And yet, as often as Ezri had told Nog that, he continued to ask questions and run his every idea past her, delivering each as enthusiastically as possible, the salesman in him shining through. As if she was actually an engineer, or possessed Jadzia's natural ability toward technical problem-solving. Even with all of the symbiont's experiences to draw upon, she wasn't going to win any physics awards.

"But you think it'll work?" he asked, turning around to look at her, his sharpened teeth bared in a sincere grin. "You don't see a problem with the numbers, do you?"

Be patient, he's under a lot of pressure.

Despite assurances to the contrary, Nog seemed to insist on holding himself personally responsible for how slowly things were going. Technically, he had taken over Miles O'Brien's job. And while there were certainly more experienced engineers in Starfleet, none of them knew the station as Nog did, and no other engineer had received his formal field training on both DS9 and the *Defiant.* He was still terrible at the administrative aspect, often relying on Kira or Jast to deal with master reports to Starfleet, and he didn't have the easy self-assurance about his ideas or work that the chief had, but he was determined, talented, and *extremely* eager.

"No, I don't see a problem with the numbers," Ezri said truthfully. She'd already forgotten the numbers. "I think you should write it up and meet with Kira about it—but if I were you, I'd wait a few days."

Nog turned back to the bridge's less than whole engineering station, nodding. "You're right. And that would give me a chance to, ah, iron out the details. I still haven't calculated the density of the subsequent particle cloud, which could interfere with shield harmonics . . ."

She listened with half an ear, her wandering thoughts moving back to Kira. Ezri wasn't one to push counseling, but she thought it'd be a good idea to seek her out later, to at least make herself available. Even with half the communications systems on the station operating sporadically, at best, word had gotten around about the murder—although she supposed not many knew that Kira had been a friend of the murdered prylar. Julian had told her that.

And so soon after losing Odo. It's so unfair. Kira projected a comfortable understanding of Odo's choice to return to the Great Link, but Ezri suspected that it still hurt her—and having to deal with the murder of a childhood friend would reinforce conscious and subconscious stresses of abandonment. That was the psychological standard, anyway; Ezri had been acting as station counselor for long enough to know that emotional reactions weren't exactly set in titanium. *I hope she'll talk to someone about it, though. Before she has time to bury the pain.*

She would have gone to see Kira already, except for the incredible workload that had practically everyone on the station occupied; as disheartening as it was, Kira undoubtedly needed Dax's engineering skills more than her ability to listen. The original plan, pushed for by the Federation and Bajor, had seemed feasible enough—take it all apart with the *Aldebaran* keeping watch, refurbish the *Defiant*'s tactical systems and armor, rewire communications and most of the subspace systems for the station, and put it all back together again in one short and brutal push. An updated *Defiant*, but more importantly, no more endlessly overlapping maintenance shutdowns for the station, no more makeshift patches between Cardassian and Federation technology that only seemed to last until it was really important for them to work. . . .

. . . and if ninety percent of the SCE techs weren't off repairing war damage, we could have gotten away with it, too. They just didn't have the staff they needed to get everything done in a reasonable amount of time.

Nog's combadge chirped, and he sat up a little straighter as he answered, drawing Ezri's attention. The obvious pride he took in his position was good to see; they'd all suffered in the war, and deserved a little happiness—

—and the strangest thing happened. She was still on her back and was looking up at Nog, and the change that came over his upside-down face—a flash of pure panic that started in his eyes and seemed to spread, contorting his rounded features—had her believing, just for a second, that he was having some kind of a convulsion.

"Nog, what is it?"

He couldn't seem to catch his breath. He stood and stumbled to communications, running his hands over the console, and as she squirmed out from beneath the flight controls, Shar's voice spilled out into the bridge.

"—is on her way, but power up *now*. I repeat, the station has gone to red alert. We need the *Defiant*'s interface on-line, and a full status report. Commander Jast is

beaming over, but the colonel says to get ready immediately, attack ships are—they're firing on the *Aldebaran!*"

Nog looked positively ill. He ran back to where he'd
been working and started digging frantically through
his tools, calling for the computer to assess the *Defiant*'s current condition. There was a sudden flurry of
movement behind them, as the three other techs on the
bridge rushed to various unpaneled consoles and
started powering things up.

". . . in-line impulse system operating at forty-two
percent. Secondary subsystems for engineering interface, reaction control, science control, and torpedo
launchers, inoperative. Primary subsystems for . . ."

As the computer's calm voice continued to list all
that was wrong with DS9's best defense, as only a
handful of engineers raced to put it back together
again, Ezri was suddenly quite sure that people were
going to die. She tapped the flight control interface and
scanned the numbers, Nog yelling for an interphasic
coil spanner over the computer's growing index of
problems.

Maybe a lot of us.

It happened faster than Shar would have thought
possible.

Only minutes ago, he'd been trying to stay awake,
vaguely wishing for the warmth of his quarters. Now he
stood at the central ops table amid flashing red lights,
relaying orders to Nog and trying to activate the display
screen at the same time, about to call for an engineering status on the shield emitters—when the station's
sensors registered a hit on the *Aldebaran.* Even as the

ship's data flow fluctuated wildly, the screen that dominated ops spun to life, displaying the fierce battle.

The trio of fighters were pulling away from their first run, flashes of brilliant light sparking from a series of shield deflections across the rapidly approaching *Aldebaran*'s bow. The *Nebula*-class starship seemed slow and lumbering as the three Jem'Hadar peeled away and looped back, strafing the saucer's underbelly, their tactical choreography almost like hunting—a pack of vicious carnivores attacking some mammoth beast.

All around Shar, techs were calling out instructions in low, tense voices, moving about purposefully and quickly, making room for the small crowd that erupted from the turbolift. Status reports started trickling in from all around the station, appearing on the table's master display. Shar ran a collation and fed it to Kira's office, channeling his body's elevated awareness and need for action—stimulated by the situation, his antennae fairly throbbed with it—into lending him greater speed.

When he looked up next, he could only see two of the darting fighters. Both twined back and forth in front of the *Aldebaran* as if taunting it, narrowly dodging a series of phaser blasts, the energy streams dissipating harmlessly into the darkness. He tapped at the table's display, looking for the third ship, but there were problems with several of the station's short-range sensors. He could only get a partial read, a suggestion of functional energy behind the *Aldebaran*'s starboard flank—

—and there was an explosion low on the ship's structure, a misty spray of light and escaping gases forming behind what could only be the *Aldebaran*'s main engineering decks. The third fighter flew down and away.

"Their shields are gone!" someone behind him shouted, and a glance at the *Aldebaran*'s interface confirmed it. A second later, the interface blanked out, but the station's sensors picked up evidence of the powerful blast, much more powerful than could have been caused by a Jem'Hadar striker's phased polaron beam. It was some type of quantum warhead, and even as Shar sent the newest data into command, Kira burst out of her office, a look of angry shock on her face.

"We've lost contact with the *Aldebaran*. Tactical, can we get targeting for quantum torpedoes?" she called out, turning to face the main screen. All three of the ships were starting another run at the *Aldebaran*. The starship was turning, but slowly, much too slowly.

Lieutenant Bowers was tapping frantically at his station's console. "Negative. Launcher sets three, four, and seven are down, and the station's internal locks are unreliable on five and six."

"Shar, establish communications with the *Defiant*, and try to get our interface with the *Aldebaran* back, at least text," Kira said. "Mr. Nguyen, take your team and get to engineering, I want you and Terek's crew on the shield-emitters. If we can get the *Aldebaran* close enough to one of the docking pylons—"

But it was already too late. Even with the visual dampening, the cascade of light that flashed through ops from the main screen was blinding. Shar was suddenly too busy struggling to compensate the station through the shockwave to see it, but enough of the sensors were working to tell him the terrible, improbable truth, as hundreds upon thousands of pieces blew outward from where the *Starship Aldebaran* had been.

No. Oh, no.

Just over nine hundred people on the *Aldebaran,* and Kira couldn't allow herself the luxury of disbelief or sorrow. It didn't matter that it shouldn't have happened, that an outgunned trio of tiny fighters shouldn't have had a chance; the ship was gone, and the second they finished dodging what was left of the *Aldebaran,* the Jem'Hadar would be back to run at the station. Their intent couldn't be clearer, and her options were limited. Shar called out that the majority of the wreckage from the starship probably wouldn't affect the station, but she barely heard him, her thoughts racing to get ahead of what was happening.

Shields practically nonexistent, weapons arrays are out—if we could commandeer the docked ships— She rejected the idea immediately, remembering what was around. Four freighters and a couple of survey ships, maybe a dozen personal craft, and even with the runabouts and the evac pods, they wouldn't get a tenth of the population out before the attack, *think, think—*

Shar's usually melodic voice was strained, rough. "Sir, we're receiving a response to our priority distress call from the *I.K.S.—*"

"How far away?" Kira interrupted, not caring who it was, hoping wildly.

"Ah, 22 minutes."

In 22 minutes, it would be over. She'd seen the report that Nog had flashed, knew that the *Defiant*'s crew wouldn't have made it to the ship yet, and it didn't matter; they had no choice. She tapped her combadge.

"Commander Jast," she said, silently hating Starfleet and herself for letting this happen, cursing the false security that they'd all been lulled into. "The *Aldebaran* has been destroyed. The *Defiant* is the station's best hope for defense; are you ready?"

Jast didn't hesitate. "We're ready."

"Do what you can," Kira said, and with a silent prayer, she turned to watch the screen, men and women calling out numbers and names behind her as they fought to keep the station safe, as pieces of the *Aldebaran* began to hammer at their shields.

A few seconds later, the Jem'Hadar started their first run at DS9.

5

After Ro's not-so-gentle persuasion, Quark had produced a Class 1 isolinear rod that he'd been storing for Istani Reyla; he had immediately followed up with an invitation to dinner, ostensibly to ensure no hard feelings, which she had refused—but pleasantly, for the same reason. She saw no reason to make an enemy of the Ferengi . . . and, she had to admit, she had a soft spot for people who didn't strictly abide by the rules.

She had just gotten back to the security office when the red alert hit, and the computer instructed her to implement emergency shelter protocols due to an unnamed threat to the station; it wouldn't or couldn't elaborate any further. She had the computer display a checklist as she calmly locked the data rod away, hoping that her staff was better prepared. They had to be—though prepared for what, exactly, she didn't know. Communications between ops and the security office were down, Shar wouldn't answer his combadge, and she didn't feel comfortable bothering anyone else during a crisis.

Doesn't matter anyway, the plan's the same for me. Direct civilians to the reinforced areas, evacuate and secure prisoners if there were any. There weren't, and a locator check for the security officers on duty informed her that she was the only one who wasn't in position.

Ro locked the office and stepped back out into the river of people rushing through the Promenade, finally unable to continue denying her own fear as she saw it all around her. A small child was sobbing somewhere in the crowd, a terrified sound of irrepressible angst, inspiring in Ro her own.

Is it war, again? Is it ever going to be over?

She was no stranger to battle. After the Dominion had effectively obliterated the Maquis, she'd led a small team of independent guerillas against the Cardassians and the Jem'Hadar, and later the Breen. Her group had held no allegiances other than to each other, earning no accolades for their efforts, nor needing any—as with the Maquis, the righteousness of the cause had been enough. She had been in as many conflicts as any Federation officer, if not more, and had done so with fewer people, less powerful weapons, and no outside support.

The difference is, I'm not in control here. I'm one of many, and the decisions aren't mine to make. It wasn't battle or even death that frightened her, it was feeling helpless. The station was under attack, and all she could do—all she was supposed to do—was try to limit casualties. And trust that someone else would make the right decisions, when trust was the one thing she'd never given lightly or easily.

However she felt about it, it was happening. Ro spotted two of her deputies working to control the crowd and moved to join them, wondering if she would ever feel like she belonged on DS9 . . . or anywhere else that required her to put her faith in others.

Bashir hurried past lines of muttering, frightened people filing through the corridors of the Habitat Ring, his emergency kit slung, his heart pounding with fear. Ezri was on the *Defiant.*

Where I should be. If they'd only called a moment earlier. He'd been seconds too late, and the first explosion had hit the station even as he'd turned away from the sealed airlock. He'd seen a half dozen *Defiant* crewmembers on his run back to the Promenade, all of them as unhappy as he was to have missed the ship's hasty departure. Unhappy, and not a little anxious; the *Defiant* had disembarked, presumably to go into battle, with a crew of techs.

Since he'd been unable to join the *Defiant*'s crew, his next priority was to coordinate with the other doctors on board, to help activate all of the contingency medical stations and prepare for trauma cases. He reached the Promenade and saw Ro Laren and her security team directing groups of civilians to the designated shelter areas Mid-Core.

As he approached Ro, the station rocked again, the thunder of another blast resounding through the hull, drawing startled cries from the hurrying crowd. The air was charged with fear, the constant bleat of alarms promoting urgency rather than calm.

"Lieutenant, do you know what's happening?" All he'd gotten from ops was the order to report to the *Defiant,* and that the station was under attack.

She seemed surprised by the question. "Don't you?"

There was no point in stating the obvious as the station trembled anew with power flux; they were being fired upon by someone, communications were down all over, and their defenses were negligible at best. And with what Ezri had been telling him about the *Defiant* . . .

"We're in trouble," Bashir said, and Ro nodded grimly. There was nothing else that needed to be said.

Ezri, be safe. The force of feeling behind the thought was so powerful that he felt short of breath, an intensity that startled him. They had slept together for the first time just before the last great battle of the war against the Dominion, and going to fight then had been difficult, fearing for her as well as himself—but things had still been so uncertain, and at least they had been together. In only a few months, so much had changed. . . .

"Ah, Doctor, I have to go make sure the shops have been evacuated—" Ro began.

"Of course. I . . . good luck, Ro. Be careful," Bashir said, and saw that he'd surprised her again, although he wasn't sure how. He didn't have time to consider it, either, or how his feelings for Ezri had complicated his life, or all of the things that could go wrong; he had his own duties to see to.

With a nod to the others, Julian turned away and ran for the infirmary, thinking that he would give anything to be on the *Defiant,* anything at all.

When Kira gave the command to engage the enemy, Nog tried to keep an open mind, to work the problems rather than consider how disastrous the situation was, but it wasn't easy. He knew better than anyone just how pitiful their defenses were right now, how many systems were down, how many weapons off-line—and with the *Aldebaran* destroyed, their chances of coming away unscathed had dropped to a negligible percentage.

Focus, stay focused, reassign pulse phasers two and four to manual, got to divert partial impulse to shields—

Commander Jast took control the second she beamed aboard, assigning positions and prioritizing system checks, but she was making decisions in part based on what he told her. Nog stepped between the engineering station and tactical, trying desperately to direct power where it was needed most, while Ezri struggled with the partially disabled communications interface—the science station was mostly dismantled, sensor arrays routed through tactical—and Prynn Tenmei sat at the helm. With the exception of the commander, Ensign Tenmei was the only person aboard who was where she was supposed to be—not a reassuring thought in spite of her piloting skills, because that was it for the bridge crew. The other techs were below, grappling with the weapons systems. The standard operational crew was forty; they had fourteen.

At least they weren't relying on the cloaking device, although that was small comfort. After the war, the Romulan government had agreed to let the *Defiant* keep it. As the Alpha Quadrant's first line of defense against anything that came through the wormhole, it only made sense—even to the characteristically skeptical Romulan Senate—to provide DS9 and the *Defiant* with every possible advantage. Unfortunately, like virtually everything else on board, the cloak wasn't even functional at the moment.

—try to transfer the transporter EPS tap to the navi-

gational deflector, I can do this, I know this ship. Another thought that wasn't particularly reassuring, considering the state of the *Defiant,* but he was too busy to come up with anything better.

The Jem'Hadar scored their first hits against the station even as Kira gave the word. Nog had had nightmares worse than what was happening, but not by much.

"Ensign, take us out," Jast said. "The armor over the warp nacelles is still temp, so try to keep the targets below and in front of us. Nog, what can we do about the lag time on beam launch?"

Nog stumbled over to tactical as Tenmei disengaged the docking clamps and tapped thrusters, the ship's AG lurching with the power flux. "Ah, not much, sir. Point six-five seconds, minimum."

Jast took it in stride. "We'll just have to fire early, then. Shields up. Stay with tactical, Lieutenant."

She spoke casually, as if the Jem'Hadar ships would hold still, waiting for the *Defiant*'s phasers to catch up. Nog had been intimidated by Jast's generally cool disposition since she arrived, but considering the situation, her calm was a definite asset.

The main screen showed a blank expanse of space until the *Defiant* swung around, just in time for them to see the station take another series of hits. Nog struggled to quash feelings of panic; all three of the attackers were apparently concentrating on the fusion reactors, at the base of the Lower Core. He could see dark streaks of polaron damage all across the section's hull, visually warped by the disrupted shields.

They'll hold, they can take a lot more than that. They could . . . except with the upgrades, a heavy percentage of the station's power was tied up in bypass circuiting, and nothing was certain; the short-range shield emitters were essentially down, running with no backup. If the strike fighters continued to hit any one area, they could inflict serious damage.

"Could," they already have. Taking out a *Nebula*-class starship hadn't proved much of a problem.

"Positions, Lieutenant. And run course probabilities. Without targeting it may be the best we can do."

Most of the directional sensors were working. Nog read the numbers aloud, tapping in trajectory calculations as he spoke. The Jem'Hadar had turned back toward the station, wheeling into a loose formation, point high.

"Dax, how's the station doing?" Jast asked.

"Unable to establish a full interface," Ezri said. "Their shields are down at least forty percent."

Jast seemed unfazed. "Let's see if we can tempt them away, people. Ensign, get us as close as you can to point at full impulse, bearing two-two-seven mark nine, and be prepared to run evasive pattern Theta 16 at my word. Lieutenant Nog, when we're 20 kilometers out to range, lay down a calculated phaser spread in front of the lead ship, firing at will. Better they think we're a bad shot than underpowered." Nog could hear the grim humor in her voice. "Who knows, enough runs and we may get lucky."

It was a clever scheme. The Jem'Hadar could be fanatic about following point, and although the computer predictions had a minimal chance of scoring a hit, the phasers would come close enough to be threatening. The evasive pattern would turn the *Defiant* back to run a two-degree parallel to its "strafing" course, keeping the well-shielded front of the ship facing the attackers.

The *Defiant* sped away from the station, angling into the path of the point ship. The instant they went to full impulse, Nog could see they were in serious trouble. At the unmanned engineering station, a bank of lights started to flash. All across the bridge, lights brightened—and abruptly dimmed, filling the tool-strewn deck with shadows.

"Sir, the mid-hull RCS thrusters are bleeding power from the electrical system!" Nog shouted. He knew the danger would be obvious to Jast; an electrical crash would shut everything down.

With a full crew, it would have been noticed immediately. *Or if I'd bothered to look closer. I should have checked that, I should have—*

"Compensate! Cut impulse to half and run a tap," Jast snapped.

"Sir, if we boost it from here without checking the source—" Nog began.

"I know," Jast said. "We risk an overload, but we don't have a choice."

Nog stepped away from tactical, but the commander was already out of her chair and headed for the engineering station. "Stay at your post, Lieutenant, I'm on it. Ensign, report."

"One hundred and ten kilometers and closing," Tenmei said tensely. "Intercept projected course in eleven seconds."

As Nog knew from experience, experience he'd hoped never to revisit, those seconds seemed to stretch into eternity, time slowing, his senses recording it all. The trio of Jem'Hadar ships streaked toward the station, their flat, insectile shapes shimmering like water mirages beneath heavy shields. The low hum of the bridge systems increased, the lights strengthening as Jast manipulated the power flow. Ezri called out the stats from DS9, confirming the loss of shield efficiency to thirty-seven percent and severe energy surges in every major system. Nog laid in the phaser directionals, intensely conscious of the sweat trickling down the back of his neck, the hot, acrid smell of scorched optical cable—and the crawl of numbers on the console that told him the *Defiant* was being targeted.

Forty . . . thirty . . . now.

Nog fired, a series of layered shots that responded with agonizing slowness to his command—and as the bright pulse bolts shot out into space, he could feel that they were lucky, the triumph blossoming in his gut, visual proof following an instant later.

Yes!

The right flank ship took a massive hit to its port side and fell away, spinning out of control as hull plates tore and atmosphere escaped. A veil of light and mist trailed behind the dying ship like a comet's tail, a pale streak lost in the brilliance of the final explosion a second later.

Everything sped up then, as if making up for the eternity of waiting, happening too fast for Nog to absorb all at once. He started to call out the information to Jast, who was still at engineering; Tenmei was shouting at the same time that the lead ship was shifting position; and, from the pulse phaser mains below, Turo Ane was trying to tell him something about the hull, her voice filtering through the com in a haze of sudden, violent static—

—because the Jem'Hadar point ship was firing, scoring a jagged hit across the *Defiant*'s bow. A terrible light filled the screen. Nog hugged his console as the gravity net pitched, as the ship bounced and jerked, and Jast let out a short, sharp scream.

The commander flew back from the engineering station in a shower of sparks and fell heavily to the deck. Nog stared at her for a half second before snapping his attention back to his screens, tapping up damage reports and checking their shields—but that half second was enough, the image of her face clear in his mind.

Commander Jast was dead.

6

The two remaining Jem'Hadar ships continued toward the station, apparently uninterested in the faltering *Defiant* as it rapidly angled away from them. The commander wasn't moving, and for a second, in spite of a thousand small indicator alarms, it seemed strangely quiet on the bridge.

Because someone should be giving orders.

Ezri was on her feet before she considered what she was doing, her heart pounding, a number of powerful memories strong in her mind—mostly from Jadzia, confident and in control, moving about the *Defiant*'s bridge, speaking as firmly as she was now.

"Nog, report."

Nog was obviously flustered, practically shouting the information. "Single intensity polaron, shields down to eighty percent! There was an electrical surge straight through the ship's structural body, warp plasma injectors are down, and we've lost communications with the station!"

Electrical surge. Ezri had crouched next to Jast and touched the woman's brow, running her finger along the central vertical ridge. A Bolian's pulse could be detected there, something she hadn't known she knew; the memory was Curzon's, vague, holding a Bolian baby at a political dinner, feeling the flutter of life through the ridge of flesh and bone. Tiris Jast had no pulse. Her eyes were wide and fixed, and there was a settling of her features that Dax had seen often enough to recognize—life had left them, transforming the strong and delicate face into a waxy likeness of Jast's, into a mask.

Even if there was *still a chance* . . . No doctor aboard, they couldn't transport her, and no one on the *Defiant* could be spared for the shuttle. As quickly as that, the decision was made; she could doubt it later. Maybe. If they were very lucky.

"Tenmei, execute evasive pattern Theta 16," Ezri said, standing, stepping in front of the captain's chair. Jadzia had commanded the *Defiant* on more than one combat mission, which made her the only person on board with the experience for it. *It'll have to be close enough.*

"Nog, shut down the bridge's engineering console, route it down to Turo. Is the shipwide working?" She was surprised at how calm she sounded, and it seemed to have a positive effect on Nog. He took a deep breath before answering.

"Negative."

"Then com them directly, tell them to put everything they can into repairing the phaser lag—we need them more than shields or thrust. And keep trying to reestablish contact with the station. Tenmei, get ready, we're about to go on the offensive."

The *Defiant* swung back toward DS9, Ezri's stomach reeling as the inertial dampeners wavered. Both of the strike ships had reached their objective and were firing, brilliant arrows of light flashing up against the dark, glowing hull of the Lower Core. The ships dropped down and split as they completed their run, each darting away in a different direction, spinning and curving between pieces of the *Aldebaran* like strange, deadly fish.

They were much smaller than the *Defiant,* and faster, but only in sprints. *If we can bear down on them one at a time, refine phaser accuracy through constant bombardment and hone in . . .* The *Defiant* would probably take heavy fire from the second ship, but it was a solid plan and they had to do something immediately. The station was practically defenseless.

"Hard to port, close in, and fire as soon as we're in range," Ezri said, feeling too many things to sort through, hidden among them a tiny astonishment as the full realization hit—she was commanding the *Defiant* by memories of Jadzia, but with a confidence all her own.

Except for the docking ring and the upper pylons, ops was situated at the point farthest from the attack on the Lower Core, but each hit resonated through all of the structure's segments. Ops trembled, lights and consoles wavering, streams of information lost as backup networks crashed—but enough came through Shar's console to show him how fortunate they were compared to other parts of the station. Damage reports from the Lower and Mid Cores were serious, bordering on critical, and the *Defiant* had only managed to destroy one of the fighters. Unless Jast stopped them, another attack could prove disastrous to the already fluttering shields.

Kira shouted orders to divert power, to shut down noncritical systems, to evacuate everyone into the Upper Core. Even occupied as he was, Shar couldn't help but notice how well Kira handled herself. Her reputation for being indomitable under pressure was well-deserved.

As the tremors subsided and the Jem'Hadar coursed away, the *Defiant* veered sharply after the point ship.

"*Defiant*'s status?" Kira called.

"Unable to lock sensors, and there was an energy surge after they were hit that wiped out the interface." Shar resisted the urge to extrapolate aloud on the state of the subspace sensors. He felt very focused, very alert, his ability to absorb and process information at its peak. He didn't glory in conflict or seek it out, but he couldn't help his body's natural response, an Andorian's response; the stimulus of the situation was now profound enough that he had no fear of injury or death. And though he was deeply anxious for the station and horrified by the loss of life that the *Aldebaran*'s destruction represented, he couldn't help his objectivity or his exhilaration.

The peace broken so soon; cruel and impractical. We're witnessing the creation of new woes. The obvious implications of the Jem'Hadar's actions had not been voiced, there was no benefit to it, but Shar silently lamented the breaking of the treaty. Wars of ignorance benefited no one.

On the main screen, the *Defiant* maneuvered into position behind the point ship and fired, multiple pulses that went wide, the striker gliding easily among the untargeted beams. The second ship was streaking back to join the battle, the *Defiant* and the point ship roughly 200 kilometers from the station at varying planes of altitude.

As the lead ship continued to elude the *Defiant*'s attack, the second ship reached its weapons range and opened fire. The *Defiant*'s rear shields sparked violently, but she held her course, closing on the target. Shar was impressed by Jast's commitment to their course of action, the *Defiant* taking several severe hits from behind as they continued their pursuit.

The tension in ops built upon itself, every spare glance on the main screen, every awareness at least partially tuned to the *Defiant*'s conflict. She fired again and again on the point ship as it swerved and dove, each series of shots coming closer, accuracy improving in costly increments as the second ship blasted mercilessly away.

Within the data stream that flowed across his console, an alarming series of numbers caught his full attention—a partial sensor read on the *Defiant* that he hoped was faulty. If it was correct, Jast was about to lose her shields. And if that happened with both Jem'Hadar still in commission, it was all over.

"Colonel, we're picking up the *Defiant,* they're losing their shields," he said, as there was another volley of shots from the second Jem'Hadar, brutal and effective that proved his words out. The *Defiant*'s shield envelope burst, the only visible sign of her imminent demise a brief, brilliant flicker of her aura—

—and the Jem'Hadar point ship exploded, becoming an expanding wave of energy and debris. Jast's gamble had paid off; the *Defiant* was certainly damaged, but even without shields, they stood a likely chance at victory over a lone strike ship. The *Defiant* sailed up and over her victory, the last Jem'Hadar ship retreating rapidly as their target turned to confront them.

Nobody cheered. People had died and there was still an enemy to deal with, but the atmosphere in ops expressed a release of tension, a partial conquest understood. Techs returned to their work with renewed fervor. Shar was warmed by the release physically, his skin flushing in reaction to the elevated bioelectrical charge in the air. His left antenna itched madly.

Colonel Kira stood a few meters away with her fists clenched, watching the screen with an expression of total concentration, her body rigid.

"They're going to attack us again," she said, almost to herself, startling Shar. Of course they were, but somehow, it hadn't occurred to him until she spoke. The ship wasn't retreating from the *Defiant;* it was coming back for another run at the station.

The Jem'Hadar had to know they wouldn't survive, they shouldn't even have made it this far. Why would they stop firing on the station now, just because they'll certainly die?

"Put everything into shields, everything," Kira shouted, as the Jem'Hadar set its course back for the station—

—and as if some unloving god had decided to put a stop to their hopes, the *Defiant* died in space. Shar didn't need to look at whatever scant information the station's sensors could tell him; it was there on the screen in front of them all.

The suddenly dark *Defiant* plummeted on momentum alone after the Jem'Hadar ship, no longer firing as the attacker closed on the station.

The money was all safe, of course. No good businessman would leave his latinum box or account access codes behind just because a few shots were fired. But in all the excitement, Quark had forgotten the kai wager sheet in the bar's hidden floor compartment. An easy mistake, considering how hectic evacuations were, securing the bar, having to keep track of each fleeing customer's bill, but a mistake all the same. He'd been two steps from his heavily fortified storeroom when he remembered, and had been forced to risk life and limb to come back for the hard copy.

At least the firing seems to have stopped. I could probably just wait it out here. The bar was silent and empty, a depressing sight but strangely peaceful. Extending the bar's hours had been a wise decision, the profit margin respectable, but he sometimes missed the quiet times, the silence of the dabo tables when the lights were low. . . .

I have got to get more sleep. Maybe his stress level was higher than he thought. The station *was* under attack, after all, and his nephew was unaccounted for—although Quark figured Nog was probably slaving away on an engineering level somewhere, wishing he had taken the advice of his elders and kept the security assignment. As for the attack, it was probably a pack of drunk Klingons, or some random terrorist element . . .

the station had been fired upon more than once in recent years, and hadn't blown up yet.

And if there was even a whisper of war in the air, I would have caught it. The proverbial "grapevine" enjoyed a healthy offshoot at Quark's, and he couldn't help overhearing a few things. Quite simply, nothing vast was brewing anywhere, or at least nothing within a troubling distance.

Quark replaced the floor panel behind the bar and stood, tucking the paper in his jacket. Kira had been adamant about no more pools when she found out he was taking bets on Winn's successor (as it had turned out, her timing couldn't have been more fortuitous; he'd given easy odds on Ungtae, who was barely in the running anymore), and since he didn't want to spend any time in a cell, he'd decided to keep that one, at least, on paper. Programs could always be traced; anyone could draw up a list, if they remembered to use DNA-resistant paper.

Although considering who would arrest me, maybe I should let myself get caught . . .

"What the hell are you doing here?"

Startled, Quark looked up—and saw the source of his budding prison fantasy glaring down at him from the balcony.

"Lieutenant Ro!" He smiled up at her, pleased with the opportunity to interact with her again . . . assuming she hadn't seen him pocket the list. "I was just making sure that everything is secured here. You know, it's my responsibility to maintain Federation and Bajoran safety standards during all emergency procedures—"

"Fine, don't tell me," she said dismissively, heading

for the stairs. "But whatever it is, it's not worth risking your life over."

Quark nodded, simulating agreement. The wager sheet was worth a few bars of gold-pressed latinum, easily. "Why are you here, if you don't mind me asking?"

"I had to check the holosuites," she said, starting down. "They're empty, by the way. Now if *you* don't mind, I think we should get—"

There was a sudden, violent quake, knocking Quark off his feet. The already dimmed lights flickered, and there was the sound of glass breaking in one of the unshielded cabinets behind him, a high, clear sound over the heavy, threatening rumble of uncertain machinery.

Please, let that be machinery!

He stayed where he was for a few seconds after the rumbling stopped, waiting for the station to evaporate around him in a ball of flame—but other than his stomach, which seemed to be in serious disagreement with his breakfast, nothing seemed to be broken.

He stood up, brushing at his coattails, suddenly quite anxious to get to a better-shielded area. "Lieutenant?"

No response. Then he heard a low groan, from the shadowy recess at the bottom of the stairs. Quark hurried to the end of the bar and out onto the main floor, worried about Ro, about the attack, wondering if he could be held liable somehow for any injury she might have incurred—

—and saw her lying on the floor, far enough from the stairs that she had to have been pitched off. Her eyes were closed and she groaned again, the sound half-conscious.

Quark hesitated, thinking it might be better if he

went to the nicely reinforced infirmary and organized a few rescue personnel to come back for her. It made more sense, really; he didn't have the appropriate training, and she *had* seemed angry that he'd risked his life to come to the bar; she certainly wouldn't want him to remain in an unsafe area. . . .

Before he could decide, the station was hit again, and more fiercely than any previous attack. Quark grabbed a table and held on as the room teetered wildly all around him. The lights went out completely as more bottles crashed behind the bar, emergency lights powering on a second later, the floor settling back to level in one sweeping, nauseating lurch. All was uncommonly quiet, even the distant blare of the red alert finally silenced.

Quark stood up, wincing at the depressingly sharp scent of spilled liquors, still clutching the table tightly with one hand as he looked around for Ro. Her body had tumbled several meters from its original position, coming to rest against a bolted chair. She'd stopped groaning.

The internal argument was brief but to the point, both positions clear. He had to get out immediately. And if he left her there, and the station took another hit like that, she was going to get hurt a lot worse.

Plus, what are the chances she could ever love the man who left her behind? And heroically saving the life of the head of security . . . contrary to popular belief, Ferengi were not cowards; the benefits just needed to outweigh the risks in some value, if not latinum. Latinum, of course, was preferable, but for Ro, he'd be content with her undying gratitude.

Quark hurried to her side and knelt down, numbly

aware that he'd hugely underestimated the seriousness of the situation.

"Lieutenant? Can you hear me?"

Ro's eyes cracked open, then closed again. Her voice was weak but clear. "Quark? Hit my head, on the stairs . . ."

"Yeah, I figured. Come on, we've got to get out of here." He slipped his arm beneath her shoulders and lifted, pulling her into a sitting position, relieved that she was conscious enough to help.

With Quark supporting her, they managed to stumble through the bar toward the door, barely staying upright as the station trembled yet again. Quark steeled his nerves with pride at his own good deed and the pleasantly firm pressure of her body leaning against his. If they survived, he had no doubt that this would be the beginning of a lucrative relationship.

7

They had run through their few ideas in thirty seconds, discarding each as quickly as they were said out loud; they just didn't have the resources or the time to implement any of them. It wasn't a matter of routing power or clever rewiring. The final hit from the strike ship had effectively destroyed the main plasma transfer conduits, from which the warp core operated. That, in turn, had instantly taken the drive off-line, creating a surge that had pushed the impulse fusion reactors into overloading ... which had basically killed absolutely everything. There was simply nothing they could do to make the *Defiant* have power that it didn't have.

Except for the viewscreen, of course, Nog thought bitterly. No gravity, no light except for a few charged emergency spots—but a working viewscreen with a near perfect picture, because holographic systems on Starfleet vessels operated from an independent power grid. Fate had apparently decided that it wasn't enough to just kill everybody; that would be too easy. No, fate had also deemed it necessary to keep the *Defiant* around as an audience for the grand finale, and had given them a primary vantage point from which to see it happen. The explosion would blow them apart, of course, but they'd get to see their friends and families die first.

Alone on the bridge, Ezri and Nog watched silently as the tiny strike ship battered the station. After gently securing Commander Jast's body, Tenmei had gone below to tell the rest of the crew what was happening . . . assuming there was anyone left to tell.

The *Defiant* continued to coast forward. DS9's shields seemed to be holding, but Nog figured it was only a matter of moments before they went—and once they were gone, the station would go even faster than that.

Ezri's strategy had almost worked—taking a beating in order to halve the attack forces wasn't necessarily inspired, but it was a sound enough plan. If the shields had lasted just another minute, it *would* have worked. . . .

Without a word, Ezri reached out and took his hand, squeezing it with her own. Nog was grateful, and glad she didn't say anything. In the face of what was happening, of the sheer enormity of the imminent apocalypse, words would be useless. The station was now obviously faltering, tilting, the translational controls probably down, the Lower Core's lights all gone.

After everything we've been through, for it to end like this . . .

He couldn't complete the thought, and as the screen suddenly flared, a wash of light enveloping the station, Nog almost convinced himself that he was seeing the end—until he realized that the brilliant blue light wasn't nearly brilliant enough to be an explosion.

The wormhole had opened, and something was coming out.

Kira felt her responsibility like a deadweight as the Jem'Hadar ship continued its attack, as the station beneath them went critical—shields down to eight percent, structural damage throughout the Lower Core, environmental systems on the brink of collapse. She should have rejected the ridiculous upgrade schedule, or demanded additional engineers, or fought harder for a second guard ship.

Should have, and didn't.

"Evacuate the station," she said, knowing the failure to be hers. "Civilian priority for runabouts and escape pods, everyone else to Docking Ring airlocks three, four, and six—make sure the freighters are full and prepped for warp, and program the ops transporter for the impulse shuttle at Upper Pylon Three. Seal off everything else."

If I had handled things better, I could have prevented this. The idea, that a trio of strike fighters could successfully disable the *Defiant*, could actually destroy the *Aldebaran* and DS9 . . . she wouldn't have believed it possible, and now, all that was left was to flee—

—and it's probably too late for us but we have to try, we have to keep trying—

There was another solid blow to the station. A second later, Lieutenant Bowers said the inevitable, horrible words Kira had dreaded hearing, the sound of them worse than she could have imagined.

"Colonel, we've lost shields."

She nodded, not trusting herself to speak as he continued.

"We can't expect more than a few minutes before a full breach in—sir! The wormhole, it's opening again!"

Kira's heart skipped a beat, sudden thoughts of the Prophets filling her with a manic hope. "On screen!"

The view was angled badly and blurred, a testimony to the station's dying power, but it was clear enough. They saw a small ship bursting out of the wormhole, riding the funnel of swirling light into the Alpha Quadrant. It streaked past the helpless *Defiant* toward the station, as small as one of the attack fighters—

Damn it, no!

It was another Jem'Hadar strike ship, and though it appeared to be damaged, much of its starboard hull black and crushed, it was obviously prepared to fight. How many more Dominion ships were waiting on the other side, they'd never know; with a second ship firing on them, there wouldn't be enough time for any kind of evacuation.

If even a quarter survive, we'll be lucky. Most—if not all—of the departing ships and escape pods would be caught in the explosion.

The station rocked, and Kira called out for Shar to send the new information to Starfleet on the long range, the thought that it was her final report a dagger to her heart. She prayed for time, furious with herself for not starting an evacuation earlier. It didn't occur her that there hadn't *been* an "earlier"; she felt too guilty and desperate to allow herself such consolation.

"Anything on sensors?" Kira asked. Perhaps the fourth ship to exit the wormhole was too damaged to fire.

"Negative, external banks are all down," Shar said. "I can attempt to transfer power from one of the auxiliary generators."

"No," she said, and raised her voice, aware that the newest strike ship would be within range in seconds. The battle was lost; it was time to let go, and hope there might still be a chance for some to survive.

"We have to evacuate now. Everyone stand down and get to the transporter—"

Lieutenant Bowers interrupted, pointing at the screen, his voice hoarse with emotion. "Colonel, the second ship!"

Kira turned, sick with sorrow; she could at least face the final moment—and watched, stunned, as the newest arrival fired upon their attacker.

"It's *fighting* them," Nog breathed.

He let go of her hand, pulling himself closer to the viewscreen, looking as shocked as Ezri felt. She barely dared to hope that the damaged ship could stop the attack; it was obviously in bad shape, only one of its weapons firing, but maybe it had a backup weapon, an override code for the attacker's ship, tractor beam capabilities . . .

. . . or some kind of warhead.

Ezri suddenly felt like her mind was being flushed with heat, the realization and the possibilities coming so fast that she could barely think. It was impossible, the strike ships were too close to the station and it had never been done—

—but if they move away... and if the command codes will work...

"Nog," she said, the hope taking a definite shape even as she spoke. "I have an idea."

The damaged striker only appeared to have one of its polaron phasers functioning, but it was as fast and agile as the attacker, managing to score several hits to the aggressor's port weapons array. The attacker stopped firing on the station, turning to dart after the damaged ship as it dropped into an evasive maneuver.

No one spoke, staring in mute disbelief as the two strike fighters engaged. They tagged each other around and beneath the station, firing and dodging. Kira refused to think about how close they were to an irreparable breach, or why the damaged Jem'Hadar ship would attack one of its own. What mattered was what was being played out in front of them.

Their protector was good, the pilot well-trained and bold, but they couldn't overcome their handicap; after a few hits from the attacking ship, its daring moves became stilted. It limped around the Lower Core, still firing—but another hit from the enemy stilled even that, knocking out its last phaser array.

The damaged fighter didn't retreat. Kira stared at the screen, unable to believe what she was seeing as it placed itself in harm's way, actually moving to block the attacker from firing on the station.

The attack ship didn't hesitate, blasting pitilessly at the interloper. Their protector suddenly barreled straight into the fire, apparently planning for a suicide collision—and streaked up and over the aggressor at the last second in an unexpected burst of energy, speeding away, heading back toward the wormhole.

Without another shot to the dying station, the point ship wheeled around and took off after it, firing intermittently. It seemed determined to finish the interloper off before doing anything else—although while the actions were clear, the motivations were anything but. Kira couldn't begin to guess at either pilot's reasoning, attack or defense.

Don't care, Prophets be praised, we're still alive—

The two ships raced toward the wormhole, the mostly undamaged attacker quickly gaining, scoring one hit, then another. They circled around, spinning back and racing forward again, gradually moving closer to the wormhole as the damaged ship worked to save itself, as the attacker tried to take it out. Their protector wasn't going to make it, it had taken too much damage—and as soon as it was gone, the point ship would be back.

Silently, Kira began to pray.

There was no way to gain access from the bridge. Nog got through to Ensign Tenmei on his combadge, filling her in as he and Ezri dropped into the turbo shaft that would take them down to deck two—one step closer to warhead control. It was a room Nog had been in only once, when Chief O'Brien had given him his first full tour of the original *Defiant.* The memory was sharp in his mind as he and Ezri hurriedly swam through the dark, the air already growing cold in the lifeless ship.

"Neat, huh?" O'Brien said, looking around at the

*tightly packed, tiny room with something like love.
"Part of the autodestruct system . . . The whole thing
can be launched from here in a worst-case combat sce-
nario, though I doubt it ever will be. Come on, let's
head back. I want to show you the pulse phaser
system. . . ."*

Not much of a memory, and although he'd studied
the schematics more than once since that long-ago day,
Nog still only had the most basic understanding of how
the deployable warhead operated. He decided that he
would gladly pay his future inheritance as the only son
of the Grand Nagus if the chief was on his way to the
control room instead of him.

The warhead module—that foremost section of the
Defiant's hull that also housed the navigational deflector—was equipped with its own impulse engines for
propulsion as well as an independent power supply,
plus a magazine of six photon torpedo warheads. As the
chief had told him, it was meant to be used only in the
most dire circumstances, which was probably why it
hadn't occurred to Nog at all—their current circumstances were probably as dire as any ever got, but he'd
just never expected to be in them.

He dredged up what he remembered, making mental
notes based on what needed to happen. This close to
the station, they would only arm one of the torpedoes,
he'd have to punch in a safe-distance shutoff and a single signature target into the guidance system. It was
dangerous, but it could work. . . .

*. . . assuming I don't mess it up, like I messed up the
repair schedule*— Nog swallowed the thought, concentrating on remembering the codes they would need,
anxious and sweating in spite of the cold.

They reached deck two, Ezri leading the way as they kicked off bottom and swam fore, the combined sound of their breathing seeming incredibly loud in the featureless dark.

"Don't worry, we're almost there," Ezri said, and the firm, calm tone of her voice made Nog feel infinitely better. Not the sweet, laughing voice of Ezri Dax, but the determined, reassuring pitch of a leader. He was too relieved to feel any surprise; a commanding officer was present and all he had to do was listen and carry out her orders.

They hurried on, Nog breathing more evenly, feeling his own spark of determination. He was still scared, and they were still probably going to die, anyway—but at least they wouldn't be sitting around waiting for it.

The damaged Jem'Hadar ship managed to draw the chase out longer than Kira would have thought possible, the pilot maneuvering well, the tiny ship like some wild animal running for its life. It had lured the aggressor away from its attack, at least—but as they looped ever closer to the wormhole, another hit spun the devastated ship around, pieces of its tattered armor bursting outward into space. It sprinted forward, back toward the station—but the enemy ship was on top of it, mercilessly blasting away, and Kira could see that it was over.

The final blow came a split second later, and the ship that had tried to protect DS9 shattered, a small but sparkling fan of wreckage and gases exploding from where it had been.

Kira's gut knotted as the people around her gasped

and cursed and softly cried out in muted despair, as the attack ship started back to finish off the station.

What did I expect, some kind of miracle, some beam of celestial light to shoot out of the Temple and save us all?

Maybe she had, maybe—

—what is that?

From offscreen, a tiny blur of motion, a glowing streak chasing after the moving strike ship. The ship apparently saw it coming at the same time she did. It picked up speed, diving down and away—and that tiny smear of light followed it, catching up—

—torpedo—

—and Kira understood what was happening just as it hit the diving Jem'Hadar ship, as the light of a small sun blossomed and expanded from the tiny craft, the light becoming everything.

"Got it, we got it!" Nog shouted, and Ezri pounded the control panel with a triumphant fist, the fire of victory surging through her heart, filling her up.

Yes!

"Hang on!" Kira shouted, and suddenly ops twisted and shook around them, people crashing into consoles and one another as the unshielded station suffered the force of the warhead explosion. Kira grabbed a railing, forgetting to breathe, seeing only the bright destruction on the screen in front of them.

Please let it be over—

—and in a few seconds, the short and violent ride ceased, the station coming to rest. For a moment, nobody moved or spoke. Kira imagined she could feel

DS9's wounds, could feel the loss of power and the compromise of integrity all around her as the people in ops slowly crawled to their feet, returning to their stations.

With a silent prayer of thanks, to the Prophets and Jast's tactical brilliance, Kira set her mind to what came next. The *Aldebaran* had been destroyed, the *Defiant* and the station had been brutalized; the treaty between the Dominion and the Federation was broken. An act of war.

We have to regroup. Jast needs to confer with Starfleet, we have to oversee the repairs, we'll need Bajor to send in more techs, and we'll have to talk about establishing a defensive line here. . . .

"Bowers, launch the *Rio Grande* and the *Sungari*. I want the *Defiant* crew beamed off before they freeze to death. And arrange for the ship to be brought back for repairs. Shar, status report." Kira suddenly welcomed the incredible amount of work ahead as the reprieve that it was; with so much to do, she wouldn't have to analyze anything for a while, or consider how much of the fault was hers. She already knew the answer, anyway.

Shar read off damage reports as the ops crew struggled to manage their posts, sending people out to assess damage and carry messages to those who had been cut off. The initial communications were daunting; the hull had been breached in several places in both the Lower and Mid Cores, most of the damage done by the aggressive point striker. Two of the fusion reactors had been impaired to the point of shut-down, reducing the station's power by a third . . . and at least thirty-four people were dead. Dozens more were unaccounted for.

Even as Shar tapped and spoke, trying to organize the flow of information, he found he couldn't stop thinking about the sensor readings that had flashed across his screen in the final seconds of the battle. They probably meant nothing, but still . . .

Kira was at the command station, her expression dismal as she scanned readouts from the Lower Core. Shar joined her, waiting until she looked up before speaking.

"Colonel—I should tell you that the internal sensor array suggested a transfer of energy to the station as the last strike ships were destroyed."

Kira frowned. " 'Suggested'?"

"It's not possible to verify any of the readings," Shar said. "And it's likely that they were all false, created by the power surge through the EPS system or—"

"How many such readings did you pick up, exactly?"

Shar shifted uncomfortably. "Seven hundred eight, sir."

Kira nodded slowly. "I see. As soon as the *Defiant* is brought in, you can try running our sensor logs against their externals, but I think you probably picked up radiation pulses from the explosions . . . or, like you said, random surges through the network itself from direct damage."

"I think so, too, sir, but I felt it was my duty to tell you."

"Thank you, Ensign. I'll include it in the master report. If that's all . . ."

Kira returned her attention to the table, and though Shar didn't know her well, he suspected that she was angry with herself over the near-success of the strike ships. It was a ludicrous notion, but she was radiating enough heat to suggest some strong emotion.

Perhaps if I engage her further, encourage her to talk about the battle . . . He had so admired her poise during the fight, he wished to offer some measure of his deference, however small. And he *was* genuinely interested in her perception of events.

"Sir, have you given any thought as to why the fourth ship attempted to protect the station?"

When she looked up again, he could see anger in her gaze—but her voice was calm and controlled, her manner almost formal. "No, I haven't. Perhaps you could hypothesize on the question for a later briefing. Right now is not a good time."

Shar nodded, wondering if he'd made a mistake in his approach. In his own culture, asking someone's opinion without offering one's own was a gesture of respect, and it had worked well with the captain of the *Tamberlaine,* a human male . . . maybe Bajorans were different. Or females.

Kira's combadge chirped.

"Colonel, this is Dax, on the *Defiant.*"

"Good to hear from you, *Defiant.* And good work. We have runabouts on the way. Tell Commander Jast and Nog to report to ops when you get here, and have Nog look at our damage reports en route. We're going to have to work out a repair schedule immediately. How's everyone on the ship?"

There was a long pause, and Ezri's voice, when she spoke again, was uncharacteristically solemn. "Two people were killed, three others wounded. Commander Jast and Turo Ane are both dead. I'm sorry, Nerys."

Shar stared at the colonel, who stared back. He could see his own feelings reflected in her face, but found no solace in the awareness that she, too, had sustained a loss.

He grasped at his training, struggling not to lash out physically in his pain, and saw in Kira the same fight—anguish warring to become violence. It was in the set of her jaw and in the tremble of her hands.

In other circumstances, discovering that they shared similar reactions to an event might have made him proud. Now, he turned and walked stiffly back to his station, understanding only that, like himself, she needed now to be left alone.

8

There were seven, including himself; each a high-ranking member of the Vedek Assembly, each of the other six as openly anxious as a vedek could be while still maintaining some semblance of piousness. It all rested in the hands of the Prophets, after all—though to look at their pinched faces, one might think otherwise. One might think, in fact, that the Prophets had deserted them, leaving each alone with his or her own fears.

Such uncertainty, because of what's happened. How difficult it must be. Yevir Linjarin understood the pain of doubt, and he ached to see it in others, particularly the six other men and women in the great chamber. That there was great change coming, there was no question, but the Prophets would provide. As They always had.

The man who'd called the meeting, Vedek Eran Dal, seated himself at the head of the long stone table, nodding to the attendant ranjen to close the doors of the great hall. The incense-scented chamber was cold, the meeting called too hastily for a single fire to have been built—although the secret nature of their small alliance surely had something to do with it. The traditional fires were lit only for the Assembly entire, and there would be no evidence of this meeting once it was dismissed.

Seated here were the seven most influential, the most doctrinally inclined, the men and women who would use their powers of persuasion to carry the rest of the Assembly in the direction best for Bajor. Kai Winn's sudden disappearance had necessitated the formation of the unnamed council; with First Minister Shakaar off-world, lobbying the Federation on Bajor's behalf, the people needed guidance, and not the endlessly turbulent sort provided by the Assembly entire, with its share of politicians and sycophants and deals.

Here, though . . . here sat the careful hands that would lead the way. The shared anxiety on their faces saddened Yevir, reminding him of the passage in Akorem's *A Poet's Flight:*

> *To doubt Their wisdom is to deny Them the pleasures of due faith, and to deny oneself the joy of being—and being, to be loved.*

When the doors had rumbled closed, Eran began to speak.

"I thank each of you for coming with such little notice. I'm sure you understand why I've called this session. Before we discuss our options, I would ask your impressions of the crisis before us."

Vedek Frelan Syla, a small, highly opinionated woman, was the first to place her hands on the table.

For reasons of poor health she had refused to be considered for the recent nomination to kai, much to everyone's relief; no one wanted another Winn Adami, and of all the possible candidates, Frelan was easily the most politically prone.

"Vedek Frelan," Eran said, opening the discussion.

"Early this morning, Deep Space 9 was attacked," she said, her statement of the obvious a clear sign that she was warming to a speech. "The last report I received from our contacts within the Militia told of sixty-one dead in all—not including the crew of the guardian starship, or the wounded—and severe damage to the power core . . . making it, I believe, the deadliest offensive yet waged against the station. Even in the time of war there was not so much damage, nor so many lives lost.

"My firm conviction is that the heresy was destroyed during the battle—and therefore that the battle itself was sanctioned by the Prophets. Did the attackers not travel through the Temple gates? I put forth that we have acted with unnecessary haste, presuming too much, and that we should now await further guidance from the Prophets."

Yevir saw, with no real surprise, that everyone now had their hands on the table, except for himself. He wanted to hear the opinions of the others before speaking; after all, it was likely they would look to him for the last word, and though he did not consider himself to be gifted politically, he knew that every notion should be heard. No one liked to feel dismissed, even if their ideas were rejected in the end. He accepted the fact of their acquiescence with no pretensions of humility, just as he accepted the reality that he would one day be kai—perhaps not after the upcoming election, but it *was* inevitable. His path was clear.

The discussion went around the table, Eran calling

each vedek by name, each stating his or her thoughts in turn, no two alike. Scio Marses believed that the matter should be opened to the Assembly, or at least the part of it that they could openly claim. Kyli Shon wanted to consult the Orb of Contemplation; Sinchante Jin, the Orb of Wisdom. Bellis Nemani insisted that they send a covert team to the station, to gather data, and Eran put forth the idea of allowing Kira Nerys into their confidence. She was, he pointed out, a devout woman, though Vedeks Kyli and Bellis disagreed strongly with the idea, reminding them all of how difficult Kira had proved to be in the past. The discussion, if not heated, was quickly becoming antagonistic. Gone were the traditional formalities of hands-on-table.

"We mustn't trust any information we don't collect for ourselves," Bellis argued. "Isn't it obvious? And Kira knew Istani, from Singha. For all we know, they were acting in collaboration—"

"—and you think she wouldn't come to the Assembly for confirmation, if she had talked with Istani?" Eran asked. "We need Kira. She runs the station and the people trust her. Granted, she can be obstinate, but her faith and loyalty to Bajor aren't in question—"

"Faith, perhaps not, but loyalty? You know the stories of her and Kai Winn," Kyli interrupted, his face flushed.

"Forget about Kira, and Istani," Frelan said. "The Prophets will show us the way, when the time is right!"

Yevir had heard enough. He placed his hands palms up on the table and closed his eyes, breathing deeply, turning his face to the high ceiling, to the sky beyond.

Their intentions are true and right, but they argue their own opinions. What is the way? How can I be a vessel of Your wishes?

He listened, to the small voice at his deepest core, the voice of his *pagh*, vaguely aware that the debate around him was finished, the angry words giving way to silence. When he opened his eyes, he saw that everyone watched him.

"Vedek Yevir, you wish to speak?" Eran asked. His tone was hushed and respectful.

"Thank you, I do." Yevir smiled, gazing at each face with warmth. "We all want to do what we think is right. Because we love the Prophets, and we love the people of Bajor. I know that each of us feels that the Prophets speak to us through our emotions, but I ask that we set aside anger and dissent at this moment, and meditate on what we share. On our love."

He had their full attention. Only a few years ago, he would have marveled at the concept that he, Yevir Linjarin, would someday lead such important people through a crisis, but all he wanted now was to share his vision.

"We have too often become entrenched in politics . . . but simply loving is also not enough. Like all matters, this is one that calls for action as well as faith. As we have all agreed, the heresy must be contained—but our course so far has not been worthy of us, and I feel regret for what has happened. I grieve; I feel shame. But I know too that the Prophets forgive us, because They know our hearts, and know that we mean only to express our love."

They were smiling back at him now. They understood, and it made him happy to see the self-doubt washed away, to see their faces shining with restored purpose. They hadn't forced Istani Reyla to run away, after all.

"What would you propose?" Eran asked.

"As you all know, I once served on the station during

my days in the Militia. I could approach Kira, and talk with her as a friend—but discreetly, a day or two from now. I wouldn't reveal so much as to burden her with the kind of decisions we're facing, of course. But if the tome is on board, and she has knowledge of it, I'm certain she would tell me."

They were nodding, pleased with the moderate and reasonable plan—and with having the immediate responsibility for what to do taken from them. It made him feel cynical to think such a thing, but he could not pretend blindness. Yevir knew each of them to be a worthy vedek, but he also knew that they missed having a kai to make the difficult decisions.

"I know it's asking a lot, but if you would place your trust in me, I believe that I could further our interests here, and thus the interests of all of Bajor," he finished, fully aware that their trust was already his. He didn't enjoy playing the politician, but there was really no choice, and he *was* deserving of their confidence. He had been chosen, after all.

As they gazed at him lovingly, he thought of the Emissary, of all he had done for Bajor—and all that Bajor was becoming because of the Emissary's work.

I won't let it fall apart because of some heretic's scratchings. I owe that to the Emissary, for choosing me, and I owe it to the Prophets, for Their boundless love—and to all of Bajor, because I am here to serve.

The seven were in agreement, all as one. Yevir would go to Deep Space 9 and make things right. He would find the heresy and burn it, and scatter the ashes so that no one else could be tainted by its evil ever again.

Hopefully, no one else would have to die. He would pray for it, anyway.

9

After a full day of triage and surgery, of making calls that meant life or death with only an educated hope that his decisions would prove sound, Bashir was exhausted . . . but as his backlog of critical cases wound down, he found himself wishing for more to do. So many lost, so many that no one had got to in time, who could have been saved; not only was it painful to review the incredible waste of life, having no pressing matter to attend to meant that there was nothing to keep him from what he thought of as the death watch—those cases for which there was no reasonable hope.

And nothing I can do, nothing at all. For all I've researched and studied, for all my abilities, I may as well wish them better.

There had been six in all. Now there were three in the infirmary's ICU, the room quiet and still but for monitor sounds and the stifled tears of the visitors. A nurse moved lightly between the beds, assuring that there would be no more pain for the dying.

Bashir stood in the doorway from surgery, looking at them, struggling to believe that he hadn't failed. He'd beaten Death throughout the day, through proper diagnosis and delegation and surgery, cases he tried to keep in mind as he gazed out at the ICU ward. Mostly he thought about the operations, because he had been able to touch the problems, to physically heal them. A sternal fracture that had caused a mediastinal bleed in a Bajoran girl, only 11 years old, healed. A compound fracture had nicked the femoral artery of a Bajoran security officer, who would have bled out if Julian's hands hadn't been fast enough. The flail chest on the visiting Stralebian boy, the open-book skull fracture of the human ensign who had been on leave from the *Aldebaran*—they all would have died if his skills had been lesser.

But that doesn't help these people, does it?

It was faulty reasoning, of course, and logically he had no cause to feel guilt. But feelings weren't necessarily logical. He couldn't blame himself for the majority of the deaths that had occurred on the station, because most of them had been instantaneous—forty-six plasma burn fatalities, a single rush of energy that probably hadn't even been experienced as pain. The rest of them had been lost to broken seals at the main Lower Core hull breach, except for two blunt trauma cases, victims of falling debris. There had been nothing that anyone could have done.

Of the nearly two hundred people injured, twenty or so had been critical, and only eleven of those had required immediate surgery or stasis. With the help of Dr.

Tarses and the Bajoran surgeon, Girani Semna, they'd gotten to everyone. Three compartment syndrome cases had been treated and released; all three would be shipping out to the advanced medicine facility at Starbase 235 for biosynthetic limbs. Except for some head traumas, a few incidentals, and those recovering from surgery, the immediate crisis was past—

—but for the three of you. Six, and now three, a death watch because I don't know enough.

In the cool, antiseptic air, the three patients were silent, sleeping or comatose. Woros Keyth, a Bajoran man who had worked in the admin offices, lay waiting for his brother to come from Bajor, to say good-bye. Keyth might have been saved, if he had been treated sooner. A subdural hemorrhage, the resulting intercranial bleed too far along by the time he'd been brought in, the brain damage irreparable. The blow was from a desk clock, of all things, when the AG had shifted; Keyth had been alone in his office, and hadn't been found for almost three hours. Too late.

Two beds away, the sleeping Karan Adabwe was watched over by her betrothed and one of her closest friends. Karan, an engineer, had been both burned and frozen, caught in the major plasma leak and exposed to an area of hull breach. It was a wonder that she was still alive, so much of her skin and muscle tissue had been affected. Her lover and a friend each held one of her poor, wretched hands, both crying, both certainly in more pain than Karan. She was beyond that, at least.

Prynn Tenmei, the new Starfleet pilot, sat next to the last case, Monyodin, a lab tech. Bashir didn't know if they'd been dating or were just friends, but either way, it was over. Monyodin was a Benzite, and had been in

Mid-Core when a cloud of chemical polymer gases had been released from a temp bank of atmospheric regulators. The alveoli of his lungs had liquefied. In a non-Benzite, Bashir would have tried stasis and an eventual transplant; for Monyodin, for any Benzite, there was no chance. With their cellular growth patterns, even external transplants rarely took. All that could be done was to make him comfortable . . . and watch him die.

It's not my fault. There's nothing that anyone could do.

It was true, and it didn't matter, not to the core of him. They were alive, but he couldn't keep them that way.

Bashir turned away, knowing that there were others to see, rounds to make, people he could still help. Knowing that the names and faces of the death watch would stay with him, as clear and crisp in his memories as he'd just seen them, until the day he died. He was aware that people on the station were starting to debate the long-term consequences of the Jem'Hadar attack, but if they could see what he had seen . . . he could personally testify to the tragedy of the short-term. It was more than enough.

". . . then perhaps I should come back at another time. How long will she be here?"

Familiar, a familiar voice. Friendly. *Shar, that's Shar* . . .

"It shouldn't be long, but I can't really say; the doctor wanted her to wake up on her own," a woman answered. "He said she could leave then, assuming her responses are normal. The concussion wasn't severe, but we don't take chances with head injuries."

"I understand. Would it be all right if I left these with you?"

Ro opened her eyes, wanting very much to see Shar, understanding from the tone of the exchange that he was about to leave. She was in the infirmary, most of the beds around her full, the woman talking with Shar one of the nurses. Ro wasn't sure what was going on, and the fact that Shar appeared to be holding a bouquet of bright green flowers only added to her disorientation.

"Shar?" She rasped, and coughed, her throat dry.

Both Shar and the Bajoran nurse turned toward her, the nurse immediately moving to her side. Ro sat up a little, light-headed but in no pain.

"What happened?" Ro asked, and coughed again. The nurse miraculously produced a container of some mildly sweet beverage and stood by while Ro drank, gratefully.

"There was an attack on the station, and you were brought to the infirmary with a head injury," the nurse said kindly. "But your readings suggest a full recovery. I'll go get the doctor."

Shar stood next to the bed as the nurse went off to find someone. He held up the rather exotic-looking bouquet of waxy, tubular blooms with a slight smile.

"These are from Quark. I saw him on the way here and he insisted that I deliver them; he said he was too busy ordering new inventory for the bar to stop in, although he might later. He says that flowers are a customary gift for the ill or diseased. These are Argelian, I think."

Ro smiled in spite of her confusion, not sure if she was more amused by Quark's gesture or Shar's uncertain explanation. "I'll be sure to thank him. Shar, what happened to the station? What happened to *me?*"

Before he could answer, Dr. Bashir appeared from another room, walking slowly and looking harried, his hair uncharacteristically rumpled. The smile he gave her seemed genuine, though. He glanced at the bed's diagnostic before moving to her other side, across from Shar. "Lieutenant, Ensign. I have a few questions, if you don't mind."

"So do I," Ro said, propping herself up on her elbows. "Chief among them, why is Quark sending me flowers?"

Bashir grinned, the expression as sincere as his smile—but she could see the strain behind it, could see that he was hiding some pain behind the sparkle. With how full the infirmary was, she guessed he'd had a rough day.

"Oh, I can imagine," he said. He opened a medical tricorder and passed the scanner over her head, his intense gaze shifting from the readout to each of her eyes as he spoke, his smile quickly fading. "Tell me, what's the last thing you remember before waking up a few minutes ago?"

She frowned, thinking. "There was . . . a murder on the Promenade. I remember meeting with you and Kira. And then I, ah, talked to Quark a little later about it, I remember that."

She'd gotten an isolinear rod from him, she'd gone to her office, and afterward . . . she recalled feelings of unease, even distress, but she couldn't pinpoint the reason. *Something about the holosuites?* "I don't know what else, I can't remember."

The doctor nodded, setting the tricorder down. "I saw you on the Promenade not long before you were brought in; I'd say you've lost less than an hour of your memory. An amnesic gap is perfectly normal with this type of concussion, nothing to worry about. Your cranial blood pressure is stable and your neurographic scan shows no disruptions. You can return to duty . . . but if you find yourself feeling nauseous or dizzy, or unwell in any way, you're to call for assistance and report back here immediately, all right?"

Ro nodded, a little surprised at his excellent bedside manner. She really hadn't interacted with him since coming to the station, and had assumed him to be generic Starfleet medical, patronizing and probably arrogant. "How did I get hurt?"

"You fell from the stairs in Quark's," Bashir said. "Quark saw it happen, and brought you here. It's lucky he did, too. With the way the station was bouncing around, you could have been seriously injured."

She started to ask about the station and the doctor hurried on, nodding toward Shar. "But I'll let your friend fill you in on all of that. If you'll both excuse me, I have rounds to make."

Ro thanked him and turned to Shar, who spent the next few minutes filling her in. She was amazed at all she had missed, and appalled by the station's death toll, not to mention the loss of the *Aldebaran*.

And Commander Jast. Hearing about her death hit Ro harder than she expected. A lot of Starfleet officers on board had a cold attitude toward Ro. Not surprising, really. She suspected most of them bitterly resented her presence on the station and were probably dismayed that Starfleet Command hadn't made a move to arrest her for her past offenses. How the provisional government had persuaded the Federation not to exercise its rights under its extradition treaty with Bajor was a mystery. The end result though, was that the Starfleet personnel on the station were forced to work alongside someone many of them believed belonged in prison. Or worse.

But Jast had been different. The commander had gone out of her way to be amicable. At first, Ro thought it was because Jast also seemed to be awkward at making friends . . . but, just in the last few days, she had been starting to feel that the commander actually liked her.

". . . and with incoming communications basically inoperative, the only messages from the Federation have been relayed through Bajor, telling us to wait," Shar continued. "Colonel Kira has all of the senior officers on standby for a briefing as soon as she gets word."

"What are we doing for defenses?" Ro asked, finally sitting up. Physically, she felt perfectly fine, but their conversation was making her stomach knot.

"The *I.K.S. Tcha'voth* got here just after the attack, and six Bajoran assault vessels arrived a few hours ago, so we aren't entirely defenseless," Shar said, "but there's great tension on the station, and the fear that war is once again imminent. It doesn't help that the wormhole has opened three times since this morning, triggered by debris from the *Aldebaran.*"

He lowered his gaze, speaking softly. "There's to be a service at 0700 tomorrow, in memory of all those lost. If you're not well enough to attend, it's going to be broadcast station-wide."

Listening to his gently lilting voice, she could sense a change in him. He was tired, she could see that, but there was more—something deeper, more fundamental.

Shar had probably liked Tiris Jast as much as Ro had, and had certainly known a majority of the station residents who had been killed. Though she wouldn't call him extroverted, exactly, Ensign ch'Thane was one of those rare people who seemed to honestly enjoy listening to and learning about others. He had quickly found himself a place in DS9's community, well-liked because, unlike herself, he never seemed to pass judgment. So different were their personalities, in fact, Ro had wondered more than once why he seemed to seek out her company. She'd finally decided that the old saying about opposites seeking out one another was probably true.

Shar was quite young and, though obviously brilliant, relatively inexperienced, both in his career and in his life. His only assignment before DS9 had been on a survey vessel, primarily collecting information on the Vorta. He'd seen little or no battle, and although he didn't seem the type to shy from it—Andorians, as a rule, were combat-ready—she doubted very much that he'd savored his first figurative taste of blood. Shar was too inherently decent, and she found herself mourning what he could not—the addition of a kind of tense wariness to his electric gray gaze, a look she knew too well from years of watching innocents return from their first real fight.

"I should return to ops," he said. "The sensor arrays are operational, but Colonel Kira wants them at peak efficiency now that we're focused on the wormhole."

Ro smiled at him. "I'm glad you came to see me, Shar," she said, and was faintly surprised at how much she meant it. He was the closest thing she had to a friend on the station.

Except for Quark, maybe, she thought, as Shar handed her the flowers. They had a pleasantly spicy scent.

"I hope that you will continue to mend properly," Shar said sincerely.

And I hope we're not about to go to war.

The unbidden thought frightened her, reminding her of all that was at stake—but it was a strangely compelling thought as well. She was only barely conscious that the prospect of battle had sparked her interest.

They made tentative plans to meet later and he departed, leaving her to consider all that had happened and to wonder what would happen next. So, the station's residents were scared, but fear wasn't all that hard to inspire in a primarily civilian population. The soldier in Ro couldn't get behind the idea that the Dominion truly wanted another war, not with what Shar had told her about the nature of the attack—and for all of Kira's faults, Ro didn't think the colonel was dense enough to think so either, not when it came to matters of conflict. Though, what Starfleet was convinced of was another thing entirely.

Forget it, Laren. None of your business. She had her own duties to worry about, reports to make and listen to, security measures to be reviewed and evaluated. And pointless as it suddenly seemed in the face of the larger tragedy, there was still that investigation into the prylar's death.

Ro stood up, Quark's flowers in hand, and though she'd already decided it wasn't her concern, she suddenly found herself wishing very much to know what Kira was thinking about, what she would say when she finally spoke to Starfleet—and what Starfleet would have to say to her.

There was more than enough room in the cargo bay for the coffins and urns and memorial plaques, but it was no less crowded for the dark and cavernous space. She'd left the main bank of lights off, the barely lit shadows much more appropriate for her lonely visit . . . and somehow, it reinforced the vague feeling that she'd never seen so many of the dead in one place. It wasn't true, of course, but the blank rows and stacks of sealed containers seemed to go on forever as they disappeared into the dark, an endless testimony to all that had gone wrong only a single day ago . . . and to her own place within that series of events that had left almost seventy of her people dead.

The memorial service had gone well, she supposed, as if any such thing could be said to describe a few simple prayers and a shocked moment of silent remembrance. It would have been better to wait a few days, but Kira knew from experience that reality assimilation often took time—which was an uncertain variable until they knew exactly why the Jem'Hadar had attacked the station. Better to say a few words when there was opportunity to say them, and hope that the survivors could manage their own personal closure in the days to come.

The service itself had been brief, the Promenade overflowing but still, everyone who could leave their work for a few moments standing en masse like a tide of lifeless dolls, watching her speak with flat and barely responsive gazes. After staying up all night walking the damaged station and personally taking reports from every section and subsection chief she could find, standing in front of the mostly silent assembly had seemed unreal, a disjointed dream filled with realistically unhappy details—the pale faces of the *Aldebaran* crew, knowing that only an assigned leave had spared them while their friends had died. The way Nog's proudly raised chin had trembled, or the soft sigh of an elderly woman who had lost her son. Kira had heard tears and seen the hard, set lines of faces that reflected emptiness, for fear that even acknowledging the pain would be too much to bear.

Kira rested her hand on the cool, smooth surface of a keepsake box, destined for a family in the Hedrikspool Province of Bajor, a few personal items that their daughter had left behind. Setrin Yeta, one of Ro's junior deputies, a bubbly redheaded girl with a high-pitched laugh. Gone. To be with the Prophets, surely, but would her family feel any less pain?

Will I? Will any of us?

Tiris and Turo Ane, Kelly and Elvim and McEwian and T'Peyn and Grehm and the list went on, some of the faces only known in passing, all of them real people with real lives, and if she had only done something more, if she'd made a decision a few seconds earlier, or later . . .

Without consciously deciding to, she had gone straight from the ceremony to the cargo bay, almost as if guided by some invisible hand. Even with all there was to do, her sense of responsibility wouldn't allow her to avoid it; to understand what had happened, to really understand what had been lost, she needed to see them. To witness the reality of them.

As she'd stepped into the bay, her early morning dream from the day before had come back to her, from what seemed to be millennia ago. It was the environment that did it, bringing a flash of imagery—a cargo bay, and she'd been surrounded by dying people on the Cardassian freighter, the fleeting glimpse of Ben as she'd walked into the light of the Prophets . . . had it been an omen, even a warning? Had she been too quick to dismiss it as a dream?

Now, she was surrounded by the dead, but she knew that there would be no saving grace at the end, no friendly voice or affirmation of divinity. She wasn't going to wake up, and although she'd been responsible for the deaths of others in her time, there was no real way to prepare for it, or work out moral rationalizations. It would always be something so vast and shocking that there was little to be done but to weather it, to let it be. There wasn't anything that could make her less responsible; better to accept the consequences and move on than to waste time wishing things were otherwise.

She walked slowly between two of the rows, letting her fingers slip across the various container tops of nondescript black metal, hurriedly replicated that afternoon. She'd had some vague idea about looking for Tiris to say good-bye, but she couldn't simply walk past the others. She thought that Jast probably would have understood.

Here were two humans bound for home, two Federation diplomatic trainees—both male, bright, fresh from the Academy and excited to study in the field, observing Cardassian aid relations. During his first day on the station, the older of the two had actually tried to flirt with her; he obviously hadn't yet learned how to read Bajoran rank insignia, and flashed a grin that told her that her eyes burned like the stars. She'd actually considered not telling him her name when he had asked, amused and secretly flattered by the ignorant attempt; in the end, she'd been unable to resist. The young man had blushed furiously and then studiously avoided her, right up until the day he'd died.

Eric, and his friend was Marten. She touched the black lines of code at the heads of their containers, wondered what Asgard and New Paris were like, the places where their families unknowingly waited for notification.

Next to them, a small, sealed pouch of liquid that would be sent to Meldrar I, blood from Starfleet Ensign Jataq'qat's heart that would be poured into the Meldrarae sea by its siblings. Jataq'qat had challenged her to a game of springball not so long ago, a date they would never keep. Kira walked on. A row away, a long line of small ceremonial urns bound for various Bajoran cities and townships, some containing earrings—the symbols of family, of the victims' devotion to the Prophets and the spiritual community to which they belonged—others with small pieces from the lives that had been taken.

She sighed, her mind so full of masked recriminations that she didn't want to think—not because she feared the pain, but because it was too distracting. Balancing between remorse and the cold, linear reality of the future was a cruel and terrible thing; she couldn't even allow herself the questionable relief of wallowing in guilt, because the station needed her, it needed her to be at the top of her game and she couldn't afford to shoulder the presumption of incompetence, no matter how much she thought she should.

"Why did you come here, Reyla," Kira said softly, her voice almost lost in the soft hum of the air coolers. She wasn't sure if it was a question, wasn't sure what she expected, but the death of her long-ago friend meant something, it had to mean something, didn't it? All of this had to mean *something*.

Kira felt her throat constrict and took several deep breaths, inhaling and exhaling heavily, clearing her mind. With each new breath, the tide of sorrow crept back, giving her room, reminding her that she was whole and alive and had a lot to do, too much to be standing around weeping in the dark.

Just as she felt herself reaching safer ground, her combadge signaled.

"Colonel Kira, there's an incoming message from Bajor, routed from the *U.S.S. Cerberus*—"

Ross's ship.

"Should I send it to your office?" It was Bowers, in ops, and he sounded tense. Everyone on the station understood that Admiral Ross's call would set them on a definite course of action, to comply with whatever the Federation decided. What that course would be, Kira wasn't certain; at one time, she would have called for immediate action, but she wasn't so quick to assume the worst as she used to be.

And not so quick to fight, if there's even a possible alternative. As far as she was concerned, the attack should be quietly investigated through diplomatic channels, at least until something solid turned up . . . and although Kira *believed* that the Federation wouldn't act rashly, that they probably wouldn't even whisper the idea of a counterattack before careful consideration, she wasn't positive. That was bad, but what really scared her was the possibility that she wouldn't have any way to influence their decision if they had, in fact, decided on some sort of retaliatory action. Deep Space 9 sat at the Alpha entrance to the wormhole, the first outpost that any Gamma traveler—or soldier—would encounter. Without question, the Dominion could not be allowed back, not if they meant to fight—but how could she allow one more life to be lost, when she might be able to prevent it?

My job here isn't about me, and it's not just about the state of the Federation. It's also about trying to do what's best for the people on this station, and for Bajor. She believed that, and it gave her strength, it was direction when she needed it—but as Bowers waited for her response, she gazed out over the sad remains of her friends, of her wards and peers and the semi-remembered faces of just a few of the thousands who depended on her, and she didn't feel it.

I'll be as strong as I need to be.

"Yes. I'm on my way," Kira said, gathering her defenses as she turned toward the doors that would lead her back to the world of the living. She didn't hurry and she didn't look back, the possibility of tears already a memory.

10

Whirling plumes of light spun up from wavering plains of fire, the radiant shapes lengthening thousands of meters until they grew too vast to sustain themselves. The funnels collapsed, disintegrating back into the amorphic ocean of red and orange before rising anew, the dance of the storms beautiful, threatening, and eternal.

After watching for what seemed like hours, Commander Elias Vaughn finally broke the silence. "Are we done yet?"

Captain Picard smiled, not looking away from the incredible lightshow. "Done watching?"

"Done looking, for the Breen. They're not here, Jean-Luc. I don't think they ever were."

Picard's smile faded. "I've come to agree with you, but we have to be thorough. Another run through the thick of it, and we'll have completed a second grid. We want to be able to declare a reasonable certainty, after all our efforts."

They stood before the viewport in the captain's ready room, the ever-shifting view of the Badlands spread out in front of them in shades of flame. For the last several days, the two men had taken to meeting there as the ship completed each run, to watch the plasma storms together.

The *Enterprise* had been searching the treacherous area for nearly three weeks, the constant atmospheric disturbances making it necessary to pilot and investigate manually, their sensors useless beyond a very short range. Vaughn had come aboard to advise the mission on Breen tactics . . . though even if their supposed presence had turned out to be true, he doubted he'd have been of much use. The captain and crew of the *Enterprise-E* were more than worthy of their distinction, and Vaughn was certain they could handle themselves against a few Breen.

It's been nice to spend some time with Picard and his people, anyway. Vaughn liked Picard, having met him on more than one occasion in the past. He'd always thought the captain bright, if a bit dry, and surprisingly well-rounded. His tactical instincts were superb, and he carried his command well, with distinction and grace. A little formal, perhaps, but not offensively so, his politeness clearly stemming from a respect for others rather than some self-promoting mechanism. But Vaughn had worked with this particular *Enterprise* crew only once before, at the Betazed emancipation over a year ago—a mission that had earned them his profound respect.

The intercom beeped, Will Riker's voice interrupting his musings. "Captain, the new course is plotted. Allowing for the predicted plasma currents, Commander

Data suggests that we begin immediately, and that we start out at one-quarter impulse for the first two million kilometers."

"Make it so," Picard said, and as the ship eased toward the shimmering Badlands, Vaughn thought again about the coded transmission he'd received only a few hours before. Even the dramatic beauty of the plasma storms wasn't enough to distract him entirely. He was bone-tired, and not from three weeks of chasing a rumor.

"I'm thinking of retiring, Jean-Luc," Vaughn said abruptly, a little surprised at his own impulsiveness as the words left his mouth. He'd been considering it for months, but hadn't planned to tell anyone until he'd decided. And he didn't even know Picard all that well. . . .

. . . *although he probably knows* me *as well as anyone.* Vaughn didn't know if that was good or bad, but it was the truth.

Picard also seemed surprised. He turned to look at Vaughn, eyebrows arched. "Really? May I ask why?"

"You may, but I'm not sure I have an answer," Vaughn said. "I suppose I could just say that I'm getting too old. . . ."

"Nonsense. You can't be much older than I am."

Vaughn smiled; he'd never looked his age. "I'm a hundred and one, actually."

Picard smiled back at him. "You wear it well. But you still have decades ahead of you, Elias."

"I suppose I mean old in spirit," Vaughn said, sighing. "Since the end of the war, I find myself thinking differently about things. After eighty years of charging off to battle . . ."

He paused, thinking. He'd never been an eloquent

man, but he wanted very much to define the path of his feelings, as much for himself as for Picard. After so long a war, so little time for pleasures or luxuries, he felt out of touch with the delicacy of his self-perceptions.

"I've always been a soldier," he said. "I was trained for it, and have excelled at it—and for a long time, I've felt my role to be an integral part of the peace process. Now, though . . . just lately, I've been thinking of the universe as an unending series of conflicts that doesn't need another aging warrior to help circumscribe them."

Vaughn shook his head, searching for more words to explain what he'd been feeling. "Wars will always be waged, I know that. But I'm starting to think of myself as a participant in war, rather than someone working toward peace. And the difference between the two is immeasurable."

Picard was silent for a moment, and they watched as the *Enterprise* slid effortlessly into the bright and turbulent space of the Badlands. Vaughn felt strangely relaxed, at ease with the captain's silence. He suspected that what he'd said was being carefully measured by Picard, scrupulously considered, and the thought was oddly comforting.

"Perhaps you need a change of vocation," Picard said finally. "Do you know the story of Marcus Aurelius?"

Vaughn smiled. A great warrior of ancient Rome, a general who'd lost his taste for battle in spite of his successes. The original soldier-philosopher of Earth. "You flatter me."

"Not at all. And I'm not suggesting that you turn to writing your meditations on war and peace . . . though perhaps that's not such a terrible idea. You have more strategic and tactical experience than any career officer I've ever known, Elias, but that doesn't mean you have to use it as a soldier would. You could write, or teach."

Picard faced him, his expression earnest. "Of course, you can do whatever you wish. But—forgive my presumption—I don't think you're the kind of man who would be content to sit back and watch the worlds go by."

Vaughn nodded slowly. "You may be right about that." He took a deep breath and expelled it heavily, finally reaching the foundation of his thought, the essence of what he was trying to express. "I don't know. I just know that I don't want to fight anymore."

Picard leaned back, looking out at the fiery storm once more. "I understand," he said softly, and Vaughn believed that he truly did. The captain's ability to empathize was perhaps his most admirable trait. It was a rarity in any species, and most particularly in upper echelon Starfleet.

The intercom signaled again. "Captain, Commander—we may have something."

That was a surprise. Vaughn left his personal thoughts behind as he followed Picard toward the door to the bridge. He'd been so sure about the Breen, had already decided that perhaps the Klingons had picked up *something,* but that "possible Breen warp signatures" wasn't it. Following the treaty, the Breen had withdrawn to their home space for the most part. But though they were certainly capable of deceit, building a military presence in hiding didn't fit with the Breen's cultural psychology. . . .

. . . *although it does fit in with a few other reports I've heard of late . . .* Reports that were still on a need-to-know basis. It was a funny thought, though Vaughn was too aware of the *Enterprise*'s current position to find any humor in it.

They stepped out onto the bridge and moved to their seats, Vaughn taking the advisory position to the captain's left. All they could see on screen was the rolling sea of unstable plasma.

"Mr. Data, report," Picard said.

The android consulted his operations console as he spoke. "Sir, the ship I am detecting is not Breen. It is a freighter, and it appears to be Cardassian in origin."

Picard frowned. From his other side, Riker spoke softly. "What's a freighter doing out here?"

Data answered him. "It is caught between two conflicted masses of pressure. Sensors indicate that the freighter is powerless, and there are no life signs aboard. Also, that they have been trapped in this area for an extended period of time."

"Estimate? How long?"

"Considering the relative consistency of both pressure fronts and initial reads on hull integrity, I would estimate that this particular eddy has existed for thirty years or more."

Picard's frown deepened. "Can you get a visual?"

"Trying, sir."

A few seconds later, the main screen's view changed, and Vaughn caught his breath, fascinated. The long, dark freighter tumbled slowly end over end against its bright backdrop, as it apparently had for decades, dead and alone. Vaughn felt his earlier exhaustion dropping away at the sight, barely noticing his relief that there was no battle to be had.

Haunted, it looks haunted.

"Captain, if you have no objection, I'd like to lead an away team to investigate," he said, not sure why he was so intrigued, not caring particularly. It seemed to be a day for impulsiveness.

Picard glanced at Vaughn and smiled, so slightly that it was barely visible. He looked back to the screen.

"Commander Data, is the ship's hull intact?"

"Yes, sir."

Meaning it's possible to initiate an atmosphere, at least temporarily. AG's a must, but we can suit it against cold, wouldn't have to wait for an environmental toxin analysis then, either. . . .

Picard nodded, and turned again to Vaughn. "Commander, I hope you'll allow Commander Riker to accompany you, and advise you in your selection of team members."

"Of course. Thank you, Captain."

Vaughn and Riker both stood, Riker asking for Data to join them, recommending that La Forge and an Ensign Dennings meet them at the transporter. Vaughn found himself unable to tear his gaze away from the exanimate freighter, and finally understood why he was so interested, the reason so fundamental but so odd that he'd almost missed it.

Somehow, looking at the lifeless freighter, he felt quite strongly that his future was inexorably tied to whatever they would find there.

I am *getting old.* Such fanciful thinking and daydreaming adventure wasn't his style. Vaughn shook himself mentally and headed for the turbolift, but in spite of his own best efforts to act his age, his excitement only grew.

Ensign Kuri Dennings was the last to arrive at the transporter room, slightly breathless in her environmental suit and obviously excited to have been asked along. As she hurriedly donned her helmet, Riker introduced her to Commander Vaughn, making a point to mention the anthropological study she'd done on Cardassia's occupation of Bajor. Vaughn asked several educated questions about the Occupation as they stepped onto the transporter pad, all of them making minor adjustments to their helmets before pressurizing their suits.

"Is everything ready?" Riker asked La Forge, his own voice sounding annoyingly strange in the confines of the headpiece. Irritating, SEWGs. No matter how streamlined the suits got, they still felt bulky and restrictive.

"Yes, sir. Our tractor beam is holding her steady. Gravity's been established, there are some emergency lights . . . though it's going to be a little cold, even with the suits. Negative 80° C at last check."

They could handle cold, but not dark. "How long will we have before the portable's cell runs low?" Riker asked.

Vaughn answered. "Considering the size of the freighter, I'd say about two hours. It's a standard cargo model, isn't it? 220?"

He directed his own question at La Forge, who nodded, looking distinctly impressed behind the thick lens of his faceplate. "That's right, Commander."

Vaughn smiled. "Sorry. I should leave the engineering matters to the expert."

Riker was also impressed, though not because of Vaughn's awareness of portable generators; Vaughn himself was an impressive man. He seemed to know a little bit about everything, but used it well, also knowing when to defer to others.

And when to shut up. The elder commander didn't seem to ramble, ever. Riker didn't know that he'd be so reserved with eighty years of war stories under his belt, and his taciturnity only added to his appeal; Vaughn wasn't mysterious, exactly, but there was an impression of great intensity behind his genial exterior, of levels operating within levels.

"Shall we?" Vaughn asked, and then nodded to Palmer at the controls. "Energize, if you please, Lieutenant."

A sparkle of light, and they were standing in the well of a large control room, littered with random debris and dusted all over with glittering frost. There were no bodies; the crew had probably sealed themselves in whatever areas were easiest to seal, to retain atmosphere for as long as possible. The freighter's bridge was cold, empty, and dimly lit by a handful of emergency lights, reminding Riker of nighttime on the mountains of Risa. He'd camped there last before the war, alone, huddled in front of a small fire as a cold plateau wind ruffled his hair. . . .

. . . *where did* that *come from?* A weird connection, to say the least. Risa was light-years away, literally and figuratively.

Vaughn stepped away from their group, surveying their surroundings. Ensign Dennings and Data both held up tricorders and started to take readings, and La Forge turned toward what had to be the engineering console with his case of adapter components, his silvery eyes glinting in the low light.

"Anything we didn't expect?" Vaughn asked, addressing no one in particular. Data answered, his voice startlingly clear. Physically, he didn't need a suit, but the helmet comlinks were still the best way for him to stay in contact with the rest of them.

"Tricorder readings are consistent with those of the *Enterprise* sensors," Data stated. "This ship was caught in a plasma storm approximately thirty-two years and four months ago. The structural damage in evidence would have made it impossible for them to break free from this pocket of space. Their power and life support would have failed in a matter of days."

"There were at least three Cardassian ships lost in the Badlands around that time," Dennings added, "but all military, no record of a freighter."

Geordi had plugged into one of the consoles and was reading from a small screen. "I think it's called the *Kamal*," he called. "Ring any bells?"

Kamala. The smell of her hair, and the way she tilted her head ever so slightly when she spoke . . . Riker blinked, taken aback by the sudden vivid memory of the empathic metamorph. He hadn't thought of Kamala in *years.*

Seems like I'm determined to let my mind wander. Deanna said I've been less focused lately, guess I should have paid more attention. . . .

He also knew from Deanna that the crew desperately needed some time off, that stresses were high and productivity low. Since the end of the war, the *Enterprise* had been inspecting defunct military installations, transporting supplies and emergency aid, chasing after possible terrorist groups—in short, wrapping up the loose ends to a war. It was almost the *Enterprise*'s turn for a much-needed break, and considering his lack of concentration, he abruptly decided that it couldn't be too soon.

Dennings was checking a padd she'd brought with her. "There *was* a transport freighter *Kamal,* but no record of it being lost. Of course, the Cardassians aren't exactly famous for sharing that kind of information. Not then, anyway."

Not much of a mystery here; the freighter had gotten stuck. For some reason it reminded him of an abandoned ship they'd come across when he'd been on the *Potemkin,* though that had been a personal craft, caught in a natural soliton wave. . . .

Snap out of it, Will!

Vaughn turned to address them, his eyes glinting with interest. "Well. I know it's not standard procedure, but if no one objects, I'd like very much to poke around a bit, see what there is to see."

He looked at Riker. "Commander, I know there are safety protocols to consider. . . ."

Riker smiled at the half question. Vaughn certainly didn't need his permission, but was gracious enough to ask, acknowledging his status as executive officer. "I think an 'unofficial' inventory would go much faster if we split up."

"I think so, too," Vaughn said, smiling in turn. "I thought I'd head for the aft cargo bays . . . perhaps we could each take a direction, and check in every fifteen minutes?"

Everyone nodded, and Riker found himself feeling relieved, looking forward to having a few moments to collect himself as he assigned sections to Dennings and Data; La Forge wanted to stay on the bridge and download whatever information he could. Riker wasn't tired, but felt as though he was suffering the symptoms of too little sleep—although of course he *had* stayed up too late, catching up on reports, and then a very late dinner with Deanna . . .

. . . curled up together afterward and talking about work, her eyes as dark and shining as when we met . . .

She'd had a sleeveless yellow dress that she often wore that first summer he'd been stationed on Betazed. He remembered the crisp feel of it brushing against his arm when they'd held hands and walked through the university's grounds, laughing about some random observation and enjoying the sun against their youthful faces—

God. He had to get some downtime, and soon.

There were dead Bajoran civilians in the cargo bays, corpses crushed beneath long-worthless boxes of supplies or sprawled atop broken sections of hull and deck. Prisoners of the Occupation, their sad, frozen bodies were too thin, a testament to the suffering they'd experienced in life—and though there were a number of Cardassian soldiers among the dead, the oppressors and villains of the Occupation, Vaughn found himself unable to work up any anger. They were all dead. The Occupation was history, and dead was dead. He wasn't always so unfeeling, so uninterested, but the reality of the *Kamal* had become a veil, a mist through which his life was being played like a holodeck program.

The memories had started small at first, shadows of experience that touched him and were gone. But the memories grew in detail as Vaughn continued to walk through the dark and cold, becoming more than vague images, becoming brighter than what was in front of him. Having never experienced a spiritual epiphany— and from the oft-heard tales of such experiences, he assumed that was what was happening—he wasn't sure what to expect, but perhaps the memories were part of it. Part of letting go . . . ?

Violence and death and rationalizations. It was hard, the truth; he'd seen and done many things that he wished he hadn't. He walked on, and the memories came faster, the intense feelings striking like lightning. People he'd loved, long ago; a dog he'd had as a child; the first time he'd kissed a girl. But overriding the touches of fond nostalgia were the battles, the substance of his life as a soldier. He couldn't stop remembering other tragedies, deaths as needless and terrible as the ones laid in front of him now. He'd witnessed innumerable wars, he'd documented the bloody aftermath on dozens of worlds—and he'd participated in more sorrows than he wanted to count.

My life has been about death. In the name of preventing it, I've killed so many, and seen so many killed. . . .

The civil war on Beta VI, where over eleven thousand men had beaten each other to death with sticks and rocks on one catastrophic afternoon, and all his team had been able to do was watch. The genocidal holocaust on Arvada III. The Tomed incident, in 2311; he'd been a lieutenant then, only in his thirties, back when he'd still believed that evil was doomed to fail simply because it was evil.

Vaughn walked slowly through connecting corridors as he'd gone through the lower cargo bays, his mind light-years from where each leaden step carried him. The desperate and hungry faces of Verillian children, orphaned by war. The mad, hopeless cries of fear and warning that had echoed down the halls of the Lethean veteran asylum. The terrible assassination of the Elaysian governor that he could have stopped, if only he'd known the truth even moments earlier. . . .

Vaughn was so caught up in the barrage of memories that he was slow to recognize the change of light. It wasn't until he stepped into the next bay that he noticed; the dim red of the emergency lighting was different here, the massive hold bathed in a purplish glow.

It wasn't as important as the images that held his mind, that battered him mercilessly as he walked inside. A dying scream. A crying woman. Friends lost. Feelings of triumph and pride, hate and fear.

The light grew brighter, illuminating the faces of the

dead cast about like debris, and Vaughn stopped walking, trapped by a lifetime of memory.

On the bridge of the *Enterprise* they had very little warning before the giant wave hit them from behind, its intense burst of radiation shattering across their shields in a sparkling halo of light. The truly powerful ones were very rare, and because the surges of energy traveled like tsunami beneath the surface of their plasma ocean, they were hard to foresee; the sensors didn't pick it up until six seconds before impact.

"Sir, there's a sudden concentration of highly charged plasma radiation behind us at mark, ah, hitting us now."

Even as the words were leaving Lieutenant Perim's mouth, the *Enterprise* was reacting, struggling to spread out the concentrated phenomenon, cutting sharply into the ship's power supply as the shields automatically prioritized their energy use.

Picard knew what it was before Perim had a chance to finish her sentence. The experienced physical effect was surprisingly mild, lights brightening suddenly and then lowering in strength, less background noise as nonessential equipment powered down, but he wasn't encouraged. A shield drain big enough to tap into something as insignificant as the lights had potentially devastating consequences.

"Engineering, report," Picard snapped, nodding to Perim at the same time. "Hail the away team, and put the freighter onscreen."

Status from Lieutenant Achen in engineering was fast and mixed. The last of the concentrated energy flux had traveled past them and wasn't dragging a secondary current, which meant they weren't in immediate danger of being hit again; all systems and their backups were suffering severe power shortages, but there was nothing irreversibly damaged except for the subspace communications array—it had been scrambled, and could take days to recalibrate and realign. Their shields were operating at substandard levels and wouldn't be up to par for several hours, which shouldn't be a problem so long as nothing else rammed them anytime soon—and the power to the tractor beam had been cut, releasing the freighter.

"No answer from the away team, sir," Perim reported, sounding tense and frustrated. "It looks like our short-range is down, too."

"Do we have transporters?" Picard asked.

"Negative, but that's temporary," said Achen. "They were just knocked off-line, so as soon as they've got enough power built up for the fail-safe, they'll automatically reinstate."

Picard watched as the magnified freighter settled across the main screen, weighing and measuring the possibilities. Nudged by the turbulence of the power wave, the freighter was slowly moving away from the *Enterprise*. Perim called out the approximate rate of four meters a second.

At their rate of movement . . . say, five to 10 minutes until they move far enough to completely dissolve the conflict of pressures, less if they're caught in a heated current.

Re-establishing a tractor lock would take too long. Factoring in the accompanying glitches to transport failure, Picard calculated that they'd need anywhere from four to nine minutes, assuming there was no trouble with the fail-safe charge.

"Get the transporters working immediately, priority one," he said. "Helm, can the sensors read anything beyond lifesigns?"

Perim shook her head, running able hands over the console pads. "Four living humanoids . . . no beacon read on Commander Data, no distinctive biosignature capacity from here."

"I can't get their combadge overrides to signal, sir," communications added.

For the well-shielded *Enterprise,* the random plasma tsunami had acted as an energy leech, no permanent damage done. But the freighter was no longer shielded by the tractor beam, had in fact been pushed toward possible danger by the beam's dying surge—and the away team might not even know it.

We can't talk to them, and at the moment, we can't pull them out. There was also no way to easily dock a shuttle, not without someone operating the freighter's lockdown controls. Blowing out a chunk of bulkhead was possible, but it would take time to do it safely.

Will was due to report within the next few minutes, and was decidedly punctual as a rule; when he realized that the *Enterprise* couldn't be contacted, he'd have the team initiate their communicator emergency signals. The transporters should be working by then.

"Prep a shuttle, and have a rescue team standing by," Picard said, not liking that he had to include it as one of the better options, knowing that he wanted as many contingency plans available as possible. "Security, send someone to transporter A, have them suited and briefed. Have Dr. Crusher standing by with a medical team as well."

Less than two minutes after the wave had come and

gone, Picard had done what he could to influence the outcome of the situation. He watched the freighter as it slowly drifted away from safety, wondering what could be keeping the away team from noticing that their tricorder readings had changed.

Kuri Dennings had been thinking about her days at the Academy as she walked, feeling fondly nostalgic and a little irritated that she couldn't seem to pay attention to her surroundings. To see an Occupation-era Cardassian freighter as it had been during those years . . . it was the chance of a lifetime, and yet she couldn't stop reminiscing about people she'd known, remembering names and faces she thought she'd forgotten. She had signaled in at fifteen minutes or so without thinking about it, too intent on her memories to care much about what everyone else was doing.

Kelison, with that silly hat he always wore to dinner, until Stanley hid it. The birds that nested outside the dorm. And Kra Celles, who could impersonate Lieutenant Ellisalda dead-on, from her facial mannerisms to that high, wavering voice. . . .

When she finally stopped walking, she realized she had found the weapons store, directly beneath the bridge. It was connected to a *yeldrin,* a kind of hand-to-hand-combat practice room common on older Cardassian ships. In the corridor between the two rooms were a dozen dead men, all Cardassian—after thirty years of weightlessness, they'd been cruelly dumped to the floor by the *Kamal*'s sudden gravity. She'd avoided looking at them, disturbed by the blank, ice-lensed gazes and stiff and awkward poses. They reminded her of the time she'd gone fishing with her brother on Catualla. They had stored their catch in a refrigeration unit that had malfunctioned, turning the fish into blocks of gray, lumpy ice. At the time, it had been funny. . . .

. . . and we joked about it, we called them ichthysicles, and Tosh was still laughing about it the last time we talked. When he called to tell me he'd met someone, a woman, and he thought he was falling in love.

A transmission in the middle of the night from her father, seven months after their vacation to Catualla. She'd been half asleep until she'd seen his face, seen the horrible struggle not to break down in the way he blinked, the way his chin trembled. He was the bravest, strongest man she'd ever known, but his son, her brother, was dead at the age of 26, victim to a freak cave-in at one of the mines he surveyed.

"Tosh is dead, baby," and he'd wept openly, tears running down his tired, tired face.

Nine years ago, but the pain was suddenly as fresh as it had been that very moment, and Dennings slumped against the icy wall of the *yeldrin* and clutched at herself weakly, trying to hold herself against the terrible pain.

Tosh is dead, baby. Tosh is dead. . . .

Ensign Dennings slid to the deck, sobbing, lost to the memory.

After Miles O'Brien had transferred to DS9, he'd kept in intermittent touch with the *Enterprise*—sometimes to say hello, to catch up with how the crew of the "D" and later the "E" were doing. In the early days he would contact La Forge just as often to complain goodnaturedly about his new job. DS9 had once been the Cardassian "Terok Nor," a uridium processing station—and, as Miles was quick to point out, Federation technology simply didn't function very well when plugged into machines built by Cardassians.

Not without a lot of rewiring, and some very imaginative bypass work. It wasn't that the technology was that much more or less advanced—only a two-point difference on the Weibrand logarithmic developmental scale, at least when the *Kamal* was built. But the fundamentals were distinct, from the positioning of warp engines to the computer's defense capabilities, and La Forge found himself appreciating O'Brien's troubles, seeing them in a whole new light. Even the mission last year to Sentok Nor hadn't prepared him for this. He was having a hell of a time figuring out how to get around in the freighter's most basic systems. It wasn't helping that he couldn't seem to get anything to power up properly.

I should get Data back up here, see if he can make sense of some of these translation disparities . . . La Forge scooped a .06 laser tip out of his tool case and sparked it, deciding to weld two of the console's EPS processing wafers together, see if he could boost efficiency—and hardly aware that he was doing it, he found himself thinking about how Leah would tackle the *Kamal.*

She'd be able to get a handle on this, no problem. Together, they'd be able to manage it easily . . . if it was the Leah he'd known on the holodeck, his own personal version of the engineer. . . .

La Forge felt a sudden flush of shame, remembering how she'd found his private program, his small fantasy of working with the brilliant engineer cruelly exposed. He'd never exploited her image, using the holographic program as a kind of confidence-builder—but he *had* made Dr. Leah Brahms much friendlier than she was comfortable with. He remembered the look on her face when he'd walked into the holosuite, too late to keep the real Leah from seeing the Leah-projection . . . he remembered the anger and embarrassment in her eyes, remembered thinking that *he* had caused those feelings, that she probably thought he was some kind of perverted miscreant when all he'd wanted was to be with her, to work side by side with a woman who respected him as much as he respected her—

La Forge frowned and shook his head, wondering why he was rehashing that particular aspect of their relationship. He'd found out she was married, she'd realized he wasn't a creep, and they'd ended up parting on friendly enough terms. . . .

This place is getting to me. Old ship, old feelings.

He'd been daydreaming since they arrived, running through all kinds of personal history as he worked. No harm done, he supposed, although he was usually better at focusing himself.

He lowered the bright torch tip to the processing chips, concentrating on the fine web of filaments. There was a spark, a wisp of smoke, the gentle swirl claiming his awareness.

—blind and alone, the smell of smoke thickening—

He'd been five years old, still too young for the VISOR implants that would allow him sight, and the fire had been started by a short in his bedroom's heating unit.

I didn't call out at first. I thought that if I stayed very still and quiet, it would go away. A blind child alone in his room at night, fists clenched and sweating, silently praying as hard as he could that there was no smoke smell, the air was clean, and that wasn't the crackle of flames, *wasn't-wasn't-wasn't*—

It wasn't until he actually felt the building heat that the little boy had screamed finally, screamed until he'd heard running footsteps, his father's gasp and mother's curse and more running. He'd burst into tears when he'd felt strong arms lift him up and away, the voice of his excellent father soft and soothing in his ear, *it's okay, Geordi, shhh, everything's okay now, shhh, my son, it's over and everything's okay . . .*

Feelings of love and remembered terror welled up in his heart and stomach, reminding him of how he'd loved them, of how dark his life had been except for their light, remembering . . .

After her hurried briefing, Deanna Troi reached the bridge as quickly as she could, the intensity of the atmosphere immediately setting her teeth on edge. The *Enterprise* was shadowing the freighter, which was apparently only minutes from hitting a strong current that would toss them, unshielded, into the whirling, deadly spumes of light. Will's report was officially overdue, and the transporters were still off-line . . . there were still too many variables for exact predictions, but simply, if they couldn't make contact with the away team soon, they would be lost.

Deeply frustrated, the captain was listening to an engineering update and leaning over the helm's console, watching stats. Deanna took her seat, breathing deeply as she opened herself up, first acknowledging and then tuning past the people directly around her. She felt for

Will, searching for the familiar presence in a radiating arc of awareness, but couldn't find him; she couldn't find anyone. She hadn't really expected to, the Badlands disrupted all sorts of sensors, even her innate empathic sense, but she'd had to try.

Having nothing to report, Deanna stayed silent, watching the freighter, hearing status revisions and possible solutions to the problem—but her concern for her lover and friends wouldn't allow her any real objectivity. She gave into it instead, recognizing her own need to feel productive in the face of such frustration.

Nothing to lose, anyway.

Deanna closed her eyes for just a few seconds, seeing herself, seeing a sense of warning expanding from her presence, mentally speaking words of alarm. *Will, you're all in danger, look out, receive, understand that you're in trouble.* She knew that it was probably useless, she wasn't much of a sender outside her own species, but her faith in their connection gave her hope—that by some chance he would feel the fear in her thoughts and understand what was happening, before it was too late.

Riker walked until the silence got to him, and then he remembered. He remembered, and was afraid.

There was death everywhere, Cardassian bodies stiffly jumbled like stick dolls and no sound but the sounds of his own body, his heart and respiration, the rustle of his uniform against the inside of his suit. It was as though the ship was holding its breath, waiting, in between what had come before and what was coming next, the silence a secret in the empty space.

Quiet and secret, secret and hidden . . .

He'd reached the living quarters. The *Kamal* had small, individual rooms for her crew, the entries dark and open, the bodies here all heaped at the end of the main corridor. He was at the opposite end, his back to a corner where another hall intersected the one filled with bodies, his hand on his phaser. He shouldn't be afraid, he knew that, and so he wouldn't draw his weapon . . . but his envelopment in the memory was complete, his outrage and horror was new.

They'd come for him at night, to perform medical experiments. Years ago. Secret experiments conducted on the sleeping crew by a secret race, the constant, random clicking of their voices or claws like insectile rain, like a black, evil thaw. They'd been solanagen-based entities, and they'd killed Lieutenant Hagler, replacing his blood with something like liquid polymer, and surgically amputated and reattached Riker's arm for no reason he could ever know or comprehend. . . .

. . . and I volunteered to stay awake, to carry the homing device so that we could seal the rift between their space and ours. I took the neurostimulant and I waited, waited for them to take me, knowing that they would dissect me awake and not care as I screamed.

Laying there in bed, seconds like hours in the dark, twitching from the hypospray, waiting in perfect silence, wondering if he'd make it back. And then the abduction, and feigning semi-consciousness as they'd clicked and muttered from the darkness, telling their secrets in an alien language. . . .

He knew he had to act, he had to do something, but

the feelings were overwhelming. Paralyzed, Riker hunched further into the corner, listening to the past.

Data stood in the *Kamal*'s communal eating area, accessing seemingly random personal information. Although he had experimented with daydreaming in the past, the spontaneous nature of the experience was unusual, particularly under the circumstances. A self-diagnostic did not inform him of any problem. Still, it was perplexing; the occurrence of memory recall did not normally interfere with his ability to function, but he found that his designated task—to observe this specified section of the Cardassian freighter—did not seem as important as the examination of his previous experiences and aspects thereof, which seemed to occur to him in no particular order.

The sentience of Lal, stardate 43657.0. Learning to dance, stardate 44390.1. Meeting Alexander, son of Worf, stardate 44246.3. Deactivating Lore, stardate 47025.4. His attempt at a romantic relationship with Ensign Jenna D'Sora, stardate 44935.6. His return to Omicron Theta, stardate 41242.4. Commanding the *U.S.S. Sutherland,* stardate 45020.4. Sarjenka, stardate 42695.3. Kivas Fajo, stardate 43872.2 . . .

Data's understanding of each memory's relevance to his current situation was lacking, and the only common element was that he seemed to be present for each one. He decided he would return to the *Kamal*'s bridge and speak to Geordi about it—but thinking of Geordi called to mind an entirely new set of experiences, and he paused to consider them, interested in his apparent ability to direct the focus of his memories.

Geordi's unnecessary funeral assemblage, stardate

45892.4. The disappearance of the *U.S.S. Hera,* on which Geordi's mother was captain, stardate 47215.5 . . .

"Captain, the transporters will be ready in two minutes or less."

The freighter would only be safe for another four minutes, at most. Not enough time for a rescue team to find anyone, and he didn't want to risk it without knowing if the away team's combadges were operating. Beyond that, it was unlikely that a transporter beam could pull them out in time, the interference of the storms too great.

Last resorts. They could try to use low-power phasers to nudge the freighter onto a new trajectory . . . but given its condition, there was no way to be sure it wouldn't cause catastrophic damage. Even if it worked, they might conceivably end up sending the freighter hurtling into the path of another plasma flare.

"Is security ready?" Picard snapped.

"Yes, sir. Mr. Dey is fully suited and standing by in transporter room A," a voice over the com called from security. "He's been briefed to objective."

Beam in, call an emergency, beam out. They'd have to hope that all the away team members still had working combadges, and weren't somehow restricted from using them. It was the last realistically possible option; if they couldn't get the team out through the steadily closing time window, there might not be any way to save them.

Something was wrong. Vaughn's internal journey through the past was starting to include events outside of his experience, or one series of events, specifically—the loss of the *Kamal,* and the deaths of the people surrounding him. The integration of memories not his own was gradual at first, but his alarm grew with each unfamiliar experience.

The woman on Panora who cursed us for letting the Jem'Hadar come. A stand of dead garlanic trees, poisoned by biogenic gas. A plasma storm, bursts of powerful energy buffeting the freighter, the impulse engines knocked out in the first wave of burning light . . .

Not me. That never happened to me.

Vaughn struggled to understand as the memories kept coming, so strong that he was nearly incapacitated. He forced himself to take a step forward, then another, practically blinded by the persistent wash of feelings and images, fewer and fewer his own.

The brilliance of exploding Jem'Hadar ships over Tiburon. The Cardassian captain shouting, ordering for power to be diverted to the shields. The controlled terror on the faces of the men guarding the prisoners, when they realized that life support had been cut by half.

The purplish light was growing in intensity, brightening, becoming bluer, and Vaughn sensed a familiar odor, comprised of unwashed bodies and desperation and overcooked soup; it was a prison smell, or that of a refugee camp. Sadly, he'd known enough of both to be certain. He took another step forward, remembering the soulless gaze of the first Borg he'd ever seen, and the soft prayers of a Bajoran couple who'd asphyxiated less than ten meters from where he now stood, and the ashy gray faces of the gasping Cardassian guards, still grasping their rifles—

—this is not some personal catharsis I'm having, I have to stop this—

—and there, at the back of the cargo bay, the source of the light. A twisting, fluid shape in an open box, less than a half meter in size, propped up on a broken crate. The object itself was barely visible behind the shining, pale blue rays of light that it emitted, the dark red of the emergency lights drowned out by its radiance. He stumbled toward it, suddenly sure that the light was creating whatever it was he was experiencing.

Dying, they were all dying, Cardassian and Bajoran alike, suffocating—

—the Cardassian Occupation. Bajoran history . . .

Orb. The Orbs of Bajor.

Another memory, but this time, there wasn't another to push it away, as though it was a memory he was supposed to have and keep. The Orbs were religious artifacts, supposed to generate spiritual visions or hallucinations of some kind; the Bajoran faithful believed that they were gifts from their gods. *Read about them somewhere . . .*

It was still the past on the *Kamal,* the strained hisses of death all around him in the cold bay, but Vaughn felt stronger, clearer. And when he reached the box, studded frosted jewels or reflecting ice, he thought for just a moment that there was someone with him, standing at his side. A tall, dark human, a man who seemed to radiate a kind of serenity as strongly as the Bajoran artifact radiated light—

—and then Vaughn closed the box's intricately carved door and he was alone, standing in the cold, silent peace of the long dead *Kamal.*

Only a few seconds later, an unfamiliar male voice

sounded in his helmet, identifying itself as a security officer and demanding that that everyone on the team trigger his or her emergency signature immediately.

Vaughn quickly hefted the box and set it by his feet before tapping the contact on the forearm of his suit, motivated by a strangely compelling certainty that the Orb was ready to leave the icy, floating tomb where it had rested for so long.

12

After some thorough scans by Dr. Crusher, the away team reported to the observation lounge for debriefing. As soon as the captain finished reviewing the final damage assessments, he would join them there.

Standing in front of the door, Deanna received a depth of chaotic and disturbed emotion, a feeling of darkness. She took a few deep breaths, relaxing, centering herself. Allowing any personal distress to enter her mind at this point would only hinder her effectiveness, which would inevitably make it harder to communicate, to listen and hear. It was a fundamental truth of effective counseling.

Still, she was concerned. The freighter had disappeared into the Badlands a full two minutes after the away team had returned, certainly close enough to trigger post-traumatic responses, but it was the discovery of an uncased Bajoran Orb that worried her. No one on the team would have been prepared for the kind of effects such an artifact produced.

She walked in and took her place at the table next to the captain's empty seat, the agitated feelings in the room assigning themselves specifically to each member of the team, except for Data. They were all confused, but in keeping with the history of the Orbs, the base feelings suggested personalized experiences. Geordi was emotionally exhausted, wrung out, but other than bewilderment and an uncharacteristic vulnerability, he was well. Kuri Dennings was similarly exhausted, but from pain. Kuri had visited Deanna a few times concerning the death of her brother, but had been handling her grief well; the raw depth of it had been revisited, and Deanna decided immediately to call in on her later.

Will . . . She could feel his strength, his desire to be brave for her, but he was struggling against a post-adrenaline low. . . . And something like self-doubt, possibly even shame.

He was scared, and quite badly.

She had to resist an urge to hone in on his feelings, to probe deeper for how the experience was affecting him. It was an important element in their relationship, to maintain a firm boundary between their private and professional lives, but there were times that she found it difficult. Now, with the crisis past, she did what she could, accepting her personal concerns for him and setting them aside for later.

She turned her attention to Commander Vaughn just as the captain walked into the room, and was surprised by what she found there. She'd come to like Elias, very much, since they had first met, and though she still didn't know him well, she appreciated the weight of the unknown responsibilities he seemed to shoulder. He was a thoughtful, intelligent man with a strong sense of decency and compassion, but he'd also been troubled since he'd come aboard for this mission. She'd sensed great uncertainty beneath his polished confidence, the kind generated by meticulous soul-searching. In that capacity, the commander was like Captain Picard... but where Jean-Luc's foundations were solid, Elias had seemed to be in doubt of the very structure of his belief system. He handled himself well, though, and as he was an extremely private man, Deanna had not approached him about it. But the highly charged energy coming from him now was so fundamentally different. . . .

. . . his doubt is essentially gone. Whatever he was struggling to decide about himself, he's decided.

She couldn't know what the decision was, but he was sending out waves of exhilaration, and she found her curiosity about the nature of this particular Orb soaring.

Vaughn waited until Picard finished telling them what had happened during their absence before delivering his simple, concise report of their ordeal aboard the freighter. Everyone on the away team, even Data, had experienced vivid and incapacitating memories while separated, which had stopped as soon as the Orb had been shielded. Data provided a brief explanation of the Orbs themselves, describing them as "energy vortices," but admitted that the Orbs Federation scientists had so far attempted to study had consistently defied a more meaningful analysis. Of the original nine, only four were accounted for. Eight had been taken by the Cardassians during the Occupation; one had remained hidden on Bajor. Three of those stolen had been returned to Bajor over the five years following the Cardassian withdrawal, but the whereabouts of the remaining five were still unknown. And given the present turmoil on Cardassia Prime, the Bajorans' expectations of recovering them anytime soon were low. A tenth Orb, previously unknown, had been discovered off-world only a year before, but that one had vanished after it had apparently fulfilled its purpose.

The captain was excited about their find, though he was outwardly calm. "It seems we've found one of the missing ones. And I think it's reasonable to speculate, from your experiences, that this is the Orb of Memory. It was originally discovered in the Denorios Belt more than 2000 years ago."

"What exactly *did* we experience?" Will asked. "How do they work?"

Captain Picard nodded toward Deanna. "Counselor?"

"As Data said, there's very little scientific information on the Orbs," she said. "Except that they transmit an energy that works directly on neural pathways, affecting chemical and electrical balances. They're quite powerful. At least one has been known to function as a time portal. In most cases, however, the effect is more . . . personal. Having an Orb experience is often life-changing for those of the Bajoran faith; many believe that it offers a line of direct communication between themselves and the Prophets, the wormhole entities said to watch over Bajor."

The discussion continued, the decision made for Data to immediately begin work on the delicate realignment of subspace communications, the captain announcing that they would be moving away from the Badlands to run full systems diagnostics and to reassess options. The *Enterprise* needed a dock so that the shield-emitters could be properly tested, and access to Starfleet command as soon as possible, to make their report. Will suggested that they plot a course for Deep Space 9, the closest starbase to their current position and conveniently owned by Bajor; they could turn over the Orb to the Bajorans and await new orders as they carried out repairs.

Deanna could feel the flagging concentration in the room and decided to speak up before the captain started assigning responsibilities. He was unaware that Will and Kuri, at least, had been adversely affected by their encounter. "Captain, Orb experiences are generally quite draining. I strongly recommend at least six hours of rest for the team members before they return to duty."

Picard nodded, the natural concern he always felt for his crew intensifying slightly. Deanna had often wondered if he knew how paternal the tenacity of his feelings were.

"There's no immediate crisis, is there? Let's make it a full night," he said lightly, and stood up, smiling. "Data, I hope you won't mind the extra hours. I'd like the rest of you to contact your teams and tell them that they'll have to do without you, that you're officially off duty until 0800 tomorrow. Rest well, everyone."

They all stood, Deanna deciding that she would walk with Kuri back to her quarters. She made eye contact with Will, and both saw and felt that he was holding up well; like Geordi, he wanted only to sleep at the moment.

Not Elias, though. He was very much awake, she could get that much from the spark in his sharp blue eyes.

"Captain, if I could have a moment . . ." he asked, and Picard nodded. Both men lingered behind as the rest of them filed out, Data telling the weary La Forge which self-diagnostics he planned to run while he worked on communications, the others silent with fatigue. The counselor felt a twinge of wistfulness as she followed, wanting very much to hear what Elias would say to the captain, if he would talk about his newfound sense of determination and purpose. Intellectually, the change was only a simple shift of attitude—but the simplest were often the most profound emotionally.

Deanna sighed inwardly before turning her full attention to Kuri Dennings's sweet, anguished heart, starting the search for the words that might help.

Commander Vaughn didn't seem to be nearly as tired as the others had—nor did he seem as tired as he'd been only a short time ago, discussing his retirement as they'd watched the storms. In fact, he seemed positively invigorated.

Perhaps I was right about that change of vocation, leading an exploration team seems to agree with him. That, or his experience inspired this somehow; he was closest to the Orb.

Picard couldn't help feeling vaguely sorry that he hadn't insisted on going along. To have found such a historically and culturally valuable object . . . it would certainly have put a spring in his own step.

"Captain, I just wanted to thank you for our conversation earlier today," Vaughn said, firmly meeting his gaze, even sounding different. Gone was the slight hesitancy, the careful measure of each sentiment expressed. "It set the stage for one of those 'powerful

156

experiences' that Deanna mentioned. I feel that things are much clearer now."

"My pleasure," Picard answered, pleasantly surprised at the man's mood for freedom of expression, part of him thinking that Vaughn was about to say he'd reconsidered retirement. Something had certainly changed; the commander no longer seemed to have that cautiously watchful quality that had drawn deep lines at the corners of his eyes and mouth.

"You seem to be in high spirits," he added, raising an eyebrow, not wanting to pry but curious about the transformation.

"I am," Vaughn said, folding his arms and leaning against the table. "The memories I experienced—I was reminded of things that I'd forgotten, of people I used to know, of events and the feelings I had when I was experiencing them. And I realized that since the end of the war, I've been . . . I've been preparing to be old, if that makes sense. Because I'm tired, I'm sick of death and the destruction that accompanies it."

Picard nodded, understanding perfectly.

"Jean-Luc, do you know why I joined Starfleet?"

Picard considered his response before answering. "I suppose I always imagined it was out of an honest sense of duty, an earnest desire to serve and defend the Federation."

Vaughn shook his head. "That was why I *stayed*. I became a floating tactical operative very early in my career because I was good at it, and I was needed. It wasn't a career path I chose; it chose *me*. And when I was on the freighter, I remembered that, and how differently it all started for me, and for a moment I felt . . . I felt like the young man that I was, when what

I really wanted to do with my life was clear in my mind."

Vaughn brushed at his neat, silvery beard, smiling. "I want to learn, Jean-Luc. I want to explore, and live in each moment, and feel excited about my experiences—not because I want to recapture that blush of youth, but because it's what I've *always* wanted, and I'm too damned old to put it off for one more minute."

"Come, my friends, 'tis not too late to seek a newer world," Picard thought, smiling back at him. "Does this mean you're leaving Starfleet?"

Vaughn shook his head. "I don't know. And the amazing thing is, I don't know if it actually matters. If what I want to do doesn't fit in with Starfleet's agenda, I'll leave."

"Bravo, Elias," Picard said warmly, amusedly considering Starfleet's reaction to the news that one of their most capable officers, with clearance that probably went higher than the captain dared to speculate, might be quitting in order to find himself. He instinctively offered his hand, which the commander promptly shook. "I'm happy for you."

"Thank you, Captain."

They decided to meet for breakfast, and Vaughn left, his shoulders definitely straighter, his head held higher than Picard had seen previously. It was a real pleasure to be witness to such a shift of spirit; discovering a renewed sense of purpose at his age—at any age, really—was cause for celebration.

Picard suddenly felt an odd wave of déjà vu, wondering when he'd witnessed such a startling transformation before. Then he remembered.

Seven years earlier, another Starfleet commander

he'd known had come to a crossroad in his life's journey, and its course also had been determined by an unexpected encounter with an Orb of Bajor.

The captain stood for a moment longer in the quiet room, thinking about Deep Space 9 and how Colonel Kira would react to their "surprise" visit. Knowing that the Cardassian relief efforts were being routed through the station, he hoped she'd be amenable to accepting unannounced guests. Now that he thought of it, he was actually looking forward to the stop; perhaps Vaughn's enthusiasm for new experience was catching. It would be interesting to see what had changed since Captain Sisko's departure, see how the staff and residents were building their post-war lives—and it would be a chance for the crew to see a few old acquaintances.

And considering that we'll be presenting them with a prominent instrument of their faith, lost for decades . . .

It was likely to be a most engaging visit.

Still thinking of the sharp new brightness in Elias Vaughn's gaze, Picard straightened his uniform and headed back to the bridge, unaware of the faint smile he wore.

13

Kira walked slowly to the briefing, collecting her thoughts, trying to relax. Her conversation with Ross hadn't gone well, but she saw no point in expressing the depth of her anger and disquiet to her crew, so she took her time. She'd gotten a lot better at controlling her temper through the years, but as tired as she was, she wanted the extra few moments to refocus. No one would like the news, and it was her job as commanding officer to provide a realistic example of calm leadership, regardless of her personal feelings.

Just before she reached the wardroom, she realized someone was walking right behind her. Startled, Kira stepped to one side and turned around—and saw nothing, a few meters of empty corridor and a wall.

Getting paranoid now, that's just wonderful. One more thing to put on her list of nervous-breakdown topics.

The meeting room seemed too empty, even though

everyone was there—Bowers, representing tactical, Nog and ch'Thane, Bashir, Dax, and Ro. No Tiris, of course . . . and Major Wayeh Surt, the Bajoran PG administrative liaison, had just gone on an indefinite leave. His wife of nearly thirty years had been one of those killed during the attack. Wayeh had offered to stay, but Kira had insisted that he go home to be with his children, promising that she'd take care of things until a replacement was found.

Maybe they should find a replacement for me, too, at least when it comes to talking with Starfleet from now on. It was one more way that Jast would be missed; the commander's ability to effectively represent the station's interests to Starfleet had never been so badly needed.

Dax threw a slight, encouraging smile at her as she moved to the head of table, but Kira couldn't manage to summon one of her own.

"I've just come from speaking with Admiral Ross," Kira said without preamble, taking her seat. "At this time, Federation and Allied forces are on full alert throughout the quadrant. After an emergency council of the Allied leaders that lasted until a few hours ago, the Federation has organized a task force to investigate yesterday's attack on the station. Members of the Romulan and Klingon governments will be joining the task force, which will leave from here, and everyone— Federation, Romulan, and Klingon—is sending military backup. Their plan is to send a well-armed contingent of ships to the Gamma Quadrant in order to make contact with possible Dominion forces."

For a few seconds, no one spoke, but she could see that their reactions were much as hers had been. Incredulity to uncertainty to frustration.

"When are they coming?" Dax asked.

"And what does this mean for us?" Nog added. "What are we supposed to be doing?"

"Three days from now, maybe four, depending on how soon they can assemble," Kira said. "Their rendezvous point is the Gentariat system, a day and a half away at high warp. And because of our current status, we're not officially expected to do anything beyond what we were already doing—repairs and upgrades, coordinating relief aid, cleaning up the mess. Bajor will be sending us several teams of Militia engineers to help—the first shuttles should arrive later today."

"Do they really think that the Dominion is about to wage another war?" Shar asked, an anxious set to his features.

"Ridiculous," Bowers said, shifting in his seat. "If they really wanted to start something, they wouldn't send only three attack ships. It was a rogue attack, we've run across that before with the Jem'Hadar."

Dax was nodding. "And there was that fourth ship, that tried to stop them. It doesn't make any sense."

"It's been suggested that the initial attack was deliberately staged, either to directly lure the Federation into battle or to distract it from noticing a buildup of forces elsewhere," Kira said woodenly, not bothering to point out the rather obvious holes in such an attack plan. She'd pointed out a few to Ross, who had countered each neatly with reminders of the Dominion's war record.

Tell them the rest, they may as well know it all. Her allegiance was to Bajor and to the people she worked with first, not to Starfleet.

"There is currently a motion before the Council to

establish an Allied peacekeeping force within the Gamma Quadrant," Kira said quietly, "which doesn't leave this room, for the time being. Officially, it's a rumor I heard."

"They can't be serious," Bashir said, his brow furrowed in disbelief. "They can't believe that the Dominion will tolerate an armed force that close to their borders even for a single day, let alone as on ongoing presence. It could spark another war."

"It's definitely not going to promote opening diplomatic relations," Ezri said. "They already don't trust us."

Kira had said pretty much the same thing to Admiral Ross, and his answer was still clear in her mind:

They broke the treaty, Colonel, and in less than three months. The Allied leaders are in full agreement on this. If the Dominion wants another war, we take it to them, and the first step is to do exactly what they've done; we're going in to assess their current capabilities, and we're going in prepared to defend ourselves.

The worst part was that she could understand that point of view. Strategically, the idea was sound, especially if they could secure the other end of the wormhole against further intrusion. Unfortunately, it was also rash and inappropriate, but she could see how the logic of defense, fueled by resentments and bitterness over a long and terrible war, could sway a crowd of politicians and admirals into making such a choice. She saw how the Klingons and the Romulans might push for an excuse to redress what they saw as deficiencies of the treaty—neither had been happy with the noninterference provisions—but Kira was stunned and not a little disappointed that the Federation was willing to spearhead it.

And there's Odo. She hadn't brought it up with Ross, aware that it would seem like an emotional argument coming from her, but she couldn't believe that Odo wasn't being figured into the equation. After his celebrated role in ending the war, he had gone back to the Link partly with the hope of teaching the Founders tolerance—and she believed that he could, that if it was possible, Odo would do it. But if the Allies undermined his efforts by sending troops, if they'd already withdrawn their faith in him, she had little doubt that he would lose tremendous ground with his people.

All of this flashed through Kira's mind in an instant, rekindling her anger, but she stamped it solidly down. She wasn't going to encourage dissent just to validate her own opinions. Besides, preaching to the converted would take energy, and she couldn't spare it.

"Admiral Ross was sympathetic, but he has his orders. I've registered my protest, and will urge the Bajoran provisional government to do the same, but there's nothing else we can do."

Again, there was a brief silence, looks of anger and worry, and Kira pushed on to station status. Whatever the Federation planned, it wasn't going to be resolved by any of them, not here and now, and there were more immediate problems to discuss.

An exhausted Nog gave them a rundown on reconstruction efforts, glumly listing the most critical first and quickly descending into a morass of minor disasters, everything from roaming power failures to industrial replicator malfunctions. Dax, back on temporary engineering duty, helpfully threw in a few that he'd forgotten before briefly touching on station morale. There wasn't much for her to say outside of the obvious; people were moving from shock into depression and anxiety.

Bowers and Shar both briefly reported on technical aspects of their respective departments—with everything powered down and no tactical capacity, not much was happening beyond hands-on manual work, cleaning, testing, or recalibrating. Bashir's medical report was even shorter, statistics and supply needs delivered in a soft, tired voice, dark circles beneath his eyes . . . and Ro basically had nothing—rehashed security measure reviews from the handling of the crisis, final effectiveness assessments, recommendations for new drill procedures. Kira was hard-pressed not to let her irritation show.

"Anything yet on the investigation into the Promenade deaths?" she asked.

"It's ongoing," Ro said blandly. "I'll file a report as soon as there's any progress."

Her tone was inflectionless, but the way she glanced away gave Kira a sense that she wasn't being entirely forthcoming.

"Do you have any leads?" Kira encouraged, hearing an edge in her voice and not able to stop it. "Anything?"

"Colonel, as soon as there's any progress, I'll file a report," Ro said, this time firmly meeting Kira's gaze, her own unflinching.

For a fraction of a second, Kira had a satisfyingly clear mental flash of throwing Ro against a wall. Aware that Bashir and Dax were exchanging a look over the tense interplay, Kira let it go—but only for the moment; it was past time for her and Ro to have a private conversation. "Fine. Let's move on."

They spent the next few minutes running through priorities and plans, Kira making her recommendations as they went along. She pushed Nog into agreeing to delegate more responsibility, and they talked about co-ordinating with the arriving technicians. Bashir and Dax were going to start collaboration on an agenda to help station residents in emotional distress. Kira emphasized the need for the station to continue coordinating Cardassian relief efforts in spite of the present situation; ships would continue to pour in for inspection and certification, and too many lives were depending on them to let that process be disrupted. The Federation-sanctioned task force wasn't mentioned again, or included as a factor in their immediate agenda; they needed to worry about making their own environment livable and working again.

The meeting was about to break when Kira remembered the one decent piece of news that Ross had given her. "I almost forgot—Starfleet commendations are pending for Nog and Prynn Tenmei—and Lieutenant Ezri Dax's name has been submitted for, let's see if I remember this right . . . the Starfleet Citation for Conspicuous Gallantry, I believe it's called."

Everyone smiled, even Ro. Dax rolled her eyes.

"I assume you'll be switching to command now—congratulations, Captain," Bashir joked, earning another round of smiles. Ezri saluted him. It wasn't much, but it was the only light moment Kira expected to have for a while, and she was grateful for it.

She hadn't planned to say anything else, but as they stood up to leave, Kira realized she wasn't quite finished.

"Listen . . . this is a difficult time, but we'll get

through it. We've come through worse. I just wanted you to know that I'm glad you're all here."

Not overly inspired, perhaps, but Kira felt better for having said it. This was her crew, these were her friends, and she'd do right by them no matter what it took.

It was late for lunch, and Quark's was mostly empty. There was still plenty of activity going on around the station, but the majority of those visiting on personal business—Quark's clientele, mostly—had decided to depart for safer seas following the attack.

They had the right idea, Kasidy thought. *The quiet is nice though, for a change.* They sat on the balcony, looking over an agreeably subdued Quark's. Kas was relieved not to be shouting over the blitz of a dabo tournament, and thought that Kira was, too; her friend was obviously in need of some peace. As it was, she'd only been able to spare enough time for a single *raktajino,* and Kasidy was ready to bet that it was the first break she'd taken in hours.

". . . but other than that, things are looking up," Kira was saying, the haggard tightness around her eyes and mouth indicating otherwise. Considering the list of the station's ongoing technical problems—and what was brewing with Starfleet—Kas wasn't surprised. "The Militia techs will stay at least a week, maybe longer."

"Things will go much faster with all the help," Kas said. She was trying to be helpful and supportive; Kira had certainly been those things for her since Benjamin had been gone, but the truth of it was, she was impatient to leave the station. If it was just her, it would be different . . . but with young Rachel Jadzia or Curzon Tye (*maybe,* she silently reminded herself; a week ago, she'd been absolutely fixed on Sylvan Jay and Joseph Cusak) to consider, her priorities had undergone a major shift. During the attack, in the reinforced corridor where she'd crouched and waited with the other frightened residents, terrified that she'd be injured in some way that might affect the baby, she'd made her decision—to turn down the next couple of assignments with the Commerce Ministry so that she could move as soon as possible. The station wasn't safe, and not far away was the quiet patch of land where home waited, sunlight streaming in the windows, an herb garden freshly planted out back. . . .

". . . don't you agree?"

Kas blinked, quickly replaying the conversation she'd missed. She'd read that a lot of women suffered lapses of concentration during pregnancy, but she couldn't blame everything on hormones. *Some friend I'm turning out to be.*

"Yes," Kas said firmly, picking up the thread again. "By the time they get here, everything will be different. They'll have to reconsider once they cool down a little, put things in perspective. Hey, look at the bright side— at the very least, there will be a few more Starfleet engineers running around for a couple of days while the brass sorts everything out. Between them and the Militia techs, the station will be taken care of, finally . . . and then maybe you can get away for a few days. Like we talked about."

Kira stared down into her cup of *raktajino,* surely lukewarm by now. "I don't know, Kas. It sounds wonderful, it really does, but you'll be getting settled in, and there's just so much for me to do now that Tiris is gone. . . ."

"Well, forget about that 'getting settled in' stuff, you know I'd love the company," Kas said firmly. "And you've been so great—without you, the house wouldn't be half finished by now. Really, you deserve to come down and spend a few days just sitting around and reading books, or wandering around in the garden. . . ."

Kira shook her head, and Kas trailed off, wondering why such a strong, brilliant woman insisted on making things so hard for herself. Kas waited until Kira looked up and held her gaze, determined to get through. She was going to push, and hope that she wasn't overstepping the bounds of their friendship.

"Nerys, the strain is showing. You haven't had a break since the day you took command. I know things are a mess right now, but you're going to have to schedule a few deep breaths now and then, or you're going to burn yourself out."

Kira looked away, and after a moment, she started to speak in a quiet, low tone, indirectly responding to Kas's question. "I hadn't seen Istani Reyla in years, or talked to her. I didn't even know she was here until after she was killed."

Kasidy already knew that Kira had been friends with the monk who'd been murdered on the Promenade, one of the Commerce secretaries had mentioned it at the morning admin meeting, but it was the first Kira had talked about it. *Probably to anyone.*

"That must have been terrible," Kasidy said softly.

Kira nodded. "I'm going to miss her. We haven't stayed close, but I'm going to miss knowing that she's out there."

"I know what that's like," Kas said, not elaborating. Kira didn't need to share, she needed to get it out.

"If she was just someone I knew from before, it would be bad enough," Kira said, finally looking at Kas again, a wrenching expression of wounded confusion in her eyes. "But she was such an amazing person—at Singha, at the labor camp where I met her . . . she was a prylar then, and she must have known what I was doing with the Resistance, but she didn't care."

Kira shook her head, wearing a faint, incredulous smile. "I mean, here was this woman who truly believed that all life was sacred, and I was just a child, and I'd already *killed* people . . . and she used to tell me the story about how the Prophets filled the oceans and painted the sky, and she taught me how to braid my hair, of all things . . . she tried to encourage me to be a child, in spite of what my life was. Or maybe because of what it was."

"What a gift," Kas said quietly, sincerely.

Kira nodded, her face working as though she were trying not to cry, but her voice was as strong and clear as ever. "Truly."

Patiently, Kasidy sipped her tea as Kira got hold of herself, aware that she would withdraw from a gush of sympathy. Considering that Nerys prided herself on her near-perfect autonomy, Kas had some idea of the effort it had taken for her to talk about her feelings.

Time to pull out the fail-safe, a simple but perfectly wonderful trick that Kas had recently discovered.

"So, are you still going to be godmother to this baby, or am I going to have to find someone else, 'cause you're too busy?" Kas asked.

The lines of tension on Kira's face almost magically

lifted, her whole demeanor changing, a more positive outlook reflected in her very posture. Kasidy had asked her almost a month ago, explaining the honorary term and receiving an enthusiastic *yes*. They'd only been close for a relatively short time, but their friendship had come to mean a lot to Kasidy. Inviting her to be godmother was Kas's first real solo decision regarding the baby, too, so it felt good to talk about it, to remind herself that she was moving forward instead of simply waiting.

"Don't you dare," Kira said. "I promise I'll take a vacation, okay?"

Kas relaxed. Just seeing Kira smiling again, really smiling, was enough to put any real concern to rest. For Kira, the birth would be doubly blessed; she'd be godmother to Kas and Ben's baby, but also an important figure to the child of the Emissary . . . although that wasn't a part of it that Kas liked to think about too much. Attention, even fame was going to be unavoidable—they were going to be living on Bajor, after all—but she meant to do what she could to see that their child was protected from the kind of religious fervor that had surrounded Ben.

Kira took another sip of her *raktajino* and grimaced, pushing the cup aside as she stood up. "I have to get back to ops. But thank you, Kas. Really."

She already seemed less exhausted, less stressed. Kas smiled, glad to have been able to help, watching Kira move down the stair spiral with a satisfied feeling. It felt good to have a close female friend again, to know that she could give support as well as be supported when things weren't ideal. It made maintaining a grounded approach to her life a lot easier. . . .

Kas happened to glance down as Kira was leaving the bar, in time to see the colonel freeze in her tracks—and shoot a startled, suspicious glance all around her. It was only for a second; Kira seemed to realize that she was in public, such as it was—only Morn at the bar, less than a dozen patrons scattered throughout the bar—and then she turned and quickly walked out before anyone noticed her behavior. But Kas had seen it, and felt her good mood stilled by that odd look. Because it meant that Nerys might be in trouble, real trouble.

Now who's paranoid? Hormones again. Kira had heard something, that was all, or . . . she only thought she had.

Kas drank the last of her tea, running through her mental packing lists, refining plans for the move . . . and found herself unable to ignore the small knot of worry that had bloomed in her mind.

Ro Laren was in the security office, absorbed in something on her desk console, the drab setting still so thoroughly *Odo* that Quark decided immediately he would give her a discount on remodeling accessories. She was simply too magnificent a gem to be surrounded by such . . . *Odo*-ness.

He straightened his coat and stepped into the office, as uncomfortable as ever in the environment of the law, but determined. He hadn't seen Ro since leaving her at the infirmary; he'd wanted to visit her, but besides having to oversee the repairs to his much-too-empty bar (Broik had actually attempted to replace some of the broken shelves with a higher grade of Foamet, trying to justify the expense in terms of durability, the witless slug), he'd felt strangely reluctant to go to her quarters.

As if she *didn't* owe him her life, and wouldn't be thrilled to see him. . . .

. . . *so why so worried?* He wasn't sure—but no, not true. He was simply a hopeless romantic, eternally doomed when it came to a pretty face and a nice set of hands, and Ro Laren made him quiver with all sorts of foolishness. Love made idiots of men, common knowledge—and thank the Great River for such stupidity, lovers loved to spend—but *being* the idiot wasn't a strong position from which to bargain. Making his intentions obvious would give her an advantage, and if he wasn't very careful, someone like Ro could embezzle his very soul. Not a big deal in and of itself; souls were too ethereal to be worth much. But his willingness to offer her genuine discounts, *that* was frightening.

When she finally looked up, the smile she favored him with very nearly paid for the flowers he'd sent. "Quark! Come in, have a seat. I was going to come by and see you later."

He smiled winningly and sat down in one of the chairs across from her, unable to remember a time when he'd been welcomed into DS9's security office. "I can't stay long. I just wanted to stop by and see how you were feeling . . . and see if you got the tube orchids."

He considered telling her how expensive they were, but decided it would be wisest to hold his tongue. She wasn't a dabo girl, after all; in fact, he suspected she was the type who didn't care about such things.

I always seem to fall hardest for the crazy ones. . . .

"I did, thank you," she said, still smiling warmly. "And I'm feeling fine, thanks to you. Dr. Bashir said that you rescued me after I was thrown off the stairs."

Quark cast his gaze modestly to the floor, saying the words he'd rehearsed in his mind on the way over. "It was a considerable risk, of course—but even with the station falling to pieces all around us, I knew I couldn't just leave you there to die. . . ."

He looked up at her, gauging her reaction. She was still smiling, still receptive; he kept going. ". . . because that would have been a tragedy beyond all measure, Laren. May I call you Laren?"

Her smile grew. "I believe you just did. Seriously, Quark, thank you. There's a good chance that you saved my life, and I'll always be grateful to you for that."

He grinned back at her, his heart singing, thinking of all the shipments that wouldn't be inspected, all the time he'd be able to save not having to sneak around to conduct business (time wasn't latinum, but they *were* interdependent), of how she'd look draped on his arm wearing something slinky—and then she opened her mouth again, and his dreams fizzled into so much smoke.

"Of course, I'm not going to let you get away with anything because of it," she continued brightly, a bit *too* brightly. "Now that I think of it, I'll have to watch you even more closely than before. We wouldn't want anyone to suspect that there was some kind of favoritism going on. Because of my appreciation for your bravery, I mean."

She was still smiling, and smiling back at her, he scrambled to salvage what he could, the 285th Rule of Acquisition running through the back of his mind like a curse. *"No good deed ever goes unpunished."* It was always the 285th that got him, he could have it tattooed on his forehead and he'd still forget it.

Think, think, you want this woman on your side— He hadn't been prepared, foolishly assuming that his selfless heroism would pay off, and—as was his everlasting luck—it had backfired. But as long as she was being amenable, he should do whatever he could to further the bond between them.

—not the flowers, and the bribe window is closed— work the Kira angle. Allying himself against the colonel might help things along; any opportunity in a storm. He'd actually come to respect Kira's shrewdness over the years, a fact that only threat of severe torture would force him to admit to the woman's face—but she was still a headache. Besides which, she made the big decisions, but it was Ro who'd be enforcing them, and therefore Ro he wanted to side with.

"You're probably right," he said, sighing. "I know the colonel would love nothing more than to catch the two of us falling short of her high moral standards."

Ro's smile faded, and he hurried on, not wanting to be *too* obvious. "Don't get me wrong—I like Kira, she's a fine commander and all that . . . but her self-righteousness can be a little trying at times."

"I don't suppose I know her well enough to say," Ro said neutrally, watching him carefully now. "Is there a point to this, Quark?"

"No, no, of course not. Making conversation, I suppose." He was about to let it drop, deciding that he'd totally misread the opportunities here, but a real curiosity struck him about the two women, something he'd wondered about since the first day Ro had come to station.

And it's not like I have anything to lose, he thought sourly.

"If it's not too personal, may I ask why you wear your earring on your left ear?" Every other Bajoran he'd ever known always wore it on the right.

Ro's smile crept back. "May I ask why you're asking?"

Quark shrugged. "Honestly, because I've noticed that it seems to bother some of the other Bajorans on board."

Particularly Kira. And "bother" was a serious understatement, but he saw no point in giving her a complex.

Ro seemed almost pleased. "That *is* honest. All right, Quark, I'll tell you. I wear it in memory of my father. He loved his culture, and in my own way, I suppose I do, too. But I've never been very religious. Not all Bajorans are, you know. Wearing my earring on the left was the best way to discourage the random vedek from wandering up to feel my *pagh* ... which, you may know, is traditionally felt by taking hold of the left ear. For different reasons, of course, the practice was also taken up by the Pah-wraith cultists. . . ."

". . . which explains why people don't like it," Quark finished, and though his hopes for having the head of security in his pocket were still dashed, his romantic interest had rekindled explosively. She'd actually gone out of her way to annoy, upset, and alienate her own kind.

What a woman.

"Right."

She didn't continue, only sat with that amused expression on her fine face, and though he felt a sudden, wild urge to profess the seriousness of his intent, Quark decided that he'd better leave before he offered her something expensive. He needed time to work out a new strategy.

"Well, I suppose I'd better let you get back to work," he said, standing. "Drop by the bar later, if you like. I'll . . . buy you a drink."

"Thank you, I'll do that," she said, and with another bright smile, she turned her attention back to whatever was on her desk monitor.

Quark walked slowly back to the bar, his heart full, his lobes tingling, Rules battling through his mind. The 94th Rule, *"Females and finances don't mix,"* was one he'd ignored to his own disadvantage on more than one occasion . . . but the 62nd Rule was louder, drowning out his concerns by its simple, love-friendly truth:

"The riskier the road, the greater the profit."

Oh, yes; quite a woman.

14

It had been some time since they'd made love, their lives too hectic, too rushed for anything but sleep... and since the attack on the station only two days before, Ezri had seemed distant, or at least preoccupied. Julian didn't mind, particularly; he'd been preoccupied himself with a second wave of minor injuries, from pulled muscles to stress headaches. And although the death watch was finally, thankfully, over, he still had the incidental cases he'd discovered while treating first-wave problems. Most had already been dealt with, but there was one he couldn't seem to "leave at the office," as it were, and he'd woken up thinking about it.

While cauterizing a scalp laceration on a Hupyrian freighter cook, a standard blood scan had picked up a fairly rare genetic disorder specific to the species—not lethal, but potentially debilitating at some future point, similar to what would have once been called rheumatoid arthritis in a human. The medical database didn't have much on it, but Julian thought he saw a few possibilities, assuming he could keep the sequences in proper order.

It was early, both of them in bed, more than an hour before he had to get up. Ezri was still asleep and Julian was working through one of his sequencing ideas, staring absently at the padd with the cook's chart. He'd gone to her quarters late the night before and they'd both been exhausted, falling comfortably asleep not long after his arrival.

Julian was just deciding that altered nucleic material re-injected into the Hupyrian's secondary pituitary-like gland might be the answer when Ezri reached out to him. The gently playful smile on her face as she touched his arm, stroking it, suggested that she'd been awake for at least a few moments.

"And what do *you* want?" he asked lightly, smiling back at her, setting the padd aside. Eight days, fourteen and a half hours, give or take a few minutes, and he carefully ignored the precise thought, reorienting his focus from the literal to the feel of her hand.

Ezri grinned, snuggling closer against him, twining her fingers through his. "What do you got?"

"I hope that's rhetorical," he said, and slid down so that he was facing her. Still holding hands, they kissed, slowly and gently, with love more than passion—at first. With his eyes closed, he still saw her, the soft warmth of her smile, the perfume of her hair and her skin enveloping him. Ezri was a physically beautiful woman, but her looks didn't matter, not here and now. It was her presence, it was the feel of them together that fired his senses, thrilling each part of him.

They shifted, breaking their kiss long enough to

reposition themselves, Julian moving over her, looking down at her sweet, flushed face, her slightly dilated eyes, as excited by the awareness of being with her as by his own physical sensations. For so long in his life he'd only known shadows of such feelings, never understanding how much more there could be, what was even possible.

He bent and kissed her again, the thinking part of him falling further away as she closed her eyes, pulling him closer ... and in another shift of limbs they were together, and it was wonderful. He watched her smile widen, heard the soft murmurings from her throat that he'd come to cherish, the tousled bangs across her brow, feeling love, feeling completely embraced by the friend he knew in her—

—and she opened her eyes, and everything changed.

For a split second, his mind couldn't grasp what he suddenly knew, but the sound of her voice brought it all together.

"Julian," she breathed, and her voice was deeper, sultry and languid. It matched the darker blue of her eyes, and of course she was Ezri ... but she was Jadzia, too. Jadzia, gazing up at him in passion's abandon.

When they finally displaced his shock, the feelings were complex, multilayered and overwhelming—fear and confusion, mainly, but there was also a sense of betrayal, glimmers of excitement, of nostalgia, of loneliness.

His response was much simpler. He instinctively pulled away from her, wanting to be covered, to protect himself. Trembling, he rolled over and sat up, pulling the rumpled bedclothes around his waist, his body forgetting the flush of sex as if no such thing existed. His thoughts were in chaos, his heart pounding. He felt like he'd been hit.

A few seconds later, a tentative hand on his shoulder, and Ezri's clear voice, gentle with concern.

"Are you okay?"

He tensed away from her, not sure how to feel about her touch for the first time since they'd become lovers.

"What just happened?" he asked, his voice harsher than he meant it to be, quite aware of what had happened, if not how. "The way you looked at me, I—what happened?"

He turned and saw Ezri, her wide, worried gaze, the curves of her face soft with compassion—

—*but maybe that's Audrid, or Emony. Or any of them.*

"I'm . . . I was—" She frowned, her body language changing abruptly. She pulled her knees to her chest and held them, staring down toward her feet.

"I'm not sure," she said, but it was all wrong. She didn't sound sorry, or afraid, or unhappy. The look on her face, the tone of her voice was deeply thoughtful.

"I was thinking about the time that you let Jadzia sleep in your cabin, on the *Defiant*," she said slowly. "Remember? When you gave up the top bunk for her . . . she thought about that later, and I was—"

She looked up at him, her expression unreadable. "I felt like Jadzia would have felt, just for a few seconds," she said intently. "I mean, it was *me*, but she was—it was different, it was—it wasn't the same, it was . . ."

She trailed off, staring into his eyes. And still, she wasn't a bit sorry, he could see it, as if she'd forgotten his reaction.

Or as if she doesn't care.

"Different," he finished, and reached down for his clothes, a rumpled heap on the floor. He stood and started to dress, not wanting to be in bed with her for where things were going.

"I'm *sorry*," she said, and surely she meant it—but was there a touch of exasperation in her tone? Could he trust that there wasn't?

"I was making love to *you*," he said angrily. Scooping up his boots, he moved to the edge of the bed and sat, not looking at her. "Can you understand that I might not want to change partners in the middle of it?"

Her voice was much cooler than his, verging on cold. "You didn't, Julian. I'm Ezri *Dax*. Can you understand *that?*"

"Right," he snapped, jerking on his second boot and standing. "Got it. Why don't you bring Tobin along next time, see how he feels? Or Lela, or Curzon?"

"Why don't you grow up," she retorted, "and try to see past yourself? I'm a joined *Trill,* and that's not going to change, ever. Why can't you see that all of me is Ezri, that I'm a whole being? That I don't have to limit myself to some species-specific concept of individuality?"

Her tone had changed from angry to near pleading, but he was too worked up to stop, unable to believe how insensitive she was being, furious at the implications of her words.

"Sorry to be so simplistic, *Dax,*" he said, regretting it even as he spoke. The look of hurt that flashed across her eyes almost quenched his anger. Almost, but even if he wanted to take it back, he wasn't sure how.

"You should leave," she said, face pale except for two hectic spots of color, high on her cheeks.

"My thoughts exactly," he said, and turned for the door. He didn't look back, and as he hit the corridor and started for his own quarters, a part of him marveled at how quickly things could change, as quickly as a look in someone's eyes.

Nog's hands were filthy, streaked with ash and blackened bits of melted polymer. He'd just finished replacing yet another in a series of torched computer boards and found himself staring down at his hands, noting each dark, chemical smudge, knowing if he raised them to his face, he would smell burning destruction. It was mindless work, shifting boards, but responsibilities were delegated for the moment, and he couldn't do much more with the *Defiant* until the shipment of parts arrived from Starbase 375. The new warhead module would have to come directly from Utopia Planitia itself, and that might take weeks. And the truth was, he'd chosen the one area no one else wanted to work in because he felt like it was the least he could do. It was the smell, he thought, that the other engineers hated so much, a reminder of what had happened. The Lower Core's atmosphere had been blasted clean through stacked filters, but the burn smell was still there, coating every twisted wire, caked on every fire-blown component.

You're not responsible, Nog, none of this is your fault.... Ezri's heartfelt words from after the briefing echoed in his mind, words he almost believed, but her voice was far away. Down in this subsection, working with a few grim-faced and silent techs in the broken spaces where forty-six people had died, a lot of things seemed far away. He knew that nobody blamed him;

earlier, after the memorial service, he'd been stopped by at least a dozen people who'd gone out of their way to tell him as much—

—but if I had organized everything better, if I'd pushed harder to get things done on time . . .

It was useless thinking. At the Academy, he'd taken PTP 1 along with everyone else—post-traumatic psych was a requisite course, even the Klingons had a version of it—and they'd hammered on the concept of useless thinking, and how guilt was essentially worthless beyond a certain point. But thinking about that only made him feel worse. Not only had he failed as an officer, contributing hugely to how effective the Jem'Hadar's attack had been, now he was wallowing in worthless guilt. Even when he'd lost his leg, he hadn't felt so terrible. At least then, he alone had been the one—

"Sir?"

Nog looked up and saw Shar standing over him, his dusky blue face uncharacteristically sober. The ensign held a tool kit.

"I thought we agreed you'd call me Nog from now on," Nog said. Maybe he'd get used to it someday, but he still didn't feel like a "sir." Particularly not today. He and Shar had actually been at the Academy at about the same time, but had never met before Shar's assignment to the station.

The Andorian nodded, speaking in his strangely formal way. "You're right, Nog, forgive me. Colonel Kira thought you might be able to use me down here."

Nog frowned. "I thought you were working on the sensor arrays."

"I was, but only because no one else was available. I miswired the secondary cilia circuits for the short-range particle samplers. It was an accident, I knew the correct sequence, but it will take several hours to re-string. The colonel said that replacing circuit boards might be easier for me."

Nog couldn't help a small smile. Shar was the most mechanically inept Andorian he'd ever met. "Okay. You can help me test these. I'll trigger, you check."

Shar crouched next to him and opened his tool kit, pulling out a diagnostic padd. Nog waited until he was situated and then started turning on the replaced boards, making minor adjustments as they went.

After a few moments, Shar broke the near-silence hesitantly. "Nog, may I ask you a question?"

"Sure."

"Were you a witness to Commander Jast's death?"

Nog had been expecting a technical question, or something about the Federation's plans, and felt new guilt crash over him, remembering that Shar had been friendly with Jast.

"Yes," Nog said dully, feeling his ears flush.

Shar looked at him curiously. "Nog, are you all right?"

"What's your question, Shar?" Nog asked, wishing he was a million light-years away, wishing he was at Vic's, balancing the books and drinking two-olive martinis, wishing he was anywhere but here.

"I only wanted to ask if you thought she died without pain," Shar said softly. "But I see now that I have upset you. I'm sorry. Were you and the commander close?"

Nog stopped working and shook his head miserably. Before he could stop himself, he blurted out the truth. "No, we weren't, but it's my fault she's dead."

Shar stared at him. "How is that possible? I thought

she was killed by an electrical surge when the *Defiant* was under attack. . . ."

Before Nog could say anything, Shar nodded his comprehension, answering himself. "You're attempting to assume responsibility because the upgrades were unfinished. I believe Colonel Kira feels the same way. Also, Lieutenant Bowers, Petty Officer Nguyen, and Nancy Sthili feel similarly, judging by their behavior. I'm fairly certain they all feel some measure of guilt for not performing more efficiently, either before or during the attack."

Nog was totally surprised. "Really? Why do *they* feel guilty?"

"Why do you?" Shar asked. "It was the Jem'Hadar who attacked us."

Nog opened his mouth to respond—and then closed it again, frowning. It wasn't as though some awesome truth had dawned on him suddenly, setting him free from all self-doubt—but he thought Shar had a point. Maybe the station could have been better prepared, but the real responsibility for what had happened didn't lay with anyone on the station.

Not with us. With them. The reminder instantly shifted his guilt, transforming it. The thought of their spiky, emotionless faces filled Nog with a powerful hatred that had become all too familiar in the last year, a mix of rage and fear unlike any he'd ever known. They were monsters, brutal, evil monsters.

"Have you ever dealt with the Jem'Hadar, face to face?" Nog asked, hardly recognizing his own voice. It was so old, so very old and wise and deadly soft. The Jem'Hadar had given him that voice.

"Not directly," Shar said. "I know something about

their chemical and genetic makeup, through some of the Vorta research we did during the war, but I've only ever seen them from a distance."

"If you're lucky, you'll never have to get any closer," Nog said. "They shouldn't exist, anyway, they aren't even a real species, they're . . ." He searched for the description he wanted and found it in a single word. "They're *abominations*. They're bred to be merciless killers, *murderers*. The Federation should have demanded their breeding programs stop when the treaty was being negotiated." It didn't even occur to him to wonder how such a thing could be enforced; he was too caught up in his own rage. "Maybe it's not so bad after all, this task force. If the Jem'Hadar attack now, they'll get wiped out."

Shar looked around suddenly, turning to face the empty, broken room behind them—and in the same instant, Nog heard something. A very faint sound of movement, like the creak of settling equipment . . .

. . . *but I've been hearing that all day, it's the supplementary bulkhead sections shifting, that's all.*

"It's just all the new materials getting settled," Nog said, surprised that Shar had noticed. He'd never heard anything about Andorians having especially good hearing.

"It's not that," Shar said, still peering around the room, his expression puzzled. After a moment, he turned back to Nog, shaking his head. "It's gone now, whatever it was. That's the third time today."

Nog frowned. "You heard something?"

Shar reached up to scratch at one of the two short, stout antennae that grew from his head like horns, pushing his thick white hair away from the base of the left one. "No, felt it. These are sensory, but not like ears. Andorians can detect some kinds of electrical fields, through changes in air density and temperature. But they're not exactly reliable . . . strong emotions, surges of adrenaline or teptaline, even an overheated piece of equipment can register analogously."

Hatred is a pretty strong emotion. Shar must have picked up his feelings about the Jem'Hadar. Interesting; Nog had met several Andorians at the Academy, but had never realized that their antennae weren't auditory. But now, as he focused his gaze past the bizarre white locks that seemed to hang randomly from Shar's head, he saw that his friend did indeed have ears.

Shar sighed. "Twice yesterday I felt something, too, and both times there didn't seem to be anything close enough to stimulate them."

"Maybe you're just getting old," Nog said, smiling so that Shar would know he was kidding. The Andorians he'd known had needed a little help when it came to humor.

Shar smiled back at him, but seemed distant as he picked up the diagnostic padd again. "Perhaps."

After a few seconds, Shar glanced up at Nog and asked, conversationally, "I've read that in popular Ferengi culture, attaining material wealth is one of life's predominant goals—is that correct?"

Nog was surprised into a chuckle. There were understatements, and then there were understatements. "Yes, I'd say that's correct."

"Would you mind if I ask, then, why you've chosen to join Starfleet?" Shar asked.

Nog shook his head. It was a personal question, but the way Shar asked made him want to answer honestly.

"I don't mind at all, but it's kind of a long story. I can tell you that it isn't easy to make a choice where, for the most part, you're going against your culture. What they expect of you, you know? My uncle insists it's just a phase—he says that many a young entrepreneur has to experience debt before he can understand the necessity of expansion planning, but I'm betting that he's wrong."

Shar nodded. "Because you feel like it's important, what Starfleet and the Federation are doing."

"Right, exactly." Shar really seemed to understand.

"I'd like to hear the long story, if you want to tell it," Shar said. "I was going to take a meal break in the next hour, at your Uncle Quark's establishment. Would you like to join me?"

Nog barely hesitated. He *was* busy, but he also instinctively liked Shar, and was grateful for the point about responsibility. And Uncle had been giving him a hard time lately about granting free favors—but also lately, Nog had come to enjoy disappointing his uncle, a fact that had pleased Father to no end the last time they'd spoken.

"You're on, Shar," Nog said.

After managing to get a few hours of sleep, Kira felt ready to sort things out with Ro. She'd meant to get to it after the briefing, but there had been too much else to do, and she'd been too exhausted. Before she'd finally collapsed for the night, she'd put it near the top of her list for the morning's agenda. A crisis was not a good time to have the social system break down; Kira needed to feel that she could depend on all of her people, and she needed Ro to understand that. After checking in with her department heads, she'd started for Ro's office, hoping that they could have a reasonable conversation about attitudes and expectations.

If not reasonable, I'll take conclusive; at least that way I'll have something *resolved before the Federation shows up.* Although they weren't behind on the current revised schedule, the first Allied ships should be arriving in three days, and neither the station nor the *Defiant* were anywhere near as functional as she'd hoped. Even with the new techs on hand, the intermittent and random crashes that seemed to be plaguing the station's every system were making everything twice as difficult as it needed to be. And it didn't help that she wasn't feeling particularly functional herself, either. If she crashed, she might end up locked in a room somewhere, mumbling to herself.

Not funny, Nerys. She felt emotionally blasted, which was bad but not paralyzing, she still felt functional and sane enough . . . but she'd had the experience four times now, of suddenly feeling that there was someone behind her. And twice, she'd felt that she was being watched when there was no one around. Shar's internal sweeps since the attack had turned up a few random energy pockets, but nothing out of the ordinary, considering the station's structural damage . . . which meant Kas was probably right to insist that she take a vacation. When she was with the resistance, she'd heard of several people in other cells who'd succumbed to paranoid episodes, eventually hurting themselves or others to avoid being caught by "them." And they probably thought they were sane, too.

In any case, one thing at a time. The big picture could be overwhelming, worrying about everything from trying to convince the Federation to stand down to her own mental quirks—and after all that had happened in the last few days . . .

. . . *just keep moving, get things sorted out. Introspection can always wait.* An attitude that generally worked well for her. She'd reached the security office, and was more than ready to establish a few ground rules.

Steeling herself against memories of Odo, and reminding herself again that Ro Laren deserved a chance to explain her position, she pasted on a friendly expression and walked in. Even knowing what she would see, Kira felt her tension level rise a notch; it was irrational, she knew, but the woman was sitting in Odo's chair.

Ro looked up from whatever she was studying and Kira saw her gaze harden slightly, her defenses obviously triggered by Kira's mere presence.

Make the effort. She had to get better at handling difficult people, now that she couldn't just throw up her hands and start shouting. Well, she still *could,* but if the last seven years had taught her anything, it was that that approach only got you so far.

Kira glanced around the office as she spoke, realizing it was still exactly as Odo had left it. "I thought I'd stop by, see if you have a few minutes to talk."

Ro nodded, waving her hand in a go-ahead gesture. "By all means."

There were other chairs in the office, but Ro's attitude made Kira feel like standing. She decided not to wait for a better opening.

"I'm going to be honest with you, Lieutenant. I'm not happy with how your posting here is working out, and I think a few changes are in order."

Ro nodded again, a sour look on her face. "I see. You're relieving me of duty. Any specific reason?"

Kira sighed inwardly, annoyed. She was trying to give her a chance. "Why do you make things so difficult, Ro? Is it me, or are you just absolutely determined to make everything impossible?"

"Of course it's not *you*," Ro snapped. "It's me, *I'm* the one with the problem, because I don't look to you every time I make a decision."

Kira stared at her. "What are you talking about?"

"I understood when I took this job that how I conduct the day-to-day operations of this office would be left to my discretion," Ro said, "but by the way you've been acting, you seem to think I'm a complete incompetent."

In spite of Ro's heated tone, Kira refused to be baited. She was being reasonable, dammit. "I know you have the skills, but you've got to understand—although there's a lot of traffic coming through here, we live in a community, and it's important that everyone at least *tries* to work together. Especially department heads and senior staff, because we have to support each other through what it takes to run DS9, *and* try to set a positive example while we're doing it."

"Does that include conversations about being transferred?" Ro asked, her face flushed.

Kira ignored her. "If you've made any effort to fit in, I haven't seen it," she said. "And you act like I'm some kind of monstrous authority figure who's out to oppress you. What will it take for you to stop turning everything into some kind of a, a contest of will?"

Ro stood up, facing her directly across the desk. "Maybe if I was human, there wouldn't be a problem."

Kira frowned. "Human? I don't see how that could—"

"Yes, you do. Without accepting the Prophets as divine, I'm not a real Bajoran, isn't that right?"

Reason only went so far. Kira could take a lot, but what Ro had just implied was insulting. Yes, she'd disliked Ro's pompous agnosticism, but had also gone entirely out of her way to be fair to Ro because of it.

"That's right, Ro," Kira said, her voice quickly raising to a near shout. "That's it exactly, I can't work with anyone who doesn't believe the same things I believe, and it has nothing to do with your constant, obvious disrespect for me as commanding officer of this station, which is both unfair and childish!"

She took a deep breath, blew it out. "Look, this obviously isn't working out. I think it would be best if you put in for a transfer, immediately."

"I couldn't do my job, so I put in for a transfer," Ro said. "That's ironic, when if you would stop second-guessing my every move, I could actually get something done."

Kira felt her anger reach a boiling point. *She wants to get booted on a disciplinary, fine—*

—when it dawned on her. From all appearances, that was exactly what Ro wanted. For some reason, she had accepted a posting she didn't actually want.

And why would she? She hasn't lived on Bajor since she was a child, she seems to despise our faith, she's either withdrawn or openly challenging most of the time—

"Why are you here, Ro?" Kira asked, her anger ebbing, remembering the Starfleet file that Jast had told her about. Ro Laren had a history of disciplinary problems, of being bright but resentful of authority, of not being a team player. But was that really the whole story? "Why did you take this job?"

Ro seemed shocked by the question, a flash of panic displacing the fury in her eyes for just a fraction of a second. For the first time Kira recognized what Ro had been doing, the bluff and bluster of insecurity and defense. She'd been a master of it herself at one time.

"Why, Ro? What do you want? What did you expect?"

Her eyes wide, Ro shook her head, and Kira could actually see her work to dredge up her anger again, could see her grabbing for something to say that would make Kira wrong, that would win the confrontation. All to avoid confronting whatever it was that was hurting her.

Kira cut her off before she got started. She had sympathy for Ro's confusion, but she didn't have all day to hold her hand through it. "Part of this job means that you will have to work with people, me included, and it means that you aren't always going to have things the way you want them. I've been there, I know it's not easy—but you have to decide what you want to do, and then do it."

"Colonel, I don't need your advice," Ro said, eyes still wide and angry.

"Lieutenant, I think you do," Kira said, and when Ro didn't respond, Kira turned and walked out.

Ro sat down after Kira left, furious, then a little less so. The question kept replaying, and she wasn't finding an acceptable answer.

Why, why did you take this job, why are you here?

Arrogant woman. Ro supposed that some part of her had been prepared for their fight since her first day on the station—but then, why did she feel so disappointed, so unhappy?

You know.

Did she? Kira was as condescending as ever, she knew that, acting as though she had personally earned Ro's respect, that she deserved it. Ro's lieutenant pin and gray special forces uniform were honorary, awarded to her—along with her assignment to DS9— by a government that, while grateful for her efforts during the war, hadn't known what else to do with her.

And Kira knows that, and she still can't stand it that I don't seek out her wisdom—

—why, then? Another part of her asked, the same part that had told her she knew why she was disappointed. *Forget Kira, she doesn't matter in this. Why are you here?*

Because. I've got nowhere else to go.

And you resent it. Why are you disappointed?

Because . . . because she had been prepared to leave the station as a result of the inevitable argument, to declare herself unappreciated and undervalued, and to seek a life for herself somewhere far from Bajor and DS9. She was angry because her little refuge of self-righteousness had been taken away, at Kira for taking it, and at herself once she understood that it had been there all along.

She hadn't belonged in Starfleet. No; that wasn't quite true, was it? She *had* felt like she belonged there once, before Garon II changed everything. And after years of running with the Maquis and then her own group of anti-Dominion fighters, she'd wanted nothing more than to return home, to the world whose air she hadn't breathed since she was a child. Word had gotten around Bajor about some of the things she and her team had accomplished during the war, and in recognition of that, the Militia had offered her a commission, hoping to make further use of her tactical experience.

But post-Occupation Bajor was an alien world to Ro; she realized almost from the start it wasn't going to work, that she no longer knew how to sit still, that she'd been living on the run and fighting for too long. Militia HQ had quickly come to the same conclusion, and informed her that her skills would better serve Bajor aboard Deep Space 9.

All I wanted was to come home . . .

And the agonizing truth was still that, unless she meant to run off and find another war, she had nowhere else to go.

I always said I wanted a life beyond the fight . . . and I finally got it, and I've been waiting for it to fall apart since day one. Wanting it to, because I no longer know how to do this.

Ro closed her eyes for a moment, recognizing her fear as useless, and understanding that Kira's question had changed things. Maybe she'd stay on the station, maybe she wouldn't, but she would no longer have the luxury of believing that it wasn't her choice to make.

Damn her.

Ro opened her eyes and looked back down at the desk screen, where the complete contents of Istani Reyla's isolinear rod were displayed—a few seemingly random numbers, with no clue as to their meaning— and abruptly realized she was more determined than ever to solve this minor mystery, to wrap up the murder of Kira's friend. She felt that she wouldn't be able to rest easy until she proved to the colonel that she was competent, until she proved to herself that she could do this job.

3, 4, 24, 1.5, 25. A code? The numbers could mean anything, but the fact that Istani had paid Quark to hide the rod—rather than storing it at the assay office—suggested to Ro that the prylar was afraid of someone finding those numbers, or finding out that she had access to them. Ro had already checked them against every combination the computer could come up with, from mathematical theorems to replicator item adaptations, but nothing she'd seen looked right.

She stared at the screen, thinking about the colonel, about sparring with Quark and Shar's friendship and Istani Reyla, and realized that for a while, at least, DS9 was going to be home. She'd lived a life of loose ends; it was time to see where the threads of these new relationships would take her, time to stop being afraid of the kind of life she'd never known.

15

"Doctor! May we join you?"

Bashir looked up and smiled, wondering why some people seemed to think that if you were reading, they weren't interrupting anything. Standing over him were Nog and Shar, both obviously taking a meal break during what must have been another difficult day. The lunchtime seating in Quark's was limited; there were a lot of people coming off shift and looking to get a little uninhibited, to talk.

Bashir set the padd aside, nodding, wistful for the second reading but happier to have company. Ezri wouldn't be by for another twenty minutes, at least. "Of course. Have a seat."

He had been fortunate enough to grab a table by the front wall, not in a main traffic area, and had been waiting for Ezri to get off her shift. When he'd called her a few hours ago, she'd agreed to talk, and he had heard relief in her voice; he'd felt some of that himself. He regretted their fight, he missed feeling that they were friends, even for a day.

"What are you reading, Doctor?" Shar asked, noticing the padd.

"Julian, please. We're not on duty. It's a letter from a friend of mine."

The Andorian smiled, nodding as he sat down. Julian hadn't spent much time with Shar, but liked him very much. A very unassuming young man—

Person, he mentally amended. Andorian biology was unique, another reason Bashir was glad Nog had asked if they could sit at his table; he'd wanted very much to ask a few questions. Except for Erib, whom he'd known at medical school, Bashir hadn't been around many Andorians.

Nog was looking at the paused text, frowning. "You're on page 256 of a *letter?* Who wrote it?"

"Garak," Bashir said, smiling again at the nervous look that suddenly appeared on Nog's face. The Cardassian tailor had intimidated a lot of people during his years on the station. Having already read the autobiographical letter once, Bashir thought that if they'd known even the half of it, they might have moved off the station themselves.

"So, what are you two up to today?" Bashir asked, picking up his glass of tea, remembering that he'd seen the two of them having dinner together last night, too.

"Ah, nothing," Nog said casually. "Just dealing with the mess in the Lower Core when Shar suggested lunch."

Nog has a new friend. The young Ferengi was trying very hard to be nonchalant, a young man's favorite game. Basir found himself feeling fondly nostalgic about O'Brien suddenly, remembering the stories they'd swapped of their reckless youth.

Back when I was a brash young officer . . . He was all of 34, not exactly ready for retirement. Now that he was thinking about it, though, he abruptly remembered one of the correlations common to all of the papers he'd read about Andorians, regarding age.

"Shar, if you don't mind me asking—how old are you?"

Shar looked up from his plate of vegetables. "Twenty-three."

"Are you married, then?"

As soon as Bashir asked, he could see that Shar was uneasy with the question, and trying to hide it. He dropped his gaze, his face flushing a darker blue; only Bashir noticed, the flush too slight to be obvious. "No, I'm not."

Shar's distinct discomfort dissuaded Bashir from pursuing the matter. Perhaps he didn't want to discuss it in front of Nog—or perhaps he didn't want to talk about it at all.

Still, 23 and not married . . .

Erib—whose full name was Shelerib th'Zharath—had avoided questions about relationships, though he'd once said that the unique biology of the Andorian species necessitated certain . . . expectations of its members. Bashir understood the biology, but not the sociology or the culture. But as interested as he was in understanding Shar's particular situation, it wasn't really any of his business.

"How would you boys like to try a little *fa'ntar?*" Quark had swept up to their table, holding a tray of glasses and a pitcher filled with a distinctly noxious-looking, deep orange brew. "It's tonight's discount special, a rare but intoxicating blend of exotic fruits and spiced leaves from—"

"—from a vat in the storeroom," Nog broke in. "Last month, you called it *tarf'an,* but it's still what you make from rotten fruit shipments, and no one ever buys it."

Quark's smile had disappeared. He leaned in, teeth bared. "You want to keep your voice down? What's wrong with you? I sell plenty, and it is rare, you can't get it anywhere but here."

Bashir shook his head. "Thanks anyway, Quark, but I think we'll probably—"

"Starfleet," Quark spat, obviously warming up for one of his tirades, still glaring at Nog. "They are sucking the Ferengi right out of you, you know that, don't you? You *never* ruin another man's sell, not unless you can profit from it. The Federation, though. They *say* that they want to help people, that they have a clear directive not to interfere with other cultures, but look at how you're turning out. And do you think they've given one thought to how another war might affect the rising tourist interest in this area?"

Quark appealed to the whole table, the very picture of sincere outrage. "I've got to say, and no offense, I'm getting pretty sick of the Federation's attitude. I mean, who made *you* keepers of the universe? What does the small business man get out of it?"

Bashir considered responding, but decided that between expressing his own opinion and prolonging the conversation, the latter would be the greater evil. Quark wasn't interested in anyone else's opinion, anyway. Besides which, Bashir suddenly felt a headache coming on.

"Uncle, please," Nog said pleadingly, growing irritated or embarrassed by the reddening of his ears. Shar didn't seem to be paying attention at all; he scratched absently at his left antenna, his expression blank.

Quark wouldn't be stopped. "I blame your father for this, Mister I'm-so-proud-you're-going-to-the-Academy. Why you chose him for your role model I'll never understand, not when you had me—"

As the last syllable left Quark's lips, Shar was suddenly in action. He lunged across the table and snatched the pitcher away from Quark, his reflexes brilliantly fast. He spun around, balancing himself in motion, and threw the contents of the pitcher at the wall behind them. He completed the action so quickly that the upset tray of glasses was still hitting the ground as the spiced fruit concoction flew—

—and before any one of them could react, the air became solid and somebody screamed.

Quark's interruption saved Shar from any more questioning by Dr. Bashir, for which he was grateful. He still hadn't decided how to respond to such inquiries, and even the thought of trying to answer them made him feel somewhat anxious.

He was still thinking of where the questioning might have led when Quark and Nog began to get angry. Shar was a little uncomfortable about the strife between the two Ferengi, but the amusement on Bashir's face suggested that there was no reason for concern.

A complicated relationship. Family dynamics often seemed so; Shar was starting to believe that it was a universal constant. There were many subtle intricacies within his own family's communication.

His left antenna itched, and he scratched it—and froze, feeling it again, the same itch and flush of heat he'd already felt several times since the attack on the station.

Someone is here.

Between their table and the wall. Shar concentrated, holding very still. Although his ability to differentiate specific energy types was limited, he couldn't help feeling that he was sensing bioelectrical energy. It was similar to the sensation of hearing two sounds of a similar pitch and volume, one made by a machine, the other by a person.

Tingling heat, and he could see that there was no one there. He thought again about the internal sweep that Colonel Kira had asked him to do, and the random pockets of collected energy he'd found.

And if someone wanted to hide . . .

All of this flashed through his mind in an instant, and he accepted it as truth by the preponderance of evidence, not the least of which was his physical reaction.

Before he could properly consider his options, the tingling started to fade, and he made his decision. As fast as he could, Shar snatched the pitcher from Quark, turned, and threw the thick liquid at what he believed to be an organic being, watching them.

A meter in front of him, the liquid hit, splashing across the head and torso of a very tall humanoid. Someone shouted as the air shimmered and curved, becoming solid, becoming a Jem'Hadar soldier.

He was imposing, his sharp, reptilian face somehow blank and malevolent at once. Quark let out a high-pitched squawk, and Bashir stood and shouted for security as Nog tried to pull Shar out of harm's way, clutching at his arm with fumbling, desperate fingers—

—but the Jem'Hadar had no weapon and only stood, watching, as fear and confusion pushed the crowd back. Shar allowed Nog to pull him away, barely able to keep himself from beating at the unexpected intruder with the empty pitcher, his body prepared to fight.

Then the Jem'Hadar spoke, and his words stilled everyone who heard them.

"I am Third Kitana'klan, here on an errand of peace," he said, his voice deep and inflectionless. "I would speak to your Colonel Kira Nerys. You can tell her that I was sent by Odo."

Ro was waiting for Kira at the entrance to the security office, her expression thankfully professional. A shrouded Jem'Hadar soldier had popped up in Quark's bar; Kira didn't have any interest in dancing around with Ro again.

"What have we got?"

"Ensign ch'Thane found him at Quark's. He's making his statement now. I've got a team working with the internal sensors, to see if there are more."

As she spoke, they started through the door that led to the holding cells, Ro leading the way. Kira was glad to see a pair of armed security guards flanking the entrance to the hallway; Ro had the presence of mind to lock down the facility, at least.

"The soldier was unarmed, and offered no resistance; he was carrying a pack of ketracel-white cartridges, but nothing else. He says his name is Kitana'klan, and asked to speak to you, claiming that he's here on a peace mission—"

Kira couldn't help a sneer as they turned into the holding cell area. *A peaceful Jem'Hadar. Right.* At least she knew now why she'd felt watched, but that small relief was heavily overshadowed by thoughts of what he could have been doing all this time; he had to have been hiding on the station since the attack.

"—and that Odo sent him."

They stopped in front of the only occupied cell, Ro nodding at the guard, excusing her with a few words of direction—but Kira barely heard them. She could only stare dumbly at the soldier, overwhelmed with feelings of loss, of anger and disbelief—and a tiny seed of hope.

Odo . . .

The Jem'Hadar stood stiffly, as if at attention. When he saw Kira, he stepped closer to the force field.

"Colonel Kira. I am Third—I am Kitana'klan," he said, his deep voice betraying no emotion. The fact that he'd faltered over his designation gave Kira pause; as long as they were supplied with white—and this one was, she could see the isogenic enzyme sputtering through a slender tube at his throat—the Jem'Hadar simply did not falter.

Just looking at him inspired a dozen unhappy memories—the first Jem'Hadar she'd ever seen, telling her that the slaughtered settlers of New Bajor had fought well, for a spiritual people; the violent and untamable Jem'Hadar child that had been found on the station— even without enemies, he'd been unable to stop fighting, or to curb his hatred for anyone who was not Jem'Hadar, Vorta, or Founder.

In that order, too. The Vorta keep them, the Founders are their apathetic gods, and everyone else deserves death. The Jem'Hadar grew from genetic envelope to maturity in a matter of days. Born to a martial code of blood lust, the vast majority died in battle before the age of ten.

Kitana'klan looked like every other Jem'Hadar she'd ever seen—tall, muscular, his heavy, pebbled gray face studded with pearly spikes like tiny claws, his eyes piercing and sharply intelligent. His vestigial tuft of long black hair was knotted in typical Jem'Hadar fashion. He stood perfectly still, staring straight ahead as she studied him. If he felt anything at all he didn't betray it, and appeared to be waiting for her to speak before saying anything else.

Where to start . . .

"Explain your presence on this station, Kitana'klan," she said finally.

"I have been sent by the changeling Odo, to serve you," he said, his gaze still fixed straight ahead.

Right, sure, that's so like Odo—

"And to learn about the cultures and lifeforms that coexist here," he continued. "I am to study everything I can about the synergy among peaceful peoples, so that I can bring this knowledge to the other Jem'Hadar. The Foun—Odo believes that this will be an initial step toward helping the Jem'Hadar evolve beyond our genetic programming."

Kira stared at him, remembering how hard Odo had fought to keep that Jem'Hadar orphan on the station, even after the "child" had proved to be incapable of forming nonaggressive tendencies.

He wanted so much to believe that the Jem'Hadar didn't have to fight, that they wouldn't *fight if given other choices, other options. . . .* Kira had strongly disagreed, and in the end, had been proved right—but suddenly, Kitana'klan's presence didn't seem so improbable. It *would* be like Odo to keep trying; his conscience had been deeply disturbed by the very existence of the Jem'Hadar, created by his people to have no aspirations higher than killing for their keepers.

"Go on," she said quietly, vaguely aware that Ro had taken the security guard's position behind her—and glad that there would be a living, breathing witness to this unprecedented conversation. She was willing to hear him out, but doubted there would be much truth in what he had to say. *The entire Dominion knew about Odo, they knew what kind of a man he was. Is. It wouldn't be all that hard to come up with a story like this one.*

But if he *was* telling the truth . . .

"The attack on your station was not sanctioned by the Founders," he said, finally turning his gaze to meet hers, and although it was exactly what she wanted to hear, she had to physically suppress a chill. His eyes were pale and unbelievably alien, incapable of any mild or gentle emotion. It was the gaze of a pure predator.

"There were a small number of Jem'Hadar who sought to redeem themselves for losing the war against the Alpha Quadrant," he continued. "They planned to destroy this station, in the hope that this might initiate hostilities once again."

"How do you know?" Ro asked abruptly. Kira didn't mind; she was wondering the same thing.

"Because I was told," Kitana'klan said, still looking at Kira. "I was overtaken by these rogue soldiers on the other side of the Anomaly—the wormhole—and they attacked me, disabling my ship. First Javal'tivon, their leader, had been my First at the end of the war; he told me of their plans so that I might understand the reason for my death."

"Quite a coincidence, you and these rogue soldiers headed for the station at the same time," Kira said.

"No. I believe that learning of my mission inspired their attack, and that they followed me from Dominion space."

Kitana'klan looked away, as if remembering, and his toneless voice grew cold and sharp. "It was their mistake to leave me still alive. A few of my crew survived, and we were able to repair the ship enough to follow after them. We defended you as best we could—but when the destruction of my ship became inevitable, I had to board this station. My instructions were clear."

"Why didn't you announce your presence then?" Kira asked. "Why have you stayed shrouded all this time?"

Kitana'klan seemed surprised by the question. "Your station had just been attacked by Jem'Hadar. I did not think I would be welcomed here."

"So you thought it would be better to skulk around, hiding in energy vents and spying on us? Exactly how long were you planning to wait?" Ro asked, and again, Kira had no objection. She'd worried about losing her mind, thanks to Kitana'klan's choice of action.

If he was bothered by Ro's obvious scorn, he gave no sign. "I was watching for a reasonable opportunity in which to present myself. Odo gave me no instruction on what to do in the event that the station was attacked by my people. . . ."

Kitana'klan lowered his gaze, almost as if ashamed. ". . . but I understand now that my decision was ill-considered, and that I have made myself untrustworthy by my actions."

Kira was unmoved by his performance, but there was a ring of truth to his story that she couldn't deny hearing.

The fourth ship was damaged. And it backs up everything about the nature of the attack.

"You said the Dominion didn't sanction the offensive. . . ." Kira prodded.

"Yes. When Odo joined the Founders, he brought with him experiences unknown to them. The Great Link is in contemplation of Odo's life; it is . . . thinking, and surely does not know even now what has happened here. At this time, the Founders wish only to remain in reflection."

Kira glanced back at Ro, and saw on her face the same skepticism that she was feeling—but she didn't seem as openly incredulous as Kira would have thought, and she realized that Ro was also uncertain. Kira didn't like the Jem'Hadar as a species, and trusted Kitana'klan about as far as she could pitch him one-handed—but his story actually made sense.

"Can you prove any of this?" she asked, turning to look at him again.

Kitana'klan shook his head. "I cannot. There was a transmission of introduction and explanation given to me by Odo, but it was destroyed along with my ship and crew."

Of course it was. He's lying.

He's telling the truth, and the Federation has to listen now; Odo sent him, Odo sent him to me.

Before she could argue with herself any further, Kitana'klan abruptly fell to his knees. Forgetting the force

S. D. PERRY

field, Kira instinctively dropped into a defensive stance, and behind her, Ro was on her feet, pulling her phaser—

—and Kitana'klan ripped at the neck of his uniform, tearing it enough to reveal his ketracel-white cartridge, a small, flat rectangle in a sewn pocket beneath his knobby collarbone. He unfastened the cartridge from the implanted throat tube and pulled it free, holding it up toward Kira.

"I was sent here to serve you. I offer you my obedience and my life."

Realistically, the gesture meant nothing. He was unarmed and in a holding cell, and Ro had said they'd taken his additional white cartridges; his life was already in her hands—but the symbolic display was effective anyway, because he was Jem'Hadar. They were merciless, competent killers, not prone to drama. Without the enzyme and trapped in the cell, he would be driven into a useless, murderous rage before dying in great pain.

"I'm not sure I want either," Kira said. She stepped back from the force field, entirely unsure of what to think. "Keep your white. I'll get back to you."

She looked at Ro, who half-shrugged, obviously as perplexed by the Jem'Hadar's behavior as Kira was.

"Have Dr. Bashir run a scan when he's done with his statement, and . . . keep a watch on him," Kira said, feeling strangely helpless. For the moment, it was as far as she was willing to go. Whether or not Kitana'klan was lying, his presence on DS9 would be a major factor in the station's future. If he was telling the truth, there would be no reason for the Allies to go into the Gamma Quadrant—and there would be a Jem'Hadar living on the station, a disruptive situation at best. If it was all a lie, if he came from one of the attack ships or from somewhere else entirely, then there was no telling what he or the Dominion was planning. In any event, it was going to take her a little time to sort through the possible consequences—and to figure out how to prove his story out, one way or the other.

Kira started to leave the area, glancing back at Kitana'klan a final time before she stepped into the corridor. He was still on his knees, and again, that feeling of helplessness hit her at the improbable sight. A Jem'Hadar soldier, claiming a mission of peace. If Odo had done this, either he had made real progress with the Founders and the Dominion . . . or his sense of humor had taken a serious turn toward the inexplicable, which Kira could not find it in herself to believe.

16

Although he'd assumed she would be seeking him out eventually—she'd already talked to everyone else on the away team—Vaughn hadn't actually decided to speak to Deanna Troi until she approached him in Ten–Forward, a full day after they'd left the *Kamal* behind. He'd been enjoying the feelings he'd been having, and felt protective of them, not sure if he wanted them analyzed. He would not have sought her out, in any case—he had too many secrets to ever feel entirely comfortable around a Betazoid, let alone someone he'd known as a friend's child—but since finding the Orb, he'd also felt open to trying new things. Like talking to a counselor.

"Elias. May I join you?" She stood in front of his table, a small one near a viewport where he'd been sitting alone, remembering all sorts of things. Outside, the Badlands erupted and shimmered wildly. Soon, they'd be on their way to DS9, leaving the plasma storms behind; he'd wanted to get his fill.

"Please," he said, gesturing at the seat across from his, thinking that Ian had been a lucky man; his daughter had grown into a bright, intelligent, lovely person.

Troi sat down, smiling somewhat shyly, a touch of color in her cheeks—and he realized that she had probably detected some of what he was feeling. Only a few days before, his mind had been too preoccupied with feelings of self-doubt and confusion to feel anything clearly.

"Is it uncomfortable for you, to sense how others perceive you?" he asked, intuitively feeling that the question would not be inappropriate.

"That depends on who it is, and in what context."

"How do you mean, context?"

Deanna grinned. "I mean, if they like me, I try to pay more attention."

"Always a good plan," Vaughn said, smiling.

"Does this mean I get to ask you a few questions?" Troi asked.

Vaughn hesitated only a second, thinking of how he'd been feeling since the freighter. Strange and chaotic, definitely, strong memories continuing to appear randomly in his thoughts—but not at all unpleasant.

"You can if you can tell me what I'm feeling right now," he replied, honestly curious as to what she would say.

Troi took a deep breath, studying him. "Confused. Elated and uncertain. Contemplative. You are out of your emotional comfort zone, but not afraid, and . . . you're still experiencing flashes of your past, aren't you?"

Vaughn nodded. "Excellent, Counselor. And I assume you know why . . ."

"The Orb experience," she said, and he sensed *her* excitement now. He could see it on her face. "It was very different for you than for the others."

"Yes, I think it was," he said lifting his glass of synthale, then putting it back down, not really in a drinking mood. "I had memories on the freighter, too, good and bad—but when it was over, when I closed the door on the Orb, I felt . . ."

He shook his head. "It's hard to explain. It wasn't so much a feeling as a comprehension, if that makes any sense. For just a second, I . . . I *remembered* who I was. Who I am. And just like that, all of my concerns and fears about the future, about *my* future— gone."

Deanna nodded, looking pleased. "Yes. I can feel some of it even now. I don't know that you had a *pagh'tem'far*—that's the Bajoran concept of a sacred vision—but I think you definitely experienced a moment of clarity, catalyzed by the Orb. Perhaps because you were already questioning some aspects of your life, and you were open to a change of direction."

He hadn't thought of it that way, assuming instead that it had been a matter of his proximity to the Orb, but she was right, of course. Ironic, that a spiritually skeptical person like himself could have such an altering experience with a religious artifact.

Although there was that Linellian fluid effigy. The dream of small death when you touched it, followed by a brief, brilliant vision of swimming through milky-white waves . . . He'd been only 24 then, charged with returning the stolen container to the embassy, and hadn't known that such peace could exist. . . .

"These memories you've been experiencing—are

they troubling to you?" Troi asked, watching him carefully.

"No," he said, thinking that her perceptions were even clearer than he'd first thought. "A little distracting, perhaps, but nothing too terrible."

Even as he said it, he realized that she, of all people, would know better. He smiled, shrugging.

"Nothing I can't handle, anyway."

Deanna leaned closer, lowering her voice slightly. "If there was anything you wanted to talk about, I could get a security clearance waiver . . ."

Vaughn felt a sudden fondness for her, wondering if she had any idea how impossible that would be for someone like him. The past was the past, but promises had been made, orders given that he could never set aside. There was a saying, something about aging tigers still having teeth . . .

. . . *and it holds true for some memories. Several of those tigers still have very sharp teeth, and claws that could inflict serious injury* . . . As long as they remained in the cage of his mind, there was no danger. He meant to keep it that way.

"Thank you, Counselor, but that's not necessary. Really, I'm all right."

At her slight frown, he thought again of how lovely she was, how compassionate, and suddenly recalled a clear image of an infant girl he'd held long ago, looking into her sweetly exotic eyes and feeling that his heart was so full it might cease to beat from the weight of his feelings. He concentrated on the memory, knowing that Ian Troi had certainly felt the same way when he'd first held Deanna, and was rewarded with another warm smile from the young woman.

"Of course you are," she said, and stood, still smiling. "Thank you, Elias. I'll leave you to your reflections."

After she was gone, Vaughn turned his attention back to the Badlands, letting himself drift again. Whether it was a Bajoran religious epiphany, or a passing mindset, or some spiritual, emotional truth that he had been destined to learn, it didn't matter; he knew what he wanted, and knew that he would figure out how to get there as he went. He'd read a saying somewhere once, about how when you knew who you were, you knew what to do; it was more true than he'd ever suspected. It made him wonder how many people in the universe simply let their lives slide into some comfortable pattern, forgetting that they could do anything they wanted to do, that they could change direction if they could remember how easy it actually was.

Isn't life a strange party, Vaughn thought, looking out at the raging storms and feeling as young and free as a child.

Vedek Yevir arrived early for the shuttle to the space station. His luggage was taken by a pleasant young man who saw that he was comfortably seated before hurrying off to attend to other duties. The young man—Kevlin Jak, he'd introduced himself as—said that the shuttle would be full, a contingent of Militia technicians having booked flight two days before in addition to a number of regular passengers. Remembering how boisterous Militia folk could be in company, even this early in the morning—he'd been one himself not so very long ago—Yevir settled into his chair and closed his eyes, taking the opportunity of his early boarding for a few moments of silent meditation. It would be his first trip back to Deep Space 9 since he'd left to pursue his calling, and although he felt mostly positive about his return, he was not calm. Even the reason for his trip could not dampen his excitement.

And why shouldn't I be excited, considering what happened for me there? Behind his closed eyes, he remembered—the touch on his shoulder, warm and strong. The soft voice, ringing with truth. The sudden complete awareness of his own path, and the tranquility that had enfolded him, that had surrounded him ever since.

It was a story he'd told time and again, to anyone who wanted to know why he'd walked away from his old life to embrace the teachings of the Prophets—and it unfolded to him now like a story, almost as if it had happened to someone else. Perhaps because he'd told it so many times, or perhaps it was because his younger self was so very different from who he was now that he could no longer relate to him. No matter; the story of his life was an inspiration, and one he was proud to own.

Yevir Linjarin, Lieutenant in the Bajoran Militia. A man barely 40 at the end of the Occupation, his family dead and gone except for an aunt he'd never known, assigned to the small but industrious Bajoran off-world operations office on Deep Space 9. He'd been a minor administrator in a sea of minor administrators following the Cardassian withdrawal, his specific task to help relocate some of the thousands of Bajorans returning home—families and individuals who'd managed to flee before or during the Occupation. It was gratifying work, he supposed, but he'd taken no real joy in it. He had been a lonely man, a man with plenty of acquaintances and no real friends, a man who ate his dinners alone. It was a gray life, not the constant celebration he'd promised himself all those years in the camps; it was the life of a survivor, who'd forgotten how to do anything but survive.

He'd had faith, of a sort, attending weekly services along with everyone else—but he'd never really felt or understood the nature of the Prophets, even after Benjamin Sisko had come to the station. His relationship with Them had been perfunctory, his feelings for the Bajoran Gods a kind of vague, mental appreciation; he likened it to the way some childless individuals felt about children—glad that they were there, but only because that was the appropriate response to children, whether or not one actually enjoyed them. The Emissary's arrival was just another "prophecy" fulfilled that would make no real difference in his life, interesting but essentially inconsequential.

Except he was *the Emissary* . . .

One day, shortly after B'hala had been rediscovered, in fact, Lieutenant Yevir had been on his gray, unassuming way to the station's Replimat for something to eat when he'd been caught in a crowd of his people— and seen light in their eyes, their faces glowing as they watched the Emissary walk among them, touching them, telling them what the Prophets whispered in his ear. Yevir hadn't known the captain beyond being someone to nod to, but on that miraculous day, he'd seen and felt the spiritual power of the man for the first time. It had radiated from him like heat, like a thousand bright colors, and Yevir had understood that something was going to happen, something vast and wonderful.

The Emissary told an aging couple not to worry about the harvest, and everyone in the crowd had known it was the truth—and suddenly, the Emissary had been standing in front of him, in front of *him*.

And he touched my shoulder, and I felt the power. "You don't belong here," he said, and I understood that my life was gray and wasted. "Go home," he said, and I knew the truth. I knew that I would serve; I knew that I had been touched by the Prophets through his hand . . . and I left the station that very night.

The story went on—there was his newfound tranquility, and his acceptance as a religious initiate back on Bajor, and his rapid rise into and through the Vedek Assembly—but it was his contact with the Emissary, that single, life-altering moment of total reality, that was the point. It was as though he'd been awakened from a very long sleep, one that had lasted his entire life, and that he would be kai one day was only a natural extension of that rapturous moment.

Is it any wonder that I'm excited to see the station again? To see the people I used to know, to walk through the same places I used to walk, but to see everything through new eyes, through eyes opened by the Prophets' love?

Just thinking of it, he was pulled from the depth of his contemplation, a slight smile touching his lips. He should enjoy his anticipation; pretending some distant calm he didn't feel was unworthy. It was funny, how he still so often worried about how a vedek *should* behave—

Yevir opened his eyes, curious. People had been boarding the shuttle for some time, their shuffle and conversation faint to his ears—but as he tuned back in to his surroundings, he realized that something had changed. An excited murmur swept through the compartment, men and women talking in rapid whispers, smiling and nodding at one another.

Kevlin Jak, the shuttle attendant, was striding past his seat. Yevir reached out and touched his arm, not even having to ask before the young man happily chattered the news.

"The son of the Emissary has just boarded," Kevlin said, his eyes wide and shining. "He asked the captain if he could sit with the other pilots in front—you know how modest he is, of course—can you believe it? The Emissary's son, on our flight!"

"It's a blessing," Yevir said, smiling at the attendant, sure now that his decision to travel to the station was the right one. He'd had doubt, that to so directly involve himself in pursuit of the heresy might not be what the Prophets wanted.

This is a sign, a portent for the righteousness of my cause. His own son, returning from the ruins to share my journey. . . .

Yevir closed his eyes again, praising Them, knowing Their wisdom in all things. The book of obscenities would be found and destroyed. The will of the Prophets would be served, in this as in all else.

Ro slowly walked the cool, quiet corridors of the Habitat Ring, deep in thought. She could have just as easily done her thinking in the security office, but something about knowing that the Jem'Hadar soldier was close by made it difficult to concentrate. She had Devro watching him at the moment, probably with one hand on his combadge and the other on his phaser, which was fine by her. She *hoped* he was scared; she'd had more than a few fights with the Jem'Hadar during the war. Letting one's guard down, even when the soldier in question was behind a good, sturdy, planar force field, was suicidal behavior.

Of course, the soldier in question seems content to stare off into space and wait for Kira to decide his fate. Kitana'klan hadn't said a word since the colonel had walked out, at least during Ro's watch. Which was also fine by her; not only could she not imagine making small talk with a Jem'Hadar, her mind had been otherwise occupied. Even as strange and possibly singular as Kitana'klan's sudden appearance was, the investigation into Istani Reyla's death was still stalled, and she was finding it more and more difficult to think about anything else.

3, 4, 24, 1.5, 25 . . . The scant information from Istani's isolinear rod had become an endlessly cycling loop, underlying everything. It was like a game, one that wasn't particularly fun but was entirely addictive: find out where the numbers go. There were three main processing cores in the station's computer network, environmental controls were polled at level four once each hour, twenty-four variations of hasperat at Quark's; the Habitat levels ran one through five, and there were twenty-five personnel and cargo transporters distributed throughout the station. As soon as she found a place for each number, the cycle started over again— three spokes within three crossover bridges, four work shifts a day, and on, and on. It was tiring and annoying, and she couldn't seem to stop; something had to fit and she knew she would find it, if she could just come up with the right combination.

After Kira's peculiar conversation with Kitana'klan, Ro had spent several frustrating hours scanning recorded images from the station's security monitors, trying vainly to trace the movements of the prylar and the mysterious thief. Thanks to the upgrades, the ODN lines for the monitors had been on a revolving track, the only constant surveillance on engineering, ops, and the Promenade—so while she'd been able to get clear images of the murder and subsequent "accidental" death, there were several time spans completely unaccounted for, most for Istani. She'd been on the station almost a full 52 hours longer than her killer.

And she spent a fair amount of that time in the Habitat Ring—but not all of it in her quarters, according to the reads from her door monitor. And there was no way to tell where, exactly. Of course. So Ro walked, counting her steps, counting doors, running through the few facts she had and theorizing wildly.

The killer had yet to be properly identified, a frustration unto itself. He had booked passage from Bajor under the name Galihie S., from the Laksie township just outside of Jalanda, and listed his reason for coming to the station as personal business—in other words, shrine services. A lot of Bajorans came to be near the Prophecy Orb. His ID card was apparently a forgery, since there was no one at the Laksie township with his name—the Bajoran net listed 227 Galihies on- or off-world, only 17 with the given initial S, and every one of those were accounted for. The woman who sat next to him on the shuttle said he was uncommunicative and seemed preoccupied. And Dr. Bashir's autopsy report listed him as a healthy Bajoran male, approximately 41.5 years of age, no distinguishing marks. He'd obviously worn an earring, probably for his entire adult life, but none had been found . . . and he hadn't eaten anything for at least 12 hours before he died. Ro had sent tissue sample scores to the Central Archives, but with their backlog, it was going to be another twenty-six hours minimum . . . and that was assuming that he was on file somewhere.

So, Istani Reyla, an archeologist with a spotlessly clean history, came to the station with something valuable, perhaps even stolen, and she'd been chased by Galihie. Istani had been working at B'hala . . . although it was hard to imagine that a prylar would take anything from the holy ruins without permission. On the other hand, why would she have any dealings with someone like Quark, unless she'd been up to something less than legal? And why would Galihie S. have gone to such pains to hide his identity, unless *he'd* meant to perform some criminal act? Maybe the two of them had been working together, some kind of smuggling operation, a partnership gone bad . . .

22, 24, 25 . . .

She was on level four of the Habitat Ring, corridor E, when the first glimmering of an idea struck her; she stopped in front of the next schematic she saw posted, scanning it. In the Bajoran alphabet, the analog of 'E' was the seventh letter; the fourth was 'C'.

So I'm at 4, 7. Istani could have meant Level 3, corridor C. Three and four, and . . . something between the 24th and 25th sets of rooms? It was simple, undoubtedly too simple, but she found herself jogging back for the turbolift, anyway, silently urging it to hurry after she pressed the call button.

It was ridiculous for her to get her hopes up, but as

she stepped off the turbolift on three and walked quickly along C, she hoped anyway. She'd been over-thinking the numbers, trying to make a complicated code out of what may have been Istani's simple re-minder to herself.

Even as she reached the rooms, she knew that she'd figured it out. Running the entire distance between the designated doors were a series of small removable maintenance panels, angling up from about a half meter off the floor to about a half meter from the height of the corridor. Environmental control overrides, for the quar-ters on this level.

Tense but exhilarated, Ro measured up what she imagined to be a meter and a half from the floor, the most obvious application of 1.5, and popped the panel loose. Behind the narrow rectangle was a circuit insert next to an empty space, room to reach in and manipu-late the wires. There was nothing else—but there *was* something behind the panel directly to the left of her first choice. The dark bundle stuffed behind the panel was perhaps the most welcome sight she'd seen in a long time.

I did it, I figured it out! She felt deeply satisfied, al-most giddy with it.

She considered running back to the office for a tri-corder for about two seconds, then reached in and care-fully pulled the bundle free; if it was a bomb or equivalent, she would at least die having solved the mystery. Narrow and weighty, about the size of two padds side by side, the object was wrapped in some kind of pounded fiber cloth.

Grinning, Ro looked up and down the corridor, wish-ing there was someone to share her excitement with before she unwrapped the package. It was a book, and a very old one, practically falling apart. The thick, leathery covers were pitted and stained, but unmarked by writing. She turned it over in her hands, brushing at the soft covers, noting the uneven ruffle of aged parchment pages sticking out.

This is from B'hala. It was too old to have come from anywhere else. In spite of her general agnosticism, Ro felt a tiny thrill, aware that she was handling something probably thousands of years old. She carefully opened it, a faint scent of cool dust emanating from the tattered but sturdy root-paper pages . . . and frowned, disappointed. Even to her untrained eye, she could tell that it was written in ancient Bajoran.

Well, obviously. It didn't matter, anyway. Although a few of the particulars had yet to be resolved, she now held the reason for Istani's murder in her hands, she was sure of it.

Except . . . why had Istani hidden the book, unless she'd thought someone would come after it? Ro turned a few of the uneven pages, saw that many were loose, and that others had been ripped out or lost to time. While it might be historically valuable—though considering the hundreds of artifacts being uncovered every day at B'hala, even that seemed unlikely—the shabby tome couldn't be worth much as a collector's piece, no matter how old it was.

Maybe it's the text itself that's valuable. A bizarre thought; anyone could copy words out of a book, or even replicate the thing. So what was so important here that two people had died for it?

Ro closed the age-worn covers and rewrapped the

book slowly, thinking about her promise to Kira. About going to her as soon as she turned anything up.

But really, I don't know what I've got here. It could be a book of recipes, for all I know—and Kira will have it translated, anyway. . . .

There had to be a translation program somewhere in the station's network; Captain Sisko had been the Emissary, after all, supposedly off living with the aliens now, and he'd spent a fair amount of time playing around with the Bajoran religion. The discovery of B'hala was even attributed to him. If she told Shar that the book was part of her investigation, which it was, and asked him to pass it quietly through the system . . .

. . . I could take the translated text to the colonel. I wouldn't be breaking any promises, just running a thorough investigation.

Her mind made up, Ro tucked the book under one arm and went to find Shar, sure that she could count on his discretion—and feeling quite pleased with her resourcefulness. She'd found the answer to Istani's death; now, all she had to do was figure out what it meant.

17

"So . . . what's up, Doc?"

Vic was smiling as though he'd told a joke, and Bashir smiled back at him, having learned a long time ago that asking the lounge singer to explain himself usually wasn't worth the effort, his references period-specific and occasionally unimaginable. Bashir liked hearing them regardless, charmed by the "hip" sound of each alien allusion.

They sat together at one of the small tables near the stage, Bashir drinking tea, Vic drinking something he called *cuppajo* that smelled very much like coffee. It was morning, the lounge empty except for a handful of casino workers at the bar who had apparently just finished their shifts. Bashir had been relieved to see that Vic was up so early; since his program had gone full-time, there was always the risk now of waking him up, or finding him preoccupied with something else.

"Lots of things, I suppose," Bashir said, noting that

his friend was making a point of not asking outright the reason for his early visit—as if he didn't already suspect. Vic Fontaine was remarkably tuned in to people when it came to relationships, particularly romantic ones, but he also didn't interject without being asked. The hologram was special, and not just because he was self-aware, or could transfer his matrix into other programs at will; Vic Fontaine knew about women and what they wanted, he knew how a man's heart worked, and he was willing to share his thoughts on either subject without seeming didactic.

Vic sipped at his *cuppajo.* "I guess so. A few people who came to last night's second set were telling me that one of those Jem'Hadar goons turned up. Bad pennies, you know?"

Bashir nodded, although he had no idea. Mid-twentieth century Earth was a complicated time. "Yes, one did, and he made some fairly amazing claims. Ezri is assessing him even as we speak, to try to see if he's telling the truth."

"Because of all that Starfleet investigation hubbub, right," Vic said. "It was the first thing I heard about when we came back on, after the power short. That and the *Aldebaran,* those poor kids."

Bashir started to ask who'd told him, but since Vic could access the station computer without much trouble, he'd probably just tapped in to see what was happening after his program had blinked. Vic was definitely exceptional. Even Miles hadn't been able to figure out how he worked, not entirely.

Bashir nodded again, thinking about how to start the conversation he wanted to have, thinking about his and Ezri's discussion the night before. They had both apologized, but hadn't talked any further about the incident itself—

"So, doll-face is running the talking cure with a Jem'Hadar," Vic said, casually leaning back in his chair. "That's quite a gig. Say, you two still making the music?"

Bashir had to smile at the man's seemingly innocent segue, matched by a guileless expression. "I think so," he said. "Things are good, overall . . . but I guess you could say we've run into a bit of dissonance."

"Stepping out bad?" Vic asked, frowning.

Bahsir shook his head, not sure. "Ah, hurt feelings bad."

"Yours or hers?"

"Both. We were—there was a problem, and she didn't seem to care about how it affected me, and I got angry about it."

Vic ran a hand through his silver hair, his handsome features set in an exaggerated wince. "Ouch. You make it up to her yet?"

Bashir sighed. "Yes. We both apologized . . . but we haven't really resolved the issue. I started to bring it up, but she changed the subject. We're having dinner tonight, though, and I thought I might try again."

Vic drank more of his beverage, a thoughtful look on his face. "Sometimes things don't get resolved until you're ready to resolve them, pallie. And even then, they don't always shake out the way you expect."

Bashir wasn't so sure he liked the sound of that. "You think she doesn't want to work this out yet?"

The singer grinned brilliantly. "Hey, you make it sound like a bad thing. The beauty of the long-term is that you get some elbow room, a little time to breathe—and taking it doesn't have to mean you're ready to call it quits."

Bashir nodded slowly, accepting the information and feeling better. Vic had a way of quickly uncovering the core of a problem; Ezri just needed some time to herself. That was fair, wasn't it?

Fair to her, since I'm the one who doesn't know what's going on.

The spurt of petty anger surprised him by its intensity, and he decided immediately that it was juvenile—but he couldn't entirely discount it. As much as he wanted everything to be good again, there was a part of him that felt *disregarded*. And childish or not, he was angry that she hadn't noticed.

I'm sorry and angry. And I want to fix it, but I don't.

"Crazy thing, love, Vic said. "All kinds of twists and turns, a real Coney ride."

Bashir thought he could grasp that one from context.

. . . and considering the subject's doubtful ability to experience guilt, the computer's interpretation of frictive patterns and syllabic emphasis points can not be relied upon to detect truthfulness (extension subtext 4).

In short, beyond the brief personal history he supplied upon request (extension subtext 2), I am unable to offer any information about Kitana'klan that he has not volunteered, or that isn't already widely understood about the Jem'Hadar's cultural psychology. . . .

Wonderful. She hadn't really thought that Ezri—or any counselor—would be able to figure out whether or not the Jem'Hadar was trustworthy in a single session, but Kira had hoped, regardless. Sighing, she scanned the rest of Ezri's summary, seeing pretty much what she expected—until they knew more, they couldn't know what to do with him. Ezri did suggest that he be moved to a secure area other than the holding cell, pointing out that even such a small extension of trust might help things along later. Assuming he was telling the truth.

Kira dropped the padd on her desk and rubbed her eyes, wishing she knew what to do about their surprise guest. Not so much what to do—putting him in one of the reinforced cargo bays, under guard, and letting Ezri work with him was a plan, at least until Admiral Ross showed up—as what to *think*. If only Kitana'klan had managed to hang on to that transmission chip from Odo—

"Nerys?"

Startled, Kira looked up—and saw a tall, dark-haired vedek standing in the doorway, smiling at her with an easy familiarity. He looked so different that it took her a second to place him, even though they'd worked together for a couple of years. Yevir Linjarin.

"Yevir—Vedek Yevir," she stumbled, and stood up, grinning. It was strange to see him wearing the robes, but they suited him. He looked tanned and healthy, and beamed with that inner radiance that so often accompanied late faith. She'd heard the stories after he'd left the station, and could see now by his open, glowing face— so different than the solemn Yevir she'd known—that he had truly been Touched.

"Please, Yevir will do just fine," he said. "It's what you always called me. May I come in? If you're busy . . ."

"No, not at all," she said, stepping around her desk to greet him. He must have come in on the early shuttle, which had docked only thirty minutes ago. "It's so good to see you!"

He opened his arms, and Kira embraced him readily, vaguely amazed to find herself hugging Yevir Linjarin. The man she remembered had been pleasant enough but extremely reserved, even awkward. It *was* good to see him; she didn't know that she had ever felt really close to him, but she had considered him a friend. And at the moment, she could use a few friends—and cynical though it made her feel, she couldn't help but think of his political standing. Reestablishing contact with a man favored to be kai someday—perhaps soon—could be beneficial for the station.

She stepped away, motioning for him to join her at the long, low couch at the office's far corner. "So, what brings you back to DS9?"

Yevir smiled, dropping comfortably onto the padded bench. "Part business, part pleasure. I don't know if you were aware of it, but I'm with the Vedek Assembly now—" At Kira's nod, he continued. "—and with everything still so unsettled on Bajor—politically, I mean, with the First Minister still on Earth, and no kai, and the provisional government caught up with the Cardassian aid project . . . well, I suppose you could say the business aspect of my visit is to see how things are going here, at least on behalf of the Assembly."

He gazed at her sorrowfully now, and with great empathy. "We were all shocked and saddened by the news of the attack, of course . . . and by the death of Istani Reyla. It must be a difficult time for you."

Kira nodded again, not sure how to respond. For the

depth of the friendship they'd had, she didn't feel right discussing her personal feelings. But he was a vedek now, and from all accounts, an inspired one. Even sitting close to him, she could feel a kind of spiritual electricity emanating from him, as though his *pagh* was too vast to be contained.

Like Benjamin, after the pagh'tem'far *that led him to B'hala.* Which was also when the Emissary had spoken to Yevir, and forever changed his life. A miracle of the Prophets.

"It's been hard for all of us," she said finally, giving in to her instincts, and to a lifetime of faith. Vedeks counseled, and she couldn't imagine hiding anything from one who had been Touched. "Reyla's senseless murder, then the attack . . . people I knew and cared about were killed. And now the Federation is coming because they believe the Dominion was behind it."

"But you don't . . . ?"

"My gut tells otherwise. And this morning we turned up a shrouded Jem'Hadar soldier hiding on the station, who insists it was a rogue aggression." Kira shook her head, feeling very tired. "Unfortunately, he's not what I'd call a credible source of information."

He continued to hold her gaze, his own soft with kindness and understanding. Again, she felt mild disbelief—Yevir Linjarin, of all people—but she also felt encouraged to continue.

"I'm feeling a lot of stress these days. It's not that any single thing I do is that hard—dealing with a difficult member of my crew, keeping the relief ships on schedule, making sure repairs are made—individually, any part of my daily routine is just something I have to get done. But when I think about running the station, I feel—overwhelmed sometimes. As though it's something much harder than the sum of those individual parts. Does that make sense?"

Yevir nodded. "It does. Because this is also your life, Nerys. And no matter how important the station is to you, you can't make it your entire life. You can't, because what will happen—what is happening—is that even the thought of it will become a terrible burden. It will make you tired and discouraged, and that's not how the Prophets meant for their children to live."

She took a deep breath and blew it out heavily, nodding. It was what Kasidy had been trying to tell her—and Ezri, and Julian, and even Tiris, in a way. Why was it so hard for her to grasp, that she needed to maintain a more balanced life?

"Forgive me for my presumptuousness," he continued quietly, "but may I say that the Prophets have blessed you with great strength and courage. Everyone I've spoken to within the Assembly agrees that you are managing Bajor's interests here wonderfully. However difficult things may be, I hope that knowing you have our full confidence is some small comfort to you."

He smiled then, his expression compassionate and caring. "As I hope our friendship will be. I know it's been a while, and that thinking of me as a vedek might take some getting used to . . . but when I heard about Reyla's death, I wanted to come and see you. It's one of my personal reasons, I suppose—to offer my prayers for you and for those recovering from the tragedies that have occurred here. I've already spoken to Vedek Capril, and he's agreed to let me lead services this evening. I hope that you'll attend; I mean to speak from *Songs of Dusk*."

A lovely, lyrical meditation on age and dying. Kira's face broke into a smile, touched by his thoughtfulness. "Of course I'll come. It's an honor for the station."

"And perhaps, afterwards, we could talk some more," he said, standing. "I have to admit, I was hoping to ask you a few questions about the Emissary. About what his life and transcendence have meant for Bajor . . . and what it was like to work with him."

Kira stood also, noting with a touch of amusement that he suddenly seemed a little shy. She could understand; although she and Captain Sisko had finally developed a good working relationship, separating her commanding officer from the Emissary . . . she supposed she'd never managed to do that, not with any consistency.

"His son was on the shuttle, you know. I took his presence as a positive omen for my—"

"Jake?" Kira couldn't help interrupting. "Jake's here on the station?" *Kas will be so happy* . . . And Nog, and Dax, and a half dozen others, not least herself.

Smiling, Yevir nodded. "I gather you didn't know he was coming."

"No, but it's wonderful news, we've really missed him around here." Kira shook her head, delighted.

"I would imagine. He *is* the son of the Emissary," Yevir said, still smiling—and although Kira didn't say anything, she felt the faintest whisper of irritation.

He's also his own person. But of course, Yevir hadn't really known Jake, or the captain, and it was only natural that he felt some reverence for the man who'd led him to the Prophets. A lot of people felt that way about the Emissary, even though Benjamin had done his best not to encourage it.

Yevir slowly raised his hand to her ear, and Kira remained motionless to allow the touch. He closed his eyes, and after a moment, the hand withdrew. He smiled gently at her. "Walk with the Prophets, Nerys."

She walked him to the door, promising again to see him at services. She was glad Yevir had come, and grateful that he'd be around for a little while . . . and Jake, returning unexpectedly—nice to have a little good news for a change.

As she returned to her desk, a loud and abrasively urgent voice squawked from her console. "Colonel Kira? This is Quark, and I have a proposal for you."

"Get off the com," Kira said, scowling. "Now."

"I wouldn't have *dared*," he intoned earnestly, "except it's come to my attention that Captain Sisko's son has come home to us, and I feel that he deserves a proper welcome back. And although I'd like to throw him a lavish party, the kind of reception he truly merits, the financial burden is really too great for a single businessman—"

"Off, Quark, I mean it," Kira warned. He was strictly prohibited from official channels unless it was an emergency.

He went on as if he hadn't heard her. "—and, of course, it would also be a chance for everyone on the station to come together, to reestablish a sense of community in these uncertain times . . . and it occurred to me that since you've always been so generous, so unstinting when it comes to providing for the emotional needs of the people who live here, I thought that you would want to lend your support to my humble gathering."

Kira sighed. She hated to admit it, and she certainly

wouldn't to him, but Quark's idea wasn't all that bad. Not a party, but . . . a connection. A reminder for everyone that they weren't alone, and that even after all they'd endured, there were still good things to share.

"Bottom-line it," she said, sighing, Quark's tone instantly hopped from wheedling to mercenary. He knew he had a sale.

But after all, he is *the son of the Emissary.* Smiling, Kira let Quark try to talk her into a few things, thinking about positive omens and old friends.

After a quick shower in his quarters, Jake put on fresh clothes—clothes that seemed too clean after B'hala—and went to see Kasidy, walking briskly along level three of the Habitat Ring and checking the numbers over each door. Level three, corridor C . . . he'd only been to her place a few times before, and when she didn't answer her door signal, he thought he'd forgotten, after all. The computer had *said* she was in her quarters, but maybe it was 0246, not 0426.

No, I remember the enviro panels, she's two doors down. I haven't been away that *long.* He signaled again, frowning, thinking that maybe he'd just missed her—

—when the door opened, revealing a bleary, tousled Kasidy Yates. He grinned as her eyes lit up, as she stepped forward and hugged him tightly.

"Jake! Why didn't you tell me you were coming?" She leaned back, gazing up into his face with a look of sheer happiness. "Did you just get in? How long are you staying? Oh, it's so good to *see* you!"

Her hair was sticking up, and Jake playfully patted it, smoothing it down. "Just wake up, Kas?"

She laughed, releasing him and stepping back,

touching her hair and straightening her loose dress. "You got me. It's what, five o'clock? I must look a mess . . . come in, come in and tell me things."

He followed her inside, happy to see that some things never changed; there were five or six empty tea cups sitting amongst several partially filled packing containers, a few random articles of clothing strewn across chairs and countertops. The woman was not a cleaner. Dad used to complain good-naturedly about it, having to pick up after her visits.

Kas settled into a chair across from the couch, and as he sat down, he saw for the first time how big she'd gotten. Her jawline had softened, the curves of her body definitely thicker, and there was a noticeable swell in her stomach. She looked fantastic, and distinctly pregnant.

"Are you going to tell me whether that's my brother or sister in there?" He asked, gesturing at her belly.

Kas laughed, touching the soft curve with both hands. "No way. It's going to be a surprise for everyone, you know that. And don't go asking Julian, he's sworn to secrecy."

"Yeah, right. I bet I can get it out of him."

She laughed again, a bright, familiar sound. "Well, if you find out, don't tell me. Now fill me in, kiddo. What's up?"

He didn't want to lie to her, he didn't want to lie to anyone, but especially Kasidy. The story he'd worked out *could* be the truth, depending on what happened after he left the station. . . .

. . . *just say it. If the prophecy turns out to be true, no one is going to be mad . . . and if it's not, there's a good chance nobody will ever know, anyway.*

"I guess I got tired of working in the dirt," he said, surprising himself by meeting her gaze evenly. "I've decided to go see Grandpa." He smiled, shrugging. "See if I can get tired of working in a kitchen for a while."

Kasidy's smile faded, but only a little. "So you're not staying?"

"I'd like to. But no, I just came to find myself a ride." He grinned at her again. "Don't worry, though, I'll be back in plenty of time to help you get ready for the baby."

She nodded. "Well, I can't say I'm not disappointed for my sake, but I know Joseph will be thrilled."

She looked at him seriously, and for just a second, her calm, caring expression was so like Dad's that he felt a chill. "And I'm glad you're going to see him for *your* sake. Family's important, Jake. So, tell me— what's B'hala like?"

Jake relaxed. He'd expected . . . actually, he wasn't sure what he'd expected, but not such an easy acceptance of his plans. It made him feel guilty, but only a little. It was best this way; if things didn't work out, he *was* going to go to Earth, and he wouldn't have to feel like a jerk for getting anyone's hopes up.

He told her a few anecdotes about B'hala, about some of the artifacts he'd handled and some of the people he'd worked with. She listened attentively, even though he caught himself telling her a funny story he'd told her before, in one of their transmissions. The fact that she laughed just as hard the second time made him feel lucky to know her; she was going to be a terrific mom.

The conversation meandered around to the house, to plans for a garden and a few questions from Kas about final touches for his room. From there, she chatted about changes in station personnel and the aftermath of the attack. He tried to appear casual and interested, but considering what he was planning—what the possible consequences could be—it was hard to sit still.

Maybe I'll leave early tomorrow. Maybe even tonight. He wanted to see a few people, Ezri and Nog and Kira at least, but only so they wouldn't feel slighted if he ended up going on to Earth. *And I won't be, because it has to be true. My father is waiting for me in the wormhole, the prophecy was clear.*

"*The son enters the Temple alone. With the Herald, he returns.*" He saw it every time he closed his eyes, felt the truth of it every time he thought the words. In the days since the prylar had given him the ancient writing, he'd been able to think of little else.

". . . and I never thought I'd end up being happy about having a Jem'Hadar on the station, but I was getting worried about Kira—"

"What? There was a Jem'Hadar, here?"

Kasidy glared at him in mock reproach. "You haven't been listening. There *is* a Jem'Hadar here, his name is Kitana—something . . . really, you'll have to get the story from someone else. All I know is that he turned up in Quark's yesterday, and that they've got him in a holding cell now."

That was news. "Did he attack anyone?"

"No, but it gives me the creeps, knowing he's been wandering around ever since their strike on the station. That's why I was worried about Kira, she was acting a little strange, and after everything she'd been through, I thought maybe she was suffering some kind of paranoia. A friend of hers was actually murdered on the

Promenade, just a few hours before the Jem'Hadar ships hit. And it turned out she thought she was being watched because she *was* being watched."

"Murdered. That's terrible," Jake said, shaking his head, feeling very much like an outsider. He'd missed all of this. "Who was it?"

"An old friend of hers who'd just come up from Bajor, a prylar. Someone stabbed her during an attempted robbery, some crazy man who grabbed her bag and then ended up falling off the second floor balcony and breaking his neck. You know, she might even have been at B'hala—she was an archeologist, I'm pretty sure. Istani Reyla?"

Stunned, Jake stared at her, at a complete loss for anything to say. Istani Reyla, murdered, here on the station. It was all he could think, and the thought repeated itself several times as Kas moved to his side, frowning, gently taking one of his hands in hers.

"You knew her."

Jake nodded mutely, new thoughts coming in, none of them comfortable. The woman who'd given him the prophecy, one that had surely been buried for thousands of years, murdered only a few days later by a thief—or someone who knew that she had taken something extremely valuable from B'hala. It couln't possibly be a coincidence—

—but you don't know *that. You don't know anything about it, and she seemed like a nice lady, but it probably doesn't have anything to do with what you're here for—*

It was the voice of rationalization and he clung to it, desperately hoping it was true and suspecting that it wasn't. He couldn't change plans, he wouldn't . . . but she was dead, somebody had *killed* her—

"Jake?"

He looked into Kasidy's worried, searching gaze and forced himself to speak, more determined than ever. If she knew what was going on, there was no way she'd let him go.

"Yeah. I didn't know her, exactly, but I met her once. She seemed really nice. It's just a surprise, you know?"

It was the best he could do, and it was enough for Kasidy. Still holding his hand, she murmured a few words of comfort and then delicately eased the conversation into less troubled waters. Jake let her, comforted by her careful maneuvering to make him feel better, telling himself that he'd be bringing Dad back to her and that everything was going to be okay, very soon.

18

"You're finished already?"

Ro Laren's first words upon answering her door. Smiling, Shar held up the wrapped Bajoran artifact in one hand, a padd with the translation in his other, and Ro quickly stepped back, motioning him inside with a somewhat anxious expression.

Shar stepped into her quarters, looking around with interest; his first invitation to see inside her rooms. Like the security office, there was not a single personal item in sight. Disappointing, but not really a surprise. The lieutenant didn't strike him as a particularly sentimental person. He didn't see Quark's flowers anywhere.

Ro took the book and its translation from him and sat down at the small table next to the replicator, scanning the padd's content numbers.

"Have a seat. Can I get you anything, a drink?" The offer was absently given, her attention fixed on the padd.

Noting how distracted she seemed, Shar shook his head. "If you'd rather, I could excuse myself so that you might have an opportunity to read the text," he said. "It seems to be of primary interest to you."

Ro looked up him and smiled, setting the padd aside. "I'm sorry, Shar. Please, sit down. I just wasn't expecting it so fast . . . how did you do it? You didn't use the main computer, did you?"

She seemed concerned by the prospect, apparently forgetting that she had specifically asked him not to upload the text. "No. It seems that one of the station's previous science officers—Jadzia Dax, in fact—made a number of improvements to a translation program the Bajoran archeologists had already been utilizing. It's been in a near-constant state of update and revision on Bajor since then. There are two vedeks on DS9 who regularly record new changes in the program for their own use. I copied the file to the terminal in my quarters and scanned the pages manually . . . though I'm afraid the translation is only about 94 percent accurate, and parts of the text are missing."

"That's all right, Shar. I appreciate what you've done . . . and knowing that I can count on your discretion."

Shar nodded. "As you said, it's evidence in an investigation. I understand your desire for caution . . . although considering the material, I'm not sure that I understand the need."

"What are your impressions of what you read?" Ro asked.

"It seems to be a book of prophecies, written in a religious context. The few I read were very old, and I don't know enough of your history to know whether or not they were accurate."

Ro nodded slowly, a look of resigned displeasure on her face. "I figured as much. We Bajorans seem to be lunatics when it comes to prophecies."

Shar wasn't clear about her meaning, but didn't think it was appropriate to ask about the evidence, which he assumed had something to do with the two Bajoran deaths on the Promenade. He was curious about her attitude, however.

"Laren, I have noted before that you don't seem to share the same religious enthusiasm as other Bajorans. Is there a particular reason?"

She didn't answer for a moment, and Shar was about to rescind his question, afraid that he'd overstepped social boundaries, when she finally spoke. He was relieved. Ro's forthright manner was one of the reasons he so enjoyed her company. It continued to mystify him that there were those on board the station who avoided her, apparently perceiving her bluntness as unfriendliness; he welcomed the opportunity to be around anyone who avoided deceit.

"I don't think that there's any one specific reason," she said. "I had a hard childhood, but so did just about every other Bajoran currently living, and it didn't stop them from believing . . . the weird thing is, I *do* believe in the Prophets. I mean, they obviously exist, and I even believe that they watch out for Bajor, after a fashion. But just because there are some mysterious beings living in the wormhole, that occasionally interfere with our people—I don't think that's enough of a reason to worship them as gods."

She smiled, a small and bitter smile. "And it doesn't help that the prevailing attitude among the faithful is that if you don't worship, there something wrong with

245

you, or that you're missing out on some great truth. Maybe I'm just contrary, but I don't like the suggestion that I'm somehow less of a person, just because I don't want to do what everyone else does. Whether or not the Prophets are gods, I'd like to feel that I'm free to make my own choice and not be judged because of it."

Her smile changed, becoming the half-whimsical expression he recognized as an attempt to lighten the severity of her statement. She used it often. "Does that make any sense at all?"

Shar's heart was pounding. He understood, better than she knew. With few changes, it was a speech he could have made concerning his own life, the feelings expressed the same as his own—the desire to be independent from what was expected, to make choices deviant from tradition. The difference was, he had never dared to speak his thoughts aloud.

Nor are you at liberty to do so now. The time, the place, even the person was inappropriate.

"It does," he said slowly. "And I support and applaud your decision, Ro Laren."

She raised her eyebrows, surprised perhaps by his sincerity, as she couldn't possibly know the cause. "Well, that makes one of you. But thank you, Shar, that's nice of you to say."

He stood, feeling a strong urge to be alone for a while, to ponder the importance and relevance of Ro's statements. It was with an effort that he remembered what else he'd meant to ask her.

"I was informed by Ezri Dax that there's to be a celebratory gathering at Quark's later this evening, about 2130 hours," he said. "The son of Captain Sisko is being welcomed back to the station, and Ezri says he's an exceptional young man. I thought I might attend . . . perhaps you'd like to meet me there? Ezri suggested that I bring a friend."

"Actually, I think I'll stay in tonight, see how much of this translation I can get through," Ro said. "But thank you for asking—and please don't talk about any of this prophecy business to anyone, all right?"

Shar nodded, and after Ro thanked him again, he left her spare quarters for the cold solitude of the corridor, feeling hopeful and reflective and very much afraid of the thoughts that their talk had inspired.

Alone in one of the engineering offices, Vaughn sat looking through files on some of the *Enterprise*'s past missions, a cup of cooling coffee at hand. The warp drive was still faltering, but they'd be headed for DS9 as soon as it was on-line; less than a day, surely. And officially, without another assignment waiting, Vaughn's time was his own.

He supposed it was awfully boring of him, but reviewing the tactical history of different commands was a pastime he'd always enjoyed, probably due to all of the years he'd spent out on loan as an adviser. Hopping from ship to ship, most without the holodeck facilities that had become standard these days, meant finding a hobby that didn't require lugging around a lot of equipment, one that he could take up anywhere.

And no matter how I've come to feel about my participation in battle as of late, I can't deny the interest. It had been his life for too long not to have become a part of him, and a change of perspective didn't mean that everything had changed; reading mission reviews relaxed and entertained him.

Only a few years out, and the *Enterprise-E* had already been involved in a number of extremely interesting tactical situations, and reading about them inspired memories of his own, conflicts and resolutions that he hadn't thought of in years. It was ironic—the Orb's influence had worn off, but his taste for reflection seemed to be growing.

He'd just finished perusing a number of entries about Picard's decision to defy the Federation's initial stance during the Ba'ku affair. It was fascinating material, but he was finding it hard to concentrate; he kept thinking about the fact that they still had no subspace communications, and what it might mean for the *Enterprise* and her passengers once they reached DS9. The coded transmission he'd received two days ago wasn't one he could talk about, but Picard would undoubtedly have been notified by now, if communications were working. Until Vaughn had official word of declassification, his hands were tied.

"Commander Vaughn?"

Vaughn looked up and saw Will Riker in the doorway. He smiled at the young man; even though he'd chosen the small office to avoid being sought out, he was happy for the reprieve from the darkening nature of his thoughts.

"There's no one around, Commander. Elias will do."

Riker smiled back at him, stepping into the small office. "Elias, then. I'm sorry to interrupt, but the captain asked me to keep you apprised of our situation."

"Which is . . .?"

"We've set a course for DS9, but the warp drive is still a concern. A diagnostic on the core shows a slight imbalance in the antideuterium levels, probably because of the extended exposure to plasma radiation. It's not serious, but Commander La Forge has recommended that we don't exceed warp four until we can dock and perform a thorough inspection. We're looking at twenty hours, maybe a little less. ETA is 1500 tomorrow."

"Have you ever been to DS9?" Vaughn asked.

The first officer nodded. "A few times. The first was just after the Cardassian withdrawal. Commander Sisko had just taken charge of overseeing Bajor's preparedness for Federation membership."

"Captain Sisko of the *Defiant?*"

Riker nodded. "He ran the station for the last . . . seven years, I guess. You never met him?"

"No. I know the name, of course." Everyone in Starfleet knew about Sisko; he'd been a key player on the frontlines, one of the Allied force leaders in the final days of the war against the Dominion.

Vaughn frowned, trying to recall something unusual he'd heard about Sisko's command. He'd had some kind of connection to the Bajoran religion, though Vaughn couldn't remember in what context. "Didn't he retire recently? Or . . . was he killed?"

"Neither, actually," Riker said. "He disappeared. I don't know the specifics, but I know that Starfleet decided not to pursue an investigation, for some reason. Something to do with Bajor . . . the Bajorans considered him to be some kind of religious figure, I believe. Maybe they're investigating, or he stepped down in private and joined their religious council. . . ."

Riker shook his head. "I'm not sure. I could have someone look it up for you."

Vaughn smiled. "Thank you, but that won't be necessary. It'll give me something to do on the way, now that we've got some extra time to kill."

"Which reminds me, the captain and I are having a working dinner in about an hour, with Commander La Forge," Riker said, "to talk over our repair schedule. He specifically asked me to invite you. It's an informal meeting in the captain's quarters. Can I tell him you'll be joining us?"

"Please do," Vaughn said. "Thank you, Will."

Riker grinned. "You're welcome, Elias."

With a nod, the first officer departed, leaving Vaughn alone once more. His curiosity piqued, he decided to see what he could find out.

"Computer—show me the current personnel file for Starfleet Captain Benjamin Sisko."

The computer's consistently efficient female voice filtered into the room. "General access to personnel files in the ship's database is limited to—"

"Whatever you have will be fine," Vaughn interrupted.

A second later, a brief history of Sisko's career popped up on the screen in front of him, a list of honors and decorations, of postings and dates—but Vaughn only saw the small head shot in the upper corner of the screen, a standard optical capture from about the time Sisko had made captain.

It's him.

When Vaughn had reached the Orb and stepped forward to close the doors of its ark, there had been someone with him for a few seconds, a calm and smiling presence he had discounted as a random Orb-induced hallucination. He saw now that it was Benjamin Sisko who had been with him on the *Kamal,* a man he'd never met or even seen before.

"Computer, show me the rest of this file, authorization Vaughn-alpha-zero-seven-zero."

"Access to specified files is restricted to Level Fourteen security clearance or above."

My, that *was* classified. "Recognize, Vaughn, Elias A., Commander, security clearance Level Twenty."

A new file hit the screen with multiple category options, everything from medical records to personal history. Vaughn called up pictures and found a good one, a full face shot taken only days before the end of the war.

Vaughn leaned back in his chair and stared at the picture, unblinking, the seconds spinning into minutes. It was definitely the same man he'd seen on the freighter, suggesting that there were forces at play that extended far beyond the reality he was most familiar with. He could only hope that they were favorable ones.

Returning to the personal history file, Vaughn opened the first chapter and started to read.

" '. . . and singing, taken to Their eternal home.' "

Finished, Yevir took a deep breath and looked out over the gathered faithful, gratified to see tears on almost every face, mingled with smiles and nods of acceptance. The piece he'd chosen to read was a powerful one, an affirmation of life and existence beyond life; it had been the perfect choice.

The Prophets guide my hand, he quickly reminded himself, knowing how easy it was to become lost in pride. It was a powerful experience for him, too, being the focal point of so much faith, even for a few moments. Every seat was taken, many standing against the back wall, and he knew from Vedek Capril that the reading had been broadcast to several private gatherings throughout the station, so that every Bajoran on board could listen.

Yevir was silent for a moment, aware of the chance he was being given—not just to comfort and lead, but also to put out a few subtle feelers for the missing book. It was hard not to be able to ask outright, but considering the nature of the text, the fewer who knew of it, the better; his small deceit was for the greater good.

"I want to thank you, to thank all of you for this opportunity," he said, nodding ever so slightly at Kira Nerys, sitting in the second row. He saw that she, too, had wept; he sincerely hoped that it wasn't her conscience that had inspired her tears. Earlier, he hadn't sensed any disingenuousness on her part, but he knew that making faulty assumptions could prove disastrous. Until he located the book, he had to remain vigilant.

"It's a particular honor for me to be able to speak to you here," he continued. "As many of you know, it was just outside this very shrine where I received the Touch that led me into the service of the Prophets, only a few years ago. The Emissary was Their tool, as he was for so many of you, for reaching me. For showing me where I belong in the grand tapestry that is our culture. It is a tapestry that we weave, with the choices that we make, with the lives that we touch—but it is incumbent upon us to always remember that it is the Prophets who provide the threads."

Nods among the gathered, smiles of acknowledgment. Yevir went on, choosing his words carefully now. "As the Emissary showed us all, one does not have to be a vedek to serve. I believe, with all my heart, that we can each do our part—and that it will take each of us doing our part to continue creating that grand tapestry. We best honor the Prophets by always seeking Their will, in every thing we do . . . by choosing love, instead of hate. By seeking to understand, instead of staying in ignorance. By rejecting all forms of heresy, raising our hands to the Prophets and turning our backs to the unclean words and thoughts that seek to pull us away from Their wisdom."

In the sea of glowing faces, Yevir saw acceptance and agreement. It was the best he could hope for; if someone listening had knowledge of the book, perhaps he had reached them. At the very least, he had made himself known to them all by leading a well-attended service. It would make his task easier, if he didn't have to introduce himself to everyone he meant to question.

"This concludes tonight's worship; thank you all for coming. *Tesra Peldor impatri bren. Bentel vetan ullon sten.* Walk with the Prophets."

He glanced at the ranjen to his left, who softly tapped the gong that signaled the end of the service. Immediately, people rose and surged forward to greet him, talking amongst themselves about their pleasure with the service, many actually reaching out to touch him. Yevir smiled and nodded as he stepped off the riser, thanking them, receiving their kindness and working to keep it from swelling his pride.

Kira was suddenly in front of him, her eyes shining. "That was beautiful," she said, briefly squeezing his hand.

"Thank you, Nerys." He leaned toward her, lowering

his voice slightly. "I hope that means that you'll buy me dinner. I haven't eaten since I got here."

Kira grinned. "Absolutely. I was just on my way to Quark's, and was going to ask if you were free. I wanted to introduce you to someone—"

There were more people eager to speak to him, standing patiently by. Yevir nodded at Kira. "I'll meet you there."

A second later she was gone, a half dozen smiling men and women pressing forward in her place to be near him. For a few seconds, he forgot about the book, forgot about Kira and the Assembly and even the Emissary, instead allowing himself to be enveloped by their faith and happiness. Surely, the Prophets wouldn't begrudge him a moment of complacency, a single moment to enjoy what his position inspired. He was only a man, after all.

Yevir opened his arms, accepting their good will, accepting their love.

19

Bashir signaled at Dax's door promptly at 2120 hours, to walk with her to the welcoming party. Ezri was still trying to make her hair do something interesting. The sound of the door's tone started her heart beating a little faster.

"Come in!"

The door opened and Bashir stepped inside, smiling when he saw her in front of the mirror. She frowned, running her fingers through her hair, brushing it forward and then pushing it back.

"It's short, Ezri," he said, moving to stand behind her, speaking to her reflection. He slid his arms around her waist, resting his chin on top of her head. It always amazed her, how well they fit together. "There's just not that much you can do with it."

Dax smiled, still fussing with her bangs, happy to be in his arms. "Says you. I'm going to dye it purple and green, and spike it like a prong flower."

She turned around, leaning back to kiss him hello before stepping away. "Are you ready yet?" she asked, teasing.

"I'm always ready," he said, his stock answer, but his smile was a little thin . . . and although she knew exactly why, she wasn't prepared to get into it. She knew he was hurt by what had happened, but his response had hurt, too, and she wanted a little more time to figure out what she wanted to tell him.

I need time to figure out what I'm trying to tell me. Since commanding the *Defiant,* she had discovered new kinds of memories, feelings of confidence and possibility that she'd never felt before. She felt strong and excited and a little bit confused, and she knew that things where changing.

But that's good, change is a good thing . . . and he loves me. He'd understand, he'd be patient and understanding—

—like he understood about Jadzia?

Dax ignored the vicious little thought, reminding herself that he'd been surprised into anger.

"Listen—about tonight . . ." Ezri smiled up at him, feeling strangely nervous. She trusted him, but was feeling a little uncertain about his mood. "Would it be okay with you if we moved dinner to tomorrow?"

Bashir's smile faded. "Why?"

"I really need to do some serious prep work, for my next session with Kitana'klan. I'd been planning to do it after our dinner, but then Kira called about Jake, and I guess he's only going to be here for a day. . . ."

At the tensing of his jaw, she gave up. "I do need the time for work, but I also want to be alone tonight. Not because of what happened yesterday, but because . . . I just do."

Bahsir stared at her, and for a moment she thought he would be angry, a thought that both distressed her and opened the door to resentment. She loved him, but she was also unhappy about his reaction to what had occurred between them. She'd reached out for understanding, for empathy and support, and he'd turned away.

"I understand," he said finally, obviously doing his best to mean it. "Tomorrow it is, then."

"Hey, we've still got a party to go to tonight, right?" Ezri smiled encouragingly at him.

"Right." His smile seemed a little forced, but she appreciated the effort.

"I love you," she said, and his face brightened a little, the lines of tension around his mouth and eyes relaxing.

"And I love you," he said, so warmly that she almost regretted changing their plans. Almost, but she had so much to think about, so much to consider. She'd known that a joined Trill had lifetimes of experience to draw upon, obviously, but except in specific instances, she hadn't really *felt* it before, not as something that could define her. But since the *Defiant* . . .

All of them, and me; Dax.

"Shall we?" Ezri asked, taking his arm, and Julian nodded, leaning down to kiss her again.

They started for Quark's, and although they walked touching and in love, their arms closely linked, smiling at one another, Ezri could feel the distance, and wondered if they'd be able to keep it from growing.

* * *

It was a beautiful thing, Quark decided, the kind of thing that made him believe in miracles.

Trays of hors d'oeuvres and sliced *hasperat* and stick sandwiches, enough to feed 600 with orders to replenish as needed. An open bar for two full hours, no maximum, and half price cost thereafter. And with shrine services ending, a wave of spiritually satisfied but certainly hungry and thirsty customers headed in his direction; all that worship could be rough on a body. It had been too short notice to get the hype up, but he was betting that at least 2,000 people would manage to drop in throughout the evening, at least for a drink. After days of drying profits, caused by those nasty Jem'Hadar driving away the last of his postwar revelers, Kira's acquiescence to a catered event—at his bar, and one that was open to the entire station—was like a blessed rain.

After a few final words to his staff—"keep it coming" prime among them—Quark stepped out from behind the bar and started encouraging the arriving patrons to eat, drink, be joyous, and then eat and drink more. He made a point of telling all who entered that everything was free, and that on such a lucky evening, they should consider trying a hand at dabo or dom-jot, perhaps even a late night game of *tongo*. As the 9th Rule promised, "Opportunity plus instinct equals profit."

He was saying as much to an elderly Bajoran woman when he saw Colonel Kira arrive, looking much happier than he'd seen her in a while. She had that bounce in her step that had been missing lately, and she actually smiled and nodded at him after looking over the accommodations. He'd had Frool hang a few streamers around the main food table, left over from Rom's going-away party. The decorations added that special festive touch, and since Rom had paid for them, it didn't cost Quark a thing to appear the consummate host; what could be better?

The bar slowly filled, more and more people wandering in, helping themselves to food and drink. When Jake Sisko and Kasidy Yates walked in together, a small cheer went up. Quark was too busy to see to them personally—that damned replicator of his was still blinking out, requiring him to constantly stay on top of his employees, keeping them running to and from the kitchen—but he had Broik go over with a glass of synthale for Jake and ginger tea for Kasidy. It was the little touches, he knew, that made Quark's the place to spend money on DS9.

Quark was fully occupied—keeping the dabo girls smiling, pushing his employees to hurry, advocating merriment—but not so engrossed that he couldn't keep his eyes and ears open. Sensing and reacting to the emotional undercurrents of his customers' interactions was the mark of any good entrepreneur. When he saw Shar come in alone, he mentioned to Morn that the new science officer probably knew all sorts of tricks for generating hair growth, and sent Morn over with a fresh pitcher of high-grade ale to share with the Andorian. When the adorable Ezri came in with her silly doctor, Quark noticed that there was definitely trouble in paradise, at least on Bashir's part. The doctor was faking his laughter, no question; Quark specifically assigned Frool to keep the doctor's whiskey glass full, as he had for so many troubled lovers through the years. Sometimes misery was even more lucrative than happiness.

Quark kept watch on the new vedek, and wasn't particularly impressed with what he saw. The mostly forgettable Yevir Linjarin had always been a man of simple, inexpensive tastes, and it seemed that getting bit by the Prophet bug hadn't changed anything. He ate a single slice of *hasperat* and drank only water, setting a bad example for his small flock of beaming followers. Kira seemed to like Yevir, though, making a point of introducing Jake and Kasidy to him soon after he walked in. Quark noticed with some interest that meeting Sisko's family was the one thing that actually wiped the pious smile from Yevir's face; nice to see a little humility in the religious, particularly those who didn't know how to enjoy free food. Rumor had it that he'd only be staying a short time on the station, at least.

In all, the party was proving to be a success, the only sour note being that Ro Laren hadn't put in an appearance. *Yet,* he reminded himself; it was still early. It was frustrating, particularly considering he had promised to buy her a drink the next time she dropped by. With Kira picking up the tab, he could have plied the lovely Laren with plenty of high quality liquor, saving himself a few slips of latinum.

Can't win 'em all, he thought, feeling uncharacteristically easygoing, ducking behind the bar to scrounge up another pitcher of Andorian ale after noting that Shar and Morn were running dry. He was in a good mood; people were eating and drinking and betting, the sound of laughter and conversation filling the air, the bill steadily climbing. Besides, Ro wasn't going anywhere; he had plenty of time to work his magic.

"Hi, Quark."

Quark stood up, pitcher in hand, and saw Jake Sisko

leaning across the bar. Quark plastered on a bright smile, a little surprised to find that he actually meant it. Not only was Jake's presence responsible for Quark's profitable night, he . . . well, Quark had a soft spot for the gangly young man. He was Nog's best friend, after all, and unlike his nephew, Jake had shown the good sense not to go into Starfleet.

"Jake! Welcome home. Enjoying your party, I hope? You should try the stick sandwiches, the fruit ones are especially crisp." They also weren't going as fast as everything else, and leftovers didn't keep.

"Thanks, but I'm not planning on—" Jake started.

"Say, where's that nephew of mine?" Quark interrupted, his grin fading. Jake Sisko was important to the people of Bajor; it would be just like Nog to destroy his only good contact.

"Ensign Chavez said he had a few more repairs to oversee in one of the defense sails, but he should be here any minute," Jake said. "Anyway, like I was saying, I wasn't planning to stay on the station—"

"Oh? Where are you going?" Quark asked eagerly. If he could talk Kira into a going-away party . . .

"Earth," Jake said, apparently frustrated about something. "And I'd actually like to travel alone for a change. So I need a ship that'll get me there. Do you have one?"

Quark stared at him for a moment, then laughed. He had more of a sense of humor than his father had, Quark had to give him that much. "Very funny."

"It's not a joke," Jake said. "And I know you had a couple of unregistered shuttles stashed in one of your cargo bays before I left for B'hala. Nog told me you picked them up cheap at an auction, after the war. Do you still have one?"

Nog had a big mouth. Quark sighed, lowering his voice slightly. There were a lot of people around. "Maybe I do. But I don't run a rental agency."

"Oh, I want to buy it. How much?"

As he spoke, Jake unfastened a small pouch from his belt and dug into it. Quark could hear the dully musical, telltale *clink* of latinum slips, the slightly deeper sound of a strip or two.

Right. Sell a shuttle for *strips.* Being the Emissary's kid apparently caused hallucinations.

"Forget it, Jake. Even if you've got a bar in there, there's no way you could afford it. Now if you don't mind, I see some empty glasses out there—"

"Wait," Jake said, and finally rummaged out a personal account card. He thumbprinted the access key and handed it over.

Quark took it from him, trying to decide if he should bother letting the kid down gently—and then he saw the number on the tiny display. Frowning, *that can't possibly be right,* he expertly tapped a few keys, *has to be in Cardassian leks, or Tarkalean notch-rocks . . .*

Gold-pressed latinum. Not just bars, but *bricks* of it, enough to buy ten shuttles. Twenty.

"Give me a couple of hours," Quark said, a little breathlessly. "You can take possession at airlock 12, 2500."

Jake plucked the card from Quark's numb fingers and slipped in back into his bag. "I'll want to see the merchandise before we agree on a price—though I'm sure it'll be fine. Nog said he checked them out, and you got a good deal."

Jake turned to walk away. Still stunned, Quark found his voice again; he had to know.

"How? How did *you* end up with that kind of latinum?"

Jake looked back at him and shrugged. "It was my dad's."

Quark shook his head. "Jake, your father worked for the *Federation*."

Jake grinned, a bright and sunny smile. "Remember how Jadzia used to win at *tongo?*"

Quark nodded, suppressing a shudder. The woman's luck had been uncanny. Six years of it, too.

Still smiling, Jake delivered the punch. "She lost most of it to Dad, wrestling him on the weekends."

Jake returned to his party, and for a moment, Quark could only stare after him, trying to think of an applicable Rule. Something about irony. He kept coming up blank, and those glasses out there weren't filling themselves.

Well, at least he'd be getting some of it back; he'd be sure to charge as much as he could get away with for the shuttle. *Sisko's kid or not, he can afford a little gouging. . . .*

Shaking his head, Quark spotted Frool and Broik loitering by the bar and went to yell at them.

Nog didn't get to Quark's until almost 2300. He'd been working with a crew of the new techs, slogging through the last bit of repair work on the weapons arrays, and had been afraid he'd missed everything; he was relieved to see that there were still plenty of people milling around.

He stopped at the bar for a root beer, eagerly looking around for Jake. Uncle was in fine form, ordering the servers around and table-hopping with a vengeance, and as Nog searched for Jake, he saw that most of his friends were still in the bar. Shar, Morn, and Ezri sat together, laughing about something, and at the table next to theirs, Kas and Kira were chatting away. Dr. Bashir was playing darts with Ensign Tenmei. A table of engineers saw Nog and waved, raising cups and glasses, and Nog held his root beer up in turn, thinking that he felt really good for the first time all day.

Hard to relax, when you know there's a murdering monster on board, an unhappy voice whispered in his mind, helpfully reminding him. It had even been hard to concentrate on work, and for the first time in months, he'd had twinges of pain in his leg.

"Hey! You made it!"

Nog turned, and saw that Jake had managed to sneak up behind him. Grinning, Nog set his drink down and impulsively hugged Jake, heartily slapping him on the back before letting go. Nog already missed him; Colonel Kira had already told him Jake was probably leaving in a day or so, off to see his grandfather.

"Sorry it took me so long," Nog said. "You wouldn't believe how much stuff there is to do around here. How's the party going? Do you want to sit down somewhere?"

Smiling, Jake jerked his head back toward the Promenade. "What do you say we go to our spot? For old times' sake?"

Nog hesitated for just a second, wondering if it was appropriate for a Starfleet lieutenant—then nodded, unable to resist. He *was* off duty. "That sounds great."

Jake glanced around the bar and then raised a finger to his lips. The old let's-keep-it-quiet sign reminded Nog of earlier times, days when his only responsibilities were going to Mrs. O'Brien's school and helping out in the bar, when his biggest worry was that Odo would catch them exploring the station's old service ducts. It was a fond, wistful feeling so sudden that it made his throat ache.

The two of them slipped quietly out of the bar, taking the long way around to the small lift that went to the second floor balcony. They headed for "their" bridge, the one that crossed between the viewport and the upstairs level of Quark's bar. Without ceremony, they flopped to the floor, sitting with their legs dangling over the edge. Although there was some noise from the bar, the Promenade itself was mostly deserted and quiet, the low, eternal hum of the station audible in the near silence.

For a moment, neither spoke, Jake gazing out the windows, Nog thinking about all the hours they had spent sitting there, talking about their plans for the future as they watched people walk the Promenade below. Jake seemed distant, and Nog supposed he was thinking about his father. It had to be hard for Jake, missing his dad. Nog missed his father, too, but Rom was on Ferenginar; he could always call him, collect, even. Rom had changed the law first thing, just so Nog would be sure to stay in touch.

"So that's what's left of the *Aldebaran*," Jake said quietly, surprising Nog. There was a wide field of scattered debris far beyond the window, glittering in the light of Bajor's distant sun. Jake had apparently been looking at the floating wreckage, not thinking about Captain Sisko.

Nog nodded. "It's been a problem, too. Some of the bigger pieces have been triggering the wormhole, and they're putting out enough radiation to confuse the sensors. The only way we can tell a ship isn't coming through is to scan for incoming neutrino bleeds, and that takes a few seconds." A few terrifying seconds, not knowing if the first wave of another Dominion aggression had just come through.

"Why don't you just blast them?" Jake asked.

"The *Defiant* is still under repair. I suppose we could use runabouts, but they aren't an immediate threat, and Starfleet will want to examine the remains once the task force gets here."

"When are they supposed to show up?"

Nog sighed. "Sometime in the next day or two, I guess. Not soon enough for me."

"Why?" Jake asked. "I thought Kira didn't want them to come at all."

"Because they'll probably take that Jem'Hadar with them when they leave," Nog said, hearing the bitterness in his voice. He couldn't help it, but wasn't sorry, either. Just because the Federation said they weren't official enemies anymore, that didn't mean they were friends . . . or that Nog had to accept one of them.

Jake frowned. "I thought—Kira told me that Odo may have sent him. And that he could end up staying, if that turns out to be true—"

"I'll quit," Nog spat. "I'll quit before I work on a station with one of those things aboard. And Odo didn't send him. There's no way he would have sent a Jem'Hadar soldier here without some kind of, of *credentials.*"

He shook his head, the anger a sharp, hot needle in his gut. "And even if he did, he wouldn't have sent *that* Jem'Hadar. If you saw him, you'd understand. He's just like the rest of them, he's a murderer, you can see it in his eyes—"

Jake put a hand on his arm. "Hey, you don't have to convince *me*."

Nog saw that he was sincere, and exhaled heavily, nodding. "Right. I'm sorry, I just—I've been thinking about it a lot, you know?"

"I understand. Maybe . . . well, I probably won't be around, but maybe you should talk about it to Ezri, or Vic—"

"What's to talk about?" Nog snapped. "They're all killers, nobody disputes that. I don't need to talk about it, I need for that thing to be off the station, and the sooner the better."

Jake nodded, his expression mild. "Yeah, okay."

They were quiet for another minute, Nog feeling somehow like he hadn't made his case properly. He *was* upset, maybe more than he should be, but he was also right, and didn't want his anger to confuse the issue. On the other hand, he hadn't seen Jake for a while, and probably wouldn't again for at least another few weeks. It would be a waste to spend their time together talking about the prisoner in the holding cell—

"I'm probably going to leave tonight," Jake said quietly, looking out again at the debris field hovering beyond the windows.

"Why? It's pretty late . . . why don't you stay for a couple of days?" Nog was a little hurt by the news, immediately wondering if Jake's decision had to do with his tirade against the Jem'Hadar.

Don't be ridiculous. He just needs some convincing.

Nog forced a grin, revealing as many teeth as possible to promote enthusiasm. "If you're here when the

Federation ships arrive, I bet we can get a dom-jot game going with some of their crew. Maybe even a tournament." Just about everyone on the station knew better than to play against them; Nog was good, but Jake was practically a master. "We make a great team."

Jake smiled, but even that seemed far away. "That's true. But there are things I need to do . . . and I'd kind of like to get away without making a big deal out of it. I mean, I've seen everyone I wanted to see. They'll understand, if I just kinda sneak out of the party early."

Jake grinned. "And I *will* be back, you know. Maybe even in time for part of that dom-jot tourney."

"I thought you were going to Earth for a couple of weeks, at least," Nog said.

Jake shrugged. "Plans change."

For just a second, Nog had the idea that Jake was concealing something, his childhood friend's expression too innocent to be genuine . . . but he dismissed the thought, deciding he was being paranoid. They weren't children anymore, trying to get away with some minor indiscretion without Odo or their fathers finding out. Besides which, he and Jake were partners; Jake wouldn't hide anything from *him*.

"Well, I hope they do," Nog said sincerely. "I miss you, Jake."

Jake nodded somberly. "I miss you, too."

After another second, Jake smiled, and batted his eyelids. "So, you want to kiss now, or what?"

Nog laughed, and punched Jake on the arm. "You should be so lucky, hew-mon."

He thought Jake would punch him back, and for a second, he had a strong flash of nostalgia for it. Even a couple of years ago, an exchange of punches would inevitably have them rolling on the floor, giggling like children as they struggled to pin each other down.

Jake suddenly looked a little down, and Nog thought he knew why. Things had changed, they'd been changing for a long time, and the reminder of how things had once been was both sweet and sad. It seemed like they'd both just figured out that they couldn't go back.

Jake started talking about B'hala, and the moment was gone. Nog wasn't sure if that was good or bad, and finally decided that it didn't matter. It was good to see his best friend again.

20

Ro wasn't as knowledgeable as some about her planet's history, but she certainly knew the high points—and it seemed that almost all of them were in the book that Istani Reyla had hidden just before her death, the events written about thousands of years before they happened.

And the way it's *written* . . . With as much truth as there was in the text, its secular nature could be considered a threat to Bajor's religious structure. Could be, although Ro wasn't sure; between the bizarre, often twisted metaphors and the occasional rantings about persecution, whoever had written it had almost certainly been insane.

Insane but eerily accurate. Eyes burning and shoulders aching, Ro flipped to the next page on the padd, fascinated and more than a little awed. The writings in the book were almost random in terms of significance, from the grand building of B'hala, to a good kava harvest in 1423—but so far as Ro knew, all of it had come to pass. She'd checked out a few things against the station's library, and hadn't managed to find a single discrepancy. A lot of the names were different, the translation program unable to decipher quite a few of them, but the descriptions of the events were so clear that it didn't matter. They were even roughly chronological, beginning with the adversarial relationship between the Prophets and the Pah-wraiths, and their war over the Celestial Temple. ("Temple" and "Prophets" seemed to be very close to the actual written words, but the term used for the Pah-wraiths translated to something like "fire-living spirits.") It continued through the dissolution of the *D'jarra* caste system with what the book called "the coming of the gray warriors."

Ro was just getting into the Occupation—the domination of the land and its children, in book-speak—when she realized she'd been sitting still for too long. She leaned back and stretched, rubbing her eyes, feeling excited and afraid and uncertain all at once.

"Computer, what time is it?"

"The time is 2512."

Ro blinked, thinking it was no wonder she was so sore. She'd been hunched over the book for well over four hours. She stood up and walked to the replicator, ordering ice water and a small fruit salad with sugared protein sauce. She ate standing up, gazing blankly at the ancient book itself, her thoughts all over the place.

Istani knew how important it was—whether the writer was crazy or not, it's a book of prophecy in which the prophecies are actually consistent and precise. She stole it from B'hala, and someone who knew it came after her and killed her for it, because . . .

Ro frowned, mentally backing up a step. How did

anyone know Istani had taken it? The prylar had gone out of her way to hide it once she reached the station—but was that because she knew it was valuable, or because she knew someone was coming for it?

She signed out of B'hala, but didn't get to the station until a day and a half later. Maybe she showed it to someone—Galihie S., for instance—before she left Bajor. And maybe Galihie wasn't all that thrilled about her keeping the book for herself. He could have been an artifact collector, or a religious fanatic, or a business partner . . . maybe he was her lover, and he killed her simply because she left him.

Until I know something about Galihie, I can only guess about why he did it. Unless—

—unless it was something in the text itself, something that Galihie didn't want to be known. Something that had happened and been written about, that could damage him somehow . . . or something that hadn't happened yet, that he'd wanted to keep hidden.

Ro carried her half-finished salad back to the table and set it aside, picking up the padd again, her aches forgotten for the moment. She skimmed through the Occupation, pausing only long enough to read about what had to be the Kendra Valley massacre before reaching a series of prophecies regarding the Dominion war . . . and a man who could only be Captain Sisko. Several pages from the book had apparently been torn out from the time period immediately following the war, but a few pages were intact. Ro skipped around, hoping that something would catch her eye—and something finally did.

Ro read and re-read the prophecy of the Avatar, her stomach knotting, feeling really afraid for the first time since picking up the translation. Two of the pages leading up to the prophecy were gone, but there was enough—and if there was even a chance that it was true. . . .

It was late, but there was no getting around it. It was time to talk to Colonel Kira.

After Quark left him at the airlock—the bartender walking away with a few more strips of latinum than he deserved—Jake stepped aboard the *Venture,* a little shocked at how easy things were turning out to be. After about an hour of hanging around with Nog, Jake had returned to his quarters and packed a few necessities, reaching the airlock without running into anyone. Quark had overcharged him, but hadn't asked any questions, either, and had managed to scrounge up a temporary registration license for a few extra strips. Although the personal craft was a little run-down accommodationwise, its warp and impulse engines were in decent shape.

It's perfect. Or good enough, anyway . . . assuming I keep the lights down. Jake sat his bag down on a padded bench, smiling as he looked around at the gaudily upholstered cabin—everything was striped purple, gold, and green, even the floors. According to Quark, the twenty-year-old Bajoran-built *Venture* had been the private shuttle of a humanoid gambler once upon a time, a woman who had made some poor investment choices during the war and had been forced to auction her assets. In spite of the opulence of the décor, tired though it was, the replicator could only churn out simple proteins and carbohydrates and the bed was a string hammock, but it would get Jake where he needed to go.

Soon, Dad.

Just thinking it gave Jake a chill. It hadn't seemed real before, working out his story back at B'hala, coming to the station and carefully stating his mistruths to the people he cared about. Throughout, it had all felt like some fantastic but distant dream. Even now, there was a dreamlike quality to the moment—he, Jake Sisko, was standing in a ship he had bought to take into the wormhole, to fulfill a prophecy written thousands of years before. "Crazy," as Vic might say, and not for the first time, Jake had to wonder if the more popular connotation didn't apply.

But if I'm wrong, so what? I'm out a few bars of latinum and maybe a little bit of hope, he reminded himself. *Nobody gets hurt.* Maybe it *was* crazy, but his feelings said otherwise. His feelings said that something big was going to happen when he reached the wormhole, because the prophecy was real. It was destiny, *his* destiny, and he wasn't going to let it pass by just because it seemed like a crazy thing to do—

—not when a woman probably died because she gave it to me, or because someone was trying to stop her from giving it to me.

No, he didn't *know* that. Maybe her death was because of something else she'd found, it was possible . . . but he couldn't begin to convince himself of it, as hard as he tried. He was appalled by her death, and he was afraid that the prophecy was the cause, and he didn't want to think that. Because he didn't know what it meant, exactly, or what he should do about it.

Nothing, for now. Later, you can think about it later. Or perhaps he could talk to his father about it, a thought that drove his fears away.

Jake walked to the pilot's seat and sat down, looking over the flight controls. For the most part, they weren't that different from those of a *Danube*-class runabout, which he had learned to pilot not long after his disastrous science project adventure in the Gamma Quadrant. Then, he and Nog had been essentially trapped on the *Rio Grande,* unable to return to DS9 to get help for Jake's father and Quark, who were being held by Jem'Hadar on the planet below. Though he'd only been a kid, Jake had sworn to learn basic piloting skills when they finally made it back to the station. He had, too, and the *Venture* was a much simpler version of the Federation ships he'd learned to pilot. There weren't any weapons or complex sensor arrays for him to worry about, and it had everything else he needed—gravity net, a single transporter, and a standard Bajoran filter/recy life-support system.

He powered up the engines and the onboard computer, and spent a few minutes punching in numbers, double and triple checking coordinate possibilities for what he had planned. He'd had some concerns about getting into the wormhole without everyone on the station knowing about it, but like everything else so far, circumstances seemed to be working in his favor. His conversation with Nog had supplied him with the information he needed, and the wreckage from the *Aldebaran* would provide the means. It was almost as though he was being helped along in his quest, as though . . . but no, that really *was* crazy.

Why? The Prophets watch out for Bajor, and he's with them. Why couldn't he be watching out for me, influencing things so that I can get to him?

It was far-fetched, but perhaps no more so than what

he was doing, no more than a dozen things he could think of that he had experienced growing up on the station. It was certainly no stranger than having one's father turn out to be the Bajoran Emissary to the Prophets.

Or having him take off to live with the Prophets, leaving me alone.

Not for much longer.

Jake plugged two flight plans into the computer, ordering the autopilot to kick in with the second one as soon as he was out of the station's sensor range. Avoiding the Klingon patrol ship would be tricky, but the debris field should be helpful there. After a few deep breaths, he transmitted the first flight plan, a mostly straight shot to Earth along a couple of major shipping lanes, to the departure log in ops. A few seconds later, he received vocal confirmation and clearance from an unfamiliar Militia officer who was working the panels. And just like that, he was ready to go.

He hesitated for a moment, the sane, rational part of his mind telling him that it still wasn't too late. He could forget all this nonsense and just head to Earth, or go back into the station and see his friends, or even return to B'hala, to the pleasant monotony of dust and data entry. But he knew better. It had been too late the instant that poor, doomed Istani Reyla had walked into the catalog room where he'd been working and handed him the prophecy of his father's return.

"Shuttle *Venture* departing from airlock 12 at 2524 hours," Jake said. "Course confirmed, bearing oh-one-five mark two."

"Received," the male voice responded, and in a

softer, quieter tone, he added, "Walk with the Prophets."

Jake felt an instant of surprise and concern as he signed off, that the officer knew something of his plans—but realized in the next second that the man was simply a Bajoran wishing him luck. It was quite doubtful that he had any idea of how appropriate the farewell was.

The shuttle lifted smoothly away from the bay and eased out into space, carrying Jake a step closer to his reunion with his father. He could hardly wait.

Kira had stayed late at the party, later than she probably should have, but she returned to her quarters feeling like she might actually get a decent night's sleep for the first time in almost a week. Even considering Kitana'klan's arrival, it had been a good day; Yevir Linjarin had conducted a beautiful, uplifting service and Jake's party had been a success, even if he had ducked out early.

He was probably tired, Kira thought, as she sat on the edge of her bed and kicked off her boots. Or just readjusting to station life, or preparing himself to leave for Earth. Any one of those would explain why he'd seemed so oddly distant. In any case, the party hadn't been just for him. She didn't expect one broadcast and a few free snacks to fix everything, or to make up for the losses that so many of the station's residents had suffered, but it been a step on the path to recovery.

She undressed, changing into a loose, woven shift before laying out clothes for the morning. Wiping her face and hands with a cleansing cloth, she thought about how even a few small things could change one's entire outlook on life. Knowing that she had Yevir's support, sharing a few glasses of spring wine with Kas, seeing the hardworking men and women of DS9 relaxing and unwinding . . . it all made her feel that she was doing her job. She felt ready for the Federation and its allies, ready to make her case and make it stick; Kitana'klan's presence helped, but more than that, the strong, positive feeling she had, that things were under control, was enough to allow her some peace. Everything would work out.

Pleasantly exhausted, Kira crawled into bed, determined not to let herself latch on to the things that had been keeping her awake. She needed to rest, and all of the sorrows and problems and complications of her life would still be around in the morning. She closed her eyes, offered a silent prayer of gratitude for the good things in her life, and was right on the verge of sleep when someone signaled at the door.

Dragging herself awake was painful. *The station had better be on fire. . . .*

"Who is it?"

"It's Ro."

Ro. Her sleepy anger dissolved and was replaced by a small knot of anxiety in her stomach; there was simply no way that Ro Laren would bother her at this hour unless it was important.

Reyla. She found something.

"Come in," Kira called, sitting up and reaching for a coverall. She pulled it on in record time and stepped out of her bedroom to greet Ro, who seemed distinctly agitated. The lieutenant was pale and disheveled, her body language uncharacteristically tense.

"I'm sorry it's so late, but I felt I needed to come to

you right away," Ro said. She held out a bulkily wrapped object, a padd sitting on top. "It's a book, and a translation. The book was Istani's. I believe she took it from B'hala, and that she was killed because of it."

Kira took them from her, frowning as she set the padd aside and unwrapped a decidedly ancient tome from a soft piece of cloth. The cover was unmarked, but the ragged pages inside were covered in Bajoran from millennia past, the ink faded with time. "Where did you get this? And why do you think someone would kill her over a book?"

"It's a book of prophecy. Istani hid it just before she was attacked, and I found it. I had it translated this afternoon—"

"This afternoon?" Kira interrupted, feeling a surge of anger. "Why didn't you come to me earlier, Ro?"

Ro shook her head. "I didn't know if it was important. I thought it was, but—maybe I should have, all right? If I made a mistake, I'm sorry. But this book . . . Colonel, the prophecies it contains have all come true. *All of them.*"

Kira's anger subsided. Bajoran history was full of prophets and prophetic writings, most notoriously contradictory, but even the best of them had only been correct part of the time. "All of them?"

"Take my word for it. Or read it yourself," Ro said. "But read the passage I have marked there, first. The first part of it's missing, but I think it's pretty clear."

Kira leaned against the divider that separated the dining area from the rest of her living room and picked up the padd, reading from where a small cursor slowly blinked.

. . . with the Herald attendant. A New Age for Bajor will begin with the birth of the alien Avatar, an age of Awareness and Understanding beyond what the land's children have ever known. The child Avatar will be the second of the Emissary, he to whom the Teacher Prophets sing, and will be born to a gracious and loving world, a world ready to Unite. Before the birth, ten thousand of the land's children will die for the child's sake. It is destined, but should not be looked upon with despair; most choose to die, and are welcomed into the Temple of the Teacher Prophets.

Without the sacrifice of the willing, the Avatar will not be born into a land of peace. Perhaps the Avatar will not be born at all; it is unclear. That ten thousand is the number, it is destined. Ten thousand must die.

Kira looked up into Ro's unsmiling face and shook her head, unable to believe it. "This isn't possible," she said.

"Colonel, I'm not prone to leaps of faith, you probably know that," Ro said. *"But so far everything in that book has come true. Everything."*

She sat down opposite Kira, her face almost sick with unhappiness. "For better or worse, I'd be the first person to disregard a Bajoran book of prophecy. But this book . . . whoever wrote it was in touch with something real. They knew about the great war, and B'hala, and the Occupation. They even knew about the Founders, and the outcome of the Dominion war. And here it says—absolutely—that 10,000 people have to die before Kasidy Yates gives birth."

Kira shook her head again, but inside, her gut was churning, explosions of darkness and fear going off in her mind and in her heart. She looked at the padd, at the book, and at Ro, still shaking her head, wanting more than anything to believe she was asleep and dreaming, painfully aware that she was wide awake.

Her earlier feelings of peace and possibility were gone, and Kira felt like she might never sleep again.

EPILOGUE

After the call from Starfleet, Ross stepped from his ready room onto the bridge, nodding at communications.

"Anything?" he asked.

Ensign Weller shook his head, certainly knowing what the question was; Ross had asked more than once in the past day since the *U.S.S. Cerberus, Prometheus*-class, had led the Federation fleet to the rendezvous in the Gentariat system. "Negative, sir. Still no acknowledgment from Captain Picard."

Damn. Lieutenant Faro had pointed out that the Badlands were notorious for garbling communications, and Ross hoped very much that he was right, that it was radiation interference keeping Jean-Luc from calling in—because the *Enterprise-E* had apparently fallen off the edge of the universe, and they couldn't wait a moment longer. The Klingon and Romulan fleets had already departed.

The admiral moved to his chair and sat, wishing that things were different, feeling sick with irresolution and dread. The nightmares from less than fifteen weeks before were still perfectly clear for him, haunting his every waking hour and many of his sleeping ones. Another war was unthinkable; the idea of new devastation raining down on societies still in ashes . . . the apocalyptic breadth of such a sin was enough to drive a man mad. Standing with Ben on Cardassia, he'd seen how easy it could be to lose one's mind from horror.

Standing with Ben on Cardassia . . .

Ross had seen many terrible things, but the sheer magnitude of the destruction and loss of life on Cardassia had been brutal beyond words. Mangled bodies littering the streets, buildings burning, the oily, grim dusk of choking smoke and dust settling over it all like a fetid shroud. It was Cardassia that Ross saw in his dreams; Cardassia was the realization of war, and he didn't know if he could bear for it to happen again.

Which is why this investigation is so very important, why it must be carried out immediately and forcefully. He could never let himself forget that the Dominion had been responsible for the holocaust he'd witnessed, and he would do everything in his power to stop them from creating another.

Violence begets violence. Peace at any cost. The two contradicted and confirmed one another, battling for higher ground, but Ross had his orders, however he felt about it; the Federation Council had spoken.

"We can't wait," Ross said, settling back into his chair, hoping beyond hope that they were doing the right thing. "Open a channel to the fleet; we're moving out."

CONTINUED IN AVATAR, BOOK TWO

Look for STAR TREK fiction from Pocket Books

Star Trek®: The Original Series

Enterprise: The First Adventure • Vonda N. McIntyre
Final Frontier • Diane Carey
Strangers From the Sky • Margaret Wander Bonanno
Spock's World • Diane Duane
The Lost Years • J.M. Dillard
Probe • Margaret Wander Bonanno
Prime Directive • Judith and Garfield Reeves-Stevens
Best Destiny • Diane Carey
Shadows on the Sun • Michael Jan Friedman
Sarek • A.C. Crispin
Federation • Judith and Garfield Reeves-Stevens
Vulcan's Forge • Josepha Sherman & Susan Shwartz
Mission to Horatius • Mack Reynolds
Vulcan's Heart • Josepha Sherman & Susan Shwartz
Novelizations
Star Trek: The Motion Picture • Gene Roddenberry
Star Trek II: The Wrath of Khan • Vonda N. McIntyre
Star Trek III: The Search for Spock • Vonda N. McIntyre
Star Trek IV: The Voyage Home • Vonda N. McIntyre
Star Trek V: The Final Frontier • J.M. Dillard
Star Trek VI: The Undiscovered Country • J.M. Dillard
Star Trek Generations • J.M. Dillard
Starfleet Academy • Diane Carey
Star Trek books by William Shatner with Judith and Garfield Reeves-Stevens
The Ashes of Eden
The Return
Avenger
Star Trek: Odyssey (contains *The Ashes of Eden*, *The Return*, and *Avenger*)
Spectre
Dark Victory
Preserver

#1 • *Star Trek: The Motion Picture* • Gene Roddenberry
#2 • *The Entropy Effect* • Vonda N. McIntyre
#3 • *The Klingon Gambit* • Robert E. Vardeman
#4 • *The Covenant of the Crown* • Howard Weinstein
#5 • *The Prometheus Design* • Sondra Marshak & Myrna Culbreath

#6 • *The Abode of Life* • Lee Correy
#7 • *Star Trek II: The Wrath of Khan* • Vonda N. McIntyre
#8 • *Black Fire* • Sonni Cooper
#9 • *Triangle* • Sondra Marshak & Myrna Culbreath
#10 • *Web of the Romulans* • M.S. Murdock
#11 • *Yesterday's Son* • A.C. Crispin
#12 • *Mutiny on the Enterprise* • Robert E. Vardeman
#13 • *The Wounded Sky* • Diane Duane
#14 • *The Trellisane Confrontation* • David Dvorkin
#15 • *Corona* • Greg Bear
#16 • *The Final Reflection* • John M. Ford
#17 • *Star Trek III: The Search for Spock* • Vonda N. McIntyre
#18 • *My Enemy, My Ally* • Diane Duane
#19 • *The Tears of the Singers* • Melinda Snodgrass
#20 • *The Vulcan Academy Murders* • Jean Lorrah
#21 • *Uhura's Song* • Janet Kagan
#22 • *Shadow Lord* • Laurence Yep
#23 • *Ishmael* • Barbara Hambly
#24 • *Killing Time* • Della Van Hise
#25 • *Dwellers in the Crucible* • Margaret Wander Bonanno
#26 • *Pawns and Symbols* • Majliss Larson
#27 • *Mindshadow* • J.M. Dillard
#28 • *Crisis on Centaurus* • Brad Ferguson
#29 • *Dreadnought!* • Diane Carey
#30 • *Demons* • J.M. Dillard
#31 • *Battlestations!* • Diane Carey
#32 • *Chain of Attack* • Gene DeWeese
#33 • *Deep Domain* • Howard Weinstein
#34 • *Dreams of the Raven* • Carmen Carter
#35 • *The Romulan Way* • Diane Duane & Peter Morwood
#36 • *How Much for Just the Planet?* • John M. Ford
#37 • *Bloodthirst* • J.M. Dillard
#38 • *The IDIC Epidemic* • Jean Lorrah
#39 • *Time for Yesterday* • A.C. Crispin
#40 • *Timetrap* • David Dvorkin
#41 • *The Three-Minute Universe* • Barbara Paul
#42 • *Memory Prime* • Judith and Garfield Reeves-Stevens
#43 • *The Final Nexus* • Gene DeWeese
#44 • *Vulcan's Glory* • D.C. Fontana
#45 • *Double, Double* • Michael Jan Friedman
#46 • *The Cry of the Onlies* • Judy Klass
#47 • *The Kobayashi Maru* • Julia Ecklar
#48 • *Rules of Engagement* • Peter Morwood

#49 • *The Pandora Principle* • Carolyn Clowes
#50 • *Doctor's Orders* • Diane Duane
#51 • *Unseen Enemy* • V.E. Mitchell
#52 • *Home Is the Hunter* • Dana Kramer Rolls
#53 • *Ghost-Walker* • Barbara Hambly
#54 • *A Flag Full of Stars* • Brad Ferguson
#55 • *Renegade* • Gene DeWeese
#56 • *Legacy* • Michael Jan Friedman
#57 • *The Rift* • Peter David
#58 • *Face of Fire* • Michael Jan Friedman
#59 • *The Disinherited* • Peter David
#60 • *Ice Trap* • L.A. Graf
#61 • *Sanctuary* • John Vornholt
#62 • *Death Count* • L.A. Graf
#63 • *Shell Game* • Melissa Crandall
#64 • *The Starship Trap* • Mel Gilden
#65 • *Windows on a Lost World* • V.E. Mitchell
#66 • *From the Depths* • Victor Milan
#67 • *The Great Starship Race* • Diane Carey
#68 • *Firestorm* • L.A. Graf
#69 • *The Patrian Transgression* • Simon Hawke
#70 • *Traitor Winds* • L.A. Graf
#71 • *Crossroad* • Barbara Hambly
#72 • *The Better Man* • Howard Weinstein
#73 • *Recovery* • J.M. Dillard
#74 • *The Fearful Summons* • Denny Martin Flynn
#75 • *First Frontier* • Diane Carey & Dr. James I. Kirkland
#76 • *The Captain's Daughter* • Peter David
#77 • *Twilight's End* • Jerry Oltion
#78 • *The Rings of Tautee* • Dean Wesley Smith & Kristine Kathryn Rusch
#79 • *Invasion!* #1: *First Strike* • Diane Carey
#80 • *The Joy Machine* • James Gunn
#81 • *Mudd in Your Eye* • Jerry Oltion
#82 • *Mind Meld* • John Vornholt
#83 • *Heart of the Sun* • Pamela Sargent & George Zebrowski
#84 • *Assignment: Eternity* • Greg Cox
#85-87 • *My Brother's Keeper* • Michael Jan Friedman
    #85 • *Republic*
    #86 • *Constitution*
    #87 • *Enterprise*
#88 • *Across the Universe* • Pamela Sargent & George Zebrowski
#89-94 • *New Earth*

#89 • *Wagon Train to the Stars* • Diane Carey
#90 • *Belle Terre* • Dean Wesley Smith with Diane Carey
#91 • *Rough Trails* • L.A. Graf
#92 • *The Flaming Arrow* • Kathy and Jerry Oltion
#93 • *Thin Air* • Kristine Kathryn Rusch & Dean Wesley Smith
#94 • *Challenger* • Diane Carey
#95-96 • *Rihannsu* • Diane Duane
    #95 • *Swordhunt*
    #96 • *The Empty Throne*

Star Trek: The Next Generation®

Metamorphosis • Jean Lorrah
Vendetta • Peter David
Reunion • Michael Jan Friedman
Imzadi • Peter David
The Devil's Heart • Carmen Carter
Dark Mirror • Diane Duane
Q-Squared • Peter David
Crossover • Michael Jan Friedman
Kahless • Michael Jan Friedman
Ship of the Line • Diane Carey
The Best and the Brightest • Susan Wright
Planet X • Michael Jan Friedman
Imzadi II: Triangle • Peter David
I, Q • Peter David & John de Lancie
The Valiant • Michael Jan Friedman
The Genesis Wave, Book One • John Vornholt
The Genesis Wave, Book Two • John Vornholt
Novelizations
Encounter at Farpoint • David Gerrold
Unification • Jeri Taylor
Relics • Michael Jan Friedman
Descent • Diane Carey
All Good Things... • Michael Jan Friedman
Star Trek: Klingon • Dean Wesley Smith & Kristine Kathryn Rusch
Star Trek Generations • J.M. Dillard
Star Trek: First Contact • J.M. Dillard
Star Trek: Insurrection • J.M. Dillard

#1 • *Ghost Ship* • Diane Carey
#2 • *The Peacekeepers* • Gene DeWeese
#3 • *The Children of Hamlin* • Carmen Carter
#4 • *Survivors* • Jean Lorrah

#5 • *Strike Zone* • Peter David

#6 • *Power Hungry* • Howard Weinstein

#7 • *Masks* • John Vornholt

#8 • *The Captain's Honor* • David & Daniel Dvorkin

#9 • *A Call to Darkness* • Michael Jan Friedman

#10 • *A Rock and a Hard Place* • Peter David

#11 • *Gulliver's Fugitives* • Keith Sharee

#12 • *Doomsday World* • David, Carter, Friedman & Greenberger

#13 • *The Eyes of the Beholders* • A.C. Crispin

#14 • *Exiles* • Howard Weinstein

#15 • *Fortune's Light* • Michael Jan Friedman

#16 • *Contamination* • John Vornholt

#17 • *Boogeymen* • Mel Gilden

#18 • *Q-in-Law* • Peter David

#19 • *Perchance to Dream* • Howard Weinstein

#20 • *Spartacus* • T.L. Mancour

#21 • *Chains of Command* • W.A. McCay & E.L. Flood

#22 • *Imbalance* • V.E. Mitchell

#23 • *War Drums* • John Vornholt

#24 • *Nightshade* • Laurell K. Hamilton

#25 • *Grounded* • David Bischoff

#26 • *The Romulan Prize* • Simon Hawke

#27 • *Guises of the Mind* • Rebecca Neason

#28 • *Here There Be Dragons* • John Peel

#29 • *Sins of Commission* • Susan Wright

#30 • *Debtor's Planet* • W.R. Thompson

#31 • *Foreign Foes* • Dave Galanter & Greg Brodeur

#32 • *Requiem* • Michael Jan Friedman & Kevin Ryan

#33 • *Balance of Power* • Dafydd ab Hugh

#34 • *Blaze of Glory* • Simon Hawke

#35 • *The Romulan Stratagem* • Robert Greenberger

#36 • *Into the Nebula* • Gene DeWeese

#37 • *The Last Stand* • Brad Ferguson

#38 • *Dragon's Honor* • Kij Johnson & Greg Cox

#39 • *Rogue Saucer* • John Vornholt

#40 • *Possession* • J.M. Dillard & Kathleen O'Malley

#41 • *Invasion! #2: The Soldiers of Fear* • Dean Wesley Smith & Kristine Kathryn Rusch

#42 • *Infiltrator* • W.R. Thompson

#43 • *A Fury Scorned* • Pamela Sargent & George Zebrowski

#44 • *The Death of Princes* • John Peel

#45 • *Intellivore* • Diane Duane

#46 • *To Storm Heaven* • Esther Friesner

#47-49 • *The Q Continuum* • Greg Cox

#47 • *Q-Space*

#48 • *Q-Zone*

#49 • *Q-Strike*

#50 • *Dyson Sphere* • Charles Pellegrino & George Zebrowski

#51-56 • *Double Helix*

    #51 • *Infection* • John Gregory Betancourt

    #52 • *Vectors* • Dean Wesley Smith & Kristine Kathryn Rusch

    #53 • *Red Sector* • Diane Carey

    #54 • *Quarantine* • John Vornholt

    #55 • *Double or Nothing* • Peter David

    #56 • *The First Virtue* • Michael Jan Friedman & Christie Golden

#57 • *The Forgotten War* • William Forstchen

#58-59 • *Gemworld* • John Vornholt

    #58 • *Gemworld #1*

    #59 • *Gemworld #2*

#60 • *Tooth and Claw* • Doranna Durgin

#61 • *Diplomatic Implausibility* • Keith R.A. DeCandido

#62-63 • *Maximum Warp* • Dave Galanter & Greg Brodeur

    #62 • *Maximum Warp #1*

    #63 • *Maximum Warp #2*

Star Trek: Deep Space Nine®

    Warped • K.W. Jeter

    Legends of the Ferengi • Ira Steven Behr & Robert Hewitt Wolfe

    The Lives of Dax • Marco Palmieri, ed.

Millennium • Judith and Garfield Reeves-Stevens

#1 • *The Fall of Terok Nor*

#2 • *The War of the Prophets*

#3 • *Inferno*

Novelizations

    Emissary • J.M. Dillard

    The Search • Diane Carey

    The Way of the Warrior • Diane Carey

    Star Trek: Klingon • Dean Wesley Smith & Kristine Kathryn Rusch

    Trials and Tribble-ations • Diane Carey

    Far Beyond the Stars • Steve Barnes

    What You Leave Behind • Diane Carey

#1 • *Emissary* • J.M. Dillard

#2 • *The Siege* • Peter David

#3 • *Bloodletter* • K.W. Jeter

#4 • *The Big Game* • Sandy Schofield

#5 • *Fallen Heroes* • Dafydd ab Hugh

#6 • *Betrayal* • Lois Tilton

#7 • *Warchild* • Esther Friesner

#8 • *Antimatter* • John Vornholt

#9 • *Proud Helios* • Melissa Scott

#10 • *Valhalla* • Nathan Archer

#11 • *Devil in the Sky* • Greg Cox & John Gregory Betancourt

#12 • *The Laertian Gamble* • Robert Sheckley

#13 • *Station Rage* • Diane Carey

#14 • *The Long Night* • Dean Wesley Smith & Kristine Kathryn Rusch

#15 • *Objective: Bajor* • John Peel

#16 • *Invasion!* #3: *Time's Enemy* • L.A. Graf

#17 • *The Heart of the Warrior* • John Gregory Betancourt

#18 • *Saratoga* • Michael Jan Friedman

#19 • *The Tempest* • Susan Wright

#20 • *Wrath of the Prophets* • David, Friedman & Greenberger

#21 • *Trial by Error* • Mark Garland

#22 • *Vengeance* • Dafydd ab Hugh

#23 • *The 34th Rule* • Armin Shimerman & David R. George III

#24-26 • *Rebels* • Dafydd ab Hugh

    #24 • *The Conquered*

    #25 • *The Courageous*

    #26 • *The Liberated*

#27 • *A Stitch in Time* • Andrew J. Robinson

Avatar • S.D. Perry

    #1 • S.D. Perry

    #2 • S.D. Perry

Star Trek: Voyager®

    Mosaic • Jeri Taylor

    Pathways • Jeri Taylor

    Captain Proton: Defender of the Earth • D.W. "Prof" Smith

Novelizations

    Caretaker • L.A. Graf

    Flashback • Diane Carey

    Day of Honor • Michael Jan Friedman

    Equinox • Diane Carey

#1 • *Caretaker* • L.A. Graf

#2 • *The Escape* • Dean Wesley Smith & Kristine Kathryn Rusch

#3 • *Ragnarok* • Nathan Archer

#4 • *Violations* • Susan Wright

#5 • *Incident at Arbuk* • John Gregory Betancourt

#6 • *The Murdered Sun* • Christie Golden

#7 • *Ghost of a Chance* • Mark A. Garland & Charles G. McGraw

#8 • *Cybersong* • S.N. Lewitt

#9 • *Invasion!* #4: *Final Fury* • Dafydd ab Hugh

#10 • *Bless the Beasts* • Karen Haber

#11 • *The Garden* • Melissa Scott

#12 • *Chrysalis* • David Niall Wilson

#13 • *The Black Shore* • Greg Cox

#14 • *Marooned* • Christie Golden

#15 • *Echoes* • Dean Wesley Smith, Kristine Kathryn Rusch &
    Nina Kiriki Hoffman

#16 • *Seven of Nine* • Christie Golden

#17 • *Death of a Neutron Star* • Eric Kotani

#18 • *Battle Lines* • Dave Galanter & Greg Brodeur

#19-21 • *Dark Matters* • Christie Golden

    #19 • *Cloak and Dagger*

    #20 • *Ghost Dance*

    #21 • *Shadow of Heaven*

Star Trek®: New Frontier

New Frontier #1-4 Collector's Edition • Peter David

    #1 •*House of Cards*

    #2 •*Into the Void*

    #3 •*The Two-Front War*

    #4 •*End Game*

#5 • *Martyr* • Peter David

#6 • *Fire on High* • Peter David

The Captain's Table #5 • *Once Burned* • Peter David

Double Helix #5 • *Double or Nothing* • Peter David

#7 • *The Quiet Place* • Peter David

#8 • *Dark Allies* • Peter David

#9-11 • *Excalibur* • Peter David

    #9 • *Requiem*

    #10 • *Renaissance*

    #11 • *Restoration*

Star Trek®: Invasion!

#1 • *First Strike* • Diane Carey
#2 • *The Soldiers of Fear* • Dean Wesley Smith & Kristine Kathryn Rusch
#3 • *Time's Enemy* • L.A. Graf
#4 • *Final Fury* • Dafydd ab Hugh
Invasion! Omnibus • various

Star Trek®: Day of Honor

#1 • *Ancient Blood* • Diane Carey
#2 • *Armageddon Sky* • L.A. Graf
#3 • *Her Klingon Soul* • Michael Jan Friedman
#4 • *Treaty's Law* • Dean Wesley Smith & Kristine Kathryn Rusch
The Television Episode • Michael Jan Friedman
Day of Honor Omnibus • various

Star Trek®: The Captain's Table

#1 • *War Dragons* • L.A. Graf
#2 • *Dujonian's Hoard* • Michael Jan Friedman
#3 • *The Mist* • Dean Wesley Smith & Kristine Kathryn Rusch
#4 • *Fire Ship* • Diane Carey
#5 • *Once Burned* • Peter David
#6 • *Where Sea Meets Sky* • Jerry Oltion
The Captain's Table Omnibus • various

Star Trek®: The Dominion War

#1 • *Behind Enemy Lines* • John Vornholt
#2 • *Call to Arms...* • Diane Carey
#3 • *Tunnel Through the Stars* • John Vornholt
#4 • *...Sacrifice of Angels* • Diane Carey

Star Trek®: The Badlands

#1 • Susan Wright
#2 • Susan Wright

Star Trek®: Dark Passions

#1 • Susan Wright
#2 • Susan Wright

Star Trek® Books available in Trade Paperback

Omnibus Editions
 Invasion! Omnibus • various
 Day of Honor Omnibus • various
 The Captain's Table Omnibus • various
 Star Trek: Odyssey • William Shatner with Judith and Garfield Reeves-
  Stevens
Other Books
 Legends of the Ferengi • Ira Steven Behr & Robert Hewitt Wolfe
 Strange New Worlds, vols. I, II, and III • Dean Wesley Smith, ed.
 Adventures in Time and Space • Mary P. Taylor
 Captain Proton: Defender of the Earth • D.W. "Prof" Smith
 New Worlds, New Civilizations • Michael Jan Friedman
 The Lives of Dax • Marco Palmieri, ed.
 The Klingon Hamlet • Wil'yam Shex'pir
 Enterprise Logs • Carol Greenburg, ed.